Maker frow
right. His instincts were starting to go haywire.

He opened a channel to Planck. "When Skullcap was making introductions earlier, was that long or short compared to what you've seen him do before?"

"He's usually pretty brief," Planck declared. "Much shorter than what he did today."

"And right now — have you ever seen him be this verbose?"

"Never."

"He's stalling," Maker said flatly, knowing it to be true. He then added Browing to their comm channel and announced, "They're up to something. Break this off *now*. We need to hustle back to the ship."

"We appreciate your sentiments," Browing interjected, cutting Skullcap off, "and wish to retire now to our ship to deliberate on what you have said."

They didn't wait for the Vacra to acknowledge what they'd said; they merely turned and started walking away. It was all Maker could do not to march double-time back to their ship.

"Adames," Maker said, hailing the *Raider*. "We're on our way back."

"So, how'd it go?" Adames asked.

"Hard to say, but something's off," Maker replied. "Just fire up the engines and get ready to take us off this rock. As a matter of fact, meet us halfway."

"You got it," the NCO answered.

Maker felt tension he wasn't aware of starting to ease, but it was a short-lived experience as roughly thirty seconds later, Adames contacted him from the ship.

"Gant," he said solemnly, "the engines are dead."

# EFFERUS

**Kid Sensation Series**
Sensation: A Superhero Novel
Mutation (A Kid Sensation Novel)
Infiltration (A Kid Sensation Novel)
Revelation (A Kid Sensation Novel)
Coronation (A Kid Sensation Novel)

**Kid Sensation Companion Series**
Amped
Mouse's Tale (An Alpha League Supers Novel)

**The Warden Series**
Warden (Book 1: Wendigo Fever)
Warden (Book 2: Lure of the Lamia)
Warden (Book 3: Attack of the Aswang)

**The Fringe Worlds**
Terminus (Fringe Worlds #1)
Efferus (Fringe Worlds #2)

**Boxed Sets**
The Kid Sensation Series (Books 1–3)
The Warden Series (Books 1–3)
Worlds of Wonder

**Short Stories**
Extraction: A Kid Sensation Story

# EFFERUS
## Fringe Worlds #2

By

## Kevin Hardman

# EFFERUS

Cover Design by Isikol

Edited by Faith Williams, The Atwater Group

This book is published by I&H Recherche Publishing.

ISBN: 978-1-937666-26-2

Printed in the U.S.A.

EFFERUS

## **ACKNOWLEDGMENTS**

I would like to thank the following for their help with this book: GOD, who has blessed me in more ways than I can count; and my family, for showing exceptional patience, love, and understanding when it comes to my writing.

# EFFERUS

Thank you for purchasing this book! If, after reading, you find that you enjoyed it, please feel free to leave a review on the site from which it was purchased.

Also, if you would like to be notified when I release new books, please subscribe to my mailing list via the following link: http://eepurl.com/C5a45

Finally, for those who may be interested, I have included my blog, Facebook, and Twitter info:

Blog: http://kevinhardman.blogspot.com/

Facebook: www.facebook.com/kevin.hardman.967

Twitter: @kevindhardman

# EFFERUS

**Efferus** -

      1. savage;

      2. wild;

      3. cruel;

      4. fierce.

# EFFERUS

## Chapter 1

Captain Ward "Warhorse" Henry — commander of the Space Navy vessel *Mantis Wing* — was sitting at a table in his meeting room when a sturdy knock sounded at the door.

"Enter," Henry said loudly. A moment later, the door slid open and Marine Lieutenant Arrogant Maker strode into the room, right on time for their meeting.

Maker marched towards the captain, stopping when he was about a foot away from the table and then snapped his hand up in a crisp salute.

Henry returned the gesture and then grumbled, "Be seated."

The captain eyed Maker warily as the Marine sat down. Frankly speaking, Henry still hadn't decided yet whether or not he liked the lieutenant, who had spent something like fifteen years as an enlisted man and then a couple of years as a civilian before being commissioned as an officer. It wasn't that the lieutenant was difficult to deal with — quite the opposite, in fact (although the same couldn't be said of the Marines under his command). He'd been on his best behavior during the past two months — ever since that wretched debacle on Terminus, when Maker had almost blown up the *Mantis*.

Somehow, despite a laundry list of felonious acts — disobeying orders, constructing and detonating a banned weapon, disabling (and almost destroying) a Navy ship in the middle of combat, etcetera — Maker had escaped court-martial. Moreover, Maker's original mission (which was to find an alien race called the Vacra) had been extended, with the crew of the *Mantis* being put at his disposal. In short, despite outranking Maker by a mile,

Captain Henry (and his crew) was subject to the lieutenant's commands.

A lot of senior officers would have chaffed at this arrangement, but not Henry. This wasn't his first rodeo; he'd actually had a number of engagements in which his ship was used to ferry lesser-ranked officers on various missions, and quite often the nature of those assignments put Henry at the beck and call of someone below his pay grade. Thus it was that he didn't have any issue with the fact that Maker pretty much decided where they went and when.

Thankfully, Maker wasn't a jerk about it. He didn't try to lord his authority over Henry like several others had done in the past. Outside of dictates about his mission, Maker left the running of the ship to the captain. Moreover, he always showed Henry the respect and deference due his rank — such as when he'd entered the room and saluted a moment earlier.

Maker took a moment to get comfortable in his chair before asking, "Where would you like to begin, sir?"

"The woman," Henry said. "She dislocated the shoulder of one of my engineers."

"Permission to speak freely, sir?"

"Always," Henry answered with a nod.

"Thank you, sir," Maker said. He placed his hands on the table with fingers interlaced and leaned forward. "Sergeant Diviana is a highly-trained operative and an intelligence agent. Your engineer got fresh with her — touched her in an ungentlemanly fashion — and she reacted."

"*Over*reacted is more like it. Granted, he shouldn't have touched her, but he didn't break anything."

"Well, from this point forward he'll understand that 'No' means 'No.' That said, I'll remind Diviana that we're all on the same side and ask that she respond less aggressively if the situation arises again."

Henry harrumphed at that last comment and Maker smiled to himself. After the job Diviana did on that engineer, the odds of a recurrence were slim indeed.

"Moving on," Henry said. "Apparently one of my crew had a run-in with the doctor assigned to your squad."

"I wouldn't describe it that way, since the doctor really didn't do anything."

"And yet my crewman ended up with almost every bone in his hand broken."

"With all due respect, sir, the guy's an idiot. He punched an augmented man in the jaw. Need I say more?" Maker asked with a shrug.

"I understand your point," Henry replied. "But still, if that Augman provoked him into throwing that punch, goaded him in some way…"

"Then you should be thanking us for revealing his stupidity. Everybody knows that Augmen are tough as nails, and throwing a jab at one is like trying to punch a steel girder. In essence, your crewman should have known better. Trying to blame my doctor for a broken hand in this instance, just because he's an Augman, is ridiculous."

"Fine. I'll make sure my crew knows that striking the good doctor with their bare hands is a bad idea."

Maker frowned, not liking the implications of the captain's statement, but before he could comment, Henry moved on to the next item on his agenda.

"Finally," the captain said, "your companion."

# EFFERUS

Maker smiled inwardly, pleased at Henry's choice of words. Most people had a tendency to categorize Erlen — the exotic alien creature to whom the captain was referring — as a pet. It was a label Maker loathed (although Erlen himself didn't seem to mind), and in the past he'd gotten into more than one altercation because of it.

Erlen was rarely far from his side, although these *tête-à-têtes* with Henry were an exception. Not because the captain had an issue with Erlen, per se, but more so because the alien's presence served no purpose in the meeting. If a person — terrestrial *or* alien — had nothing to offer, Henry didn't see the need to have them taking up space.

At the moment, the captain was launching into the current issue related to Erlen.

"It seems your *friend*," he said, "had a brush with Lieutenant Kepler."

Maker let out a slight groan. *Kepler again.* That guy was constantly finding a way to be a thorn in his side.

"There was an incident," Maker acknowledged, then began struggling to keep a grin off his face as he remembered the particulars.

"As I understand it, your alien confederate spat some kind of compound on Kepler's shoes. It immediately glued him to the spot. It adhered so completely, in fact, that my crew had to cut away that section of flooring in order to remove Kepler's footwear."

Maker finally gave up on trying to contain the smile that had been slowly overtaking his features. "But on the bright side, there was no violence involved."

"Maybe by your standards, but I consider any act that harms this vessel as violence with respect to my *ship*."

"Yes, sir," Maker acknowledged, sobering almost instantly. "I'll make sure the incident isn't repeated."

"I think that would be best — unless you want your friend confined to quarters."

"Understood. Will there be anything else, sir?"

"No, we're done. Dismissed."

Maker stood, coming to attention. He gave the captain a snappy salute which was hastily returned, then turned and strode from the room.

## Chapter 2

Upon exiting Henry's meeting room, Maker found his second-in-command, Hector Adames, waiting for him just outside the door. The Marine Master Sergeant was a seasoned NCO (non-commissioned officer), a battle-hardened soldier, and one of Maker's oldest friends; he fell into step beside Maker almost instinctively.

"So, how'd it go?" Adames asked as they walked down the passageway.

"About as well as can be expected," Maker replied. "We both essentially agreed to try to keep our people in check."

"That's good, considering his people got the worst of it."

"Don't forget about his ship. He wasn't wild about the cute little joke Erlen played on Kepler. In fact, he was more concerned about that incident than any fisticuffs."

"Well, a crewman's a lot easier to replace than a ship. Cheaper, too."

Maker nodded, then slowed to a halt as they came to an intersection between their passageway and another corridor — this one fairly congested. Members of the *Mantis* crew shuffled by, eyeing the two Galactic Marines warily; they all knew "Maniac" Maker now (by reputation, if not personally), and after recent events most of them felt his nickname — as well as his other sobriquet, "Madman" Maker — was truly deserved.

Maker ignored them, turning to face Adames directly. "Speaking of ships, how are things coming with our new vessel?"

"All reports indicate she's ready to go. You just have to give the word."

"Consider it given."

Adames raised an eyebrow. "Does that mean…?"

"Yes," Maker said, nodding. "We're ready to go to Plan B."

"Sounds good. I'm assuming you'll want to inspect the ship."

"Let's brief the rest of the squad first — say in about an hour?"

"That works. See you then," Adames said. As he turned to walk away, he tilted his chin towards the area behind Maker. "Watch your six."

Slightly alarmed, Maker did an immediate about-face, and found himself facing the person he least wanted to see.

Lieutenant Kepler.

# EFFERUS

## Chapter 3

Kepler was a tall, well-muscled fellow who hailed from a family with a strong tradition of military service. Young and well-groomed, he wore the uniform well — so well, in fact, that they could have used his image on recruiting posters. On top of all that, from what Maker could discern, Kepler was actually a competent officer and good at his job.

In short, under other circumstances, Maker was certain that he and Kepler could actually have been friends. As it was, however, Kepler was working overtime to prove himself Maker's archenemy, and might have actually earned the title if the spot wasn't already taken. (Although it certainly didn't keep him from getting honorable mention.)

The source of Kepler's animus was a mission Maker had undertaken years earlier, the very assignment that had resulted in mankind's first contact with the Vacra. Kepler's cousin — a young officer named Greeley — was one of many people who died during that initial encounter on a ship called the *Orpheus Moon*. (In fact, not counting Erlen, Maker had been the sole survivor that fateful day — a fact that had made him infamous.)

Moreover, Kepler was just one of thousands who somehow blamed Maker for what happened back then. One of the people jumping on the bandwagon was Greeley's father, an admiral in the Space Navy (and a powerful enemy to have). It was Admiral Greeley who had gotten Kepler a last-minute transfer to the *Mantis*, where he had proceeded to make life as onerous as possible for Maker and his team.

At the moment, Kepler was in the midst of giving Maker a menacing look as he closed the distance between them.

"You owe me a new pair of shoes," Kepler growled when he got close, leaning well into Maker's personal space.

"Fine," Maker said flatly. "I'll forward you the money for a new pair."

"And you'd better start keeping your people in line."

"Already taken care of," Maker said softly.

"And you need to start keeping that pet of yours on a leash."

"It's been addressed."

Maker had maintained a mild tone while responding to Kepler, hoping that — with nothing to stoke his ire — the man would quickly move on. Instead, Kepler launched into a laundry list of minor offenses allegedly committed by Maker or those under his command, citing them all in petty detail.

As before, Maker continued to respond docilely, almost robotically. Mentally, however, he rolled his eyes, wondering how long he should put up with Kepler's antics on this particular occasion. Despite Kepler's attempts to appear threatening, Maker wasn't at all intimidated; he'd already proved himself capable of handling the younger man in hand-to-hand fashion on more than one occasion. He just didn't like the idea of things escalating to the point where he and another human being were at each other's throats — especially with a *real* enemy like the Vacra out there.

In addition, it was a lot easier to just let Kepler vent on these occasions. It didn't cost Maker anything —

it certainly didn't hurt his pride — and if it kept a lid on this particular powder keg, then it was worth a little verbal kowtowing.

Thus, it was with a sense of relief that Maker recognized that Kepler seemed to be winding down.

"—our step," Kepler was saying as Maker tuned back in, "because you've been on thin ice for a long time with a lot of people."

"I understand," Maker said. "That's not really news."

Kepler's eyes narrowed in anger, letting Maker know that what he'd thought was an innocuous comment had somehow lit a fuse within the man.

"Oh?" Kepler remarked quizzically. "Then maybe it'll be news to you that almost everyone on the ship feels the same way about your entire detachment."

Now it was Maker's turn to narrow his eyes, as Kepler's comments made a number of things clear. Here was the source of the conflict between his people and Henry's crew. He should have realized a lot sooner that there was more to it that simply being confined together in close quarters for an extended period.

"Look," Maker said firmly, "I don't care what you say about me — you can spread rumors until you're blue in the face — but leave my squad out of it. Inciting the rest of the *Mantis* crew to harass them is unfounded. They weren't there when your cousin died. They had nothing to do with it."

"Birds of a feather," Kepler muttered as he shrugged. Then he pushed past Maker, intentionally and forcefully bumping the latter's shoulder as he went by.

Maker sighed despondently, watching Kepler walk away and wishing there were some way to resolve his differences with the younger man. Shaking his head glumly, he turned and headed towards his cabin.

# EFFERUS

## Chapter 4

Erlen was lying on the floor, playing with a rubber ball, when the door to their quarters slid open and Maker entered. The alien swiftly and agilely rose up on all fours, a questioning growl rumbling softly from his throat.

"All is forgiven," Maker said. "But do me a favor. Stay away from Kepler from now on."

Erlen tilted his head slightly, then let out a noncommittal yawning sound that conveyed a maybe-I will-maybe-I-won't attitude.

Maker stared at his companion for a moment, wondering if he should press the issue. About the size of an oversized dog, Erlen looked like the sleek, hybrid offspring of a spider monkey and a salamander (and perhaps a few other species). Confining him to quarters would be one way to make sure the alien didn't cross paths with Kepler. However, it would surely cause Erlen to become irritated and surly.

"Regardless," Maker finally added, "try not to produce any more compounds that affect the ship adversely. The captain would prefer not to have to carve out pieces of the *Mantis* every time you open your mouth."

Erlen's response was a weird, high-pitched cough, followed by him spitting a weird glob of purple onto the cabin floor. Almost immediately, the substance began bubbling and hissing angrily, like acid, and issuing forth an ominous cloud of blue steam.

The scene only lasted a few seconds — not even long enough for Maker to comment on what was occurring. At the end of that time, the purple glob had dissolved and the blue steam had dissipated. More surprisingly, the area of the floor where the alien had spat looked exactly as it had before — completely unmarred.

"Funny," Maker said sarcastically, noting that Erlen was giving him what appeared to be a cocksure look.

This was, of course, the alien's way of showing that not every biological amalgam he produced was caustic. Truth be told, Erlen was a living chemical factory. He could metabolize, synthesize, and reproduce almost any element he encountered (as well as a few outside the realm of human experience). And, while he typically sampled items by licking them, his paws — which were home to razor-sharp, retractable claws — also contained dry papillae on their pads that allowed him to "taste" objects simply by touching them.

Maker decided to let his alien companion have the last word, so to speak; he had a briefing to get ready for.

With that in mind, he pulled out his p-comp and tapped in a few commands on the screen of the palm-sized computer. Almost immediately the lights in the cabin dimmed, and a moment later a holographic star chart appeared in the middle of the room, the image broadcast by a projector in the ceiling.

The chart displayed a large array of stars and planets spread across a broad area which Maker was intimately familiar with: Gaian Space — that portion of the cosmos primarily occupied and controlled by *Homo sapiens*. It consisted of several discrete regions that branched out almost spherically from a central core. The heart of this expanse was the Hub — the multitude of worlds that served as the cultural, financial, and governmental nerve center of the human race.

Next to the Hub was the middle region known as the Mezzo, worlds that were generally considered the industrial arm of humanity, the suppliers of raw materials. Outside of the Mezzo was the Rim, which was typically thought of as two sections: the Inner Rim and the Outer Rim.

Following the Rim was the Fringe, the outermost edge of the Gaian Expanse and human settlement. It was an area that had garnered a reputation for attracting the wrong elements of society — unsavory individuals and men of questionable character — because of a dearth of law enforcement in the region.

Finally, other than those sectors known to be home to other sentient species, areas beyond the Fringe (most of which were uncharted and unexplored) were known simply as the Beyond or X-Space. Few people ventured Beyond without a very compelling reason.

Maker tapped the p-comp screen and the image changed, zooming in on a sleepy little solar system in the Beyond that consisted of three small planets circling a mid-sized star — the current location of the *Mantis*. Their pursuit of the Vacra had taken them well into undiscovered country, probably farther than most of the ship's crew had ever been (and certainly farther than most of them were comfortable with).

For a moment, Maker felt sympathy for the *Mantis* crew. They were originally only supposed to go to a planet called Terminus, nominally located on the outer edge of the Fringe (but which, in his own opinion, was actually situated in the Beyond). The change in mission parameters had taken them much deeper into the Beyond than they had probably ever contemplated, and for a greater length of time. But that was the military for you:

orders and mission directives could transition in the blink of an eye. Plus, where the Vacra were concerned, all bets were off.

*Speaking of the Vacra...* Maker touched the p-comp screen once more, altering the projected image once again. Now on display was a member of an alien species — an insectoid decked out in full body armor. From both personal experience and the design of the armor, Maker knew exactly what they looked like under the protective metal suit: compound eyes, antennae, a six-limbed thorax, abdomen... All in all, they resembled ants to a large extent (if ants were bipedal and grew to man-sized height).

This was the Vacra, the enemy he'd been tasked with finding. However, the image in front of Maker wasn't just any run-of-the-mill member of that species; this was Skullcap, one of the Vacran leaders.

Although most of the Vacra looked almost like clones (and possibly were), Skullcap was easily identifiable because of three features. First was the source of his nickname: the bony cranium of some wild, horned animal had been grafted on top of his armored helmet. Second, he had a ring of skulls from various species embedded in the armor encircling his neck. Finally, there was the fact that one of his middle arms was severely deformed. Maker smiled to himself, thinking back to how Skullcap had actually lost the original limb during their first, bloody encounter four years earlier. The Vacran's body had seemingly tried to regrow the arm, but the replacement was stunted and disfigured.

However, despite the physical flaw, Skullcap was still exceedingly dangerous, both in hand-to-hand combat and as a military tactician. He was, in fact, the primary reason why Lieutenant Kepler couldn't capture the number one spot on Maker's personal hate parade. The slot was already occupied.

*Where are you?* Maker wondered to himself as he stared at the image of Skullcap, while Erlen growled menacingly at the projection. Maker's alien companion had special reason to hate the Vacra. For some reason, the insectoids had made Erlen the object of their desire, and it was clear that one of their primary goals was capturing him.

Maker glanced at Erlen. To call the alien "special" was clearly an understatement, but for the umpteenth time, Maker had to admit that the Vacra seemingly knew more about his extraterrestrial friend than he did. In truth, Maker had to admit that he knew very little.

Erlen had been entrusted to him as a newborn by the indigenous race of a far-flung alien world. All Maker had really been able to glean from them was the fact that Erlen hailed from a planet called Niota. Beyond that (and the fact that the Niotan was somehow very important), the aliens who had made Erlen his ward had imparted very little information to Maker, although there admittedly had been something of a language barrier.

There were, no doubt, a lot of questions about Erlen, and at some juncture Maker would probably have to try to find the answers to them. At the moment, however, dealing with the Vacra took priority over everything else.

With that in mind, Maker turned off the holographic display.

"Come on," he said to Erlen. "Let's take a walk."

# EFFERUS

## Chapter 5

They ended up in the landing bay, the result of Maker wanting to lay eyes on the new ship his crew would be using. Although he had told Adames he'd check it out after their upcoming briefing, the lack of anything meaningful to do in the interim had led to an early inspection.

As he and Erlen walked through the area, Maker took note of the various vessels present: fighters, personnel carriers, and so on. He also couldn't help noticing how everyone — pilots, navigators, maintenance crew — all hustled out of their path, like a bunch of hens that suddenly found a chicken hawk in their midst. In addition to Maker's own notoriety, Erlen had become infamous in his own right. Thus, the two of them together were typically shunned even more than Maker was when alone.

Their destination was at the rear of the bay: a small, weathered cruiser that had last seen action as a pirate ship. In fact, the vessel had been part of a buccaneer convoy that had recently made the foolish mistake of attacking the *Mantis*, apparently thinking it would be easy prey.

The raiders had overreached badly. Maybe they had underestimated the offensive capabilities of Space Navy ships. Maybe they had misidentified the spacecraft altogether. Or maybe they had simply thought that the *Mantis* was lost or disabled in some way — why else would a Terran vessel (even a military one) be this far out in the Beyond?

Regardless of the reason, the decision had proved costly. Of the half-dozen ships the corsairs had attacked with, two were destroyed outright and another two crippled beyond repair. The fifth — the cruiser now sitting in the landing bay and which Maker had commandeered and rechristened as the *Midnight Raider* — had had its engines disabled during the battle. The final ship had turn tail and run, belching smoke from a couple of holes in its hull before activating its jump drive and leaping away through hyperspace to parts unknown.

In addition to salvaging the cruiser, the *Mantis* had also taken on some unexpected cargo: the pirate crews from the two crippled ships, as well as that of the now-named *Raider*. Needless to say, the brig of the *Mantis* was now stuffed to capacity.

As they approached the *Raider*, something seemed off to Maker, and his brow crinkled as he concentrated, trying to pinpoint the problem. The door to the ship was open, but that wasn't uncommon; they were hastily making repairs and modifications to the ship, so there was always someone around doing something. And that's when it hit him as to what was different: from what he could see, there was no one working on the ship at the moment.

Usually Maker could count on seeing a flurry of activity around the vessel — machinists, welders, and so on, all flitting about like maternity ward nurses fretting over a colicky newborn. (Upon learning the next phase of Maker's plans for finding the Vacra, Captain Henry had made restoring the *Raider* a singular priority and authorized repair crews to work on it around the clock.) On this occasion, there didn't seem to be anyone around, lending credence to Adames' earlier statement that the overhaul of the ship was complete.

Almost on a whim, Maker eschewed the idea of going inside the vessel immediately, choosing instead to do a quick walk-around of the exterior, with Erlen padding along beside him. As he eyed the ship, Maker had to admit that Henry's people did good work; not only had they repaired all damage inflicted by the *Mantis*, but they had made such distinct alterations in the physical appearance of the *Raider* that anyone familiar with the original vessel wouldn't recognize it now.

Satisfied with what he'd seen thus far, Maker headed to the ship's door. Once there, he saw movement in the interior, a clear indication that someone was inside. Maker knew, without guessing, who it was. He coughed softly, deliberately announcing his presence as he stepped through the entryway.

The person inside — a Marine, based on the uniform — had his back to the door as he inspected a control panel set in a wall of the ship. He didn't even bother turning around as Maker entered, preferring instead to shout "Welcome, el-tee," over his shoulder. "You, too, Erlen."

Maker chuckled. "How'd you know it was us, Wayne?"

Now it was the young man's turn to snicker. "Saw you scrutinizing the ship on the external cameras," he said as he finally turned around. "Well, what do you think?"

"Looks good," Maker acknowledged truthfully. "Excellent, in fact."

Edison Wayne beamed with pride at the comment. Although the crew of the *Mantis* had done most of the work, Wayne was the person Maker had actually put in charge of overseeing repairs to the *Raider* — and with good reason. The young Marine was an engineering genius, a true prodigy with an unrivaled knack for invention and innovation. As evidence of his brilliance, floating next to Wayne was an odd, cylindrical object about a foot in height, with a makeshift head and arms attached. This was Jerry — a robot that he had built from scraps.

"Glad to hear you approve," Wayne said, turning Maker's mind back towards the *Raider*. "She's been almost completely refit and refurbished. We've repaired the damage, reinforced the hull, upgraded the weapons and shields, installed a new jump drive…"

Maker nodded in approval as Wayne ticked off the list of improvements. The offensive and defensive capabilities of the *Raider* had been enhanced considerably, in his opinion. Still, whether it was enough to take on the Vacra was an open-ended question.

"Sounds like you've got this baby in fighting trim," Maker commented as Wayne finished his narrative.

"Thanks, sir," Wayne said. "The trick — at least on the exterior — was overhauling the ship while maintaining the appearance of a seasoned frigate."

Maker understood what Wayne was getting at: out at the Fringe and Beyond, a ship that looked too new might draw unwarranted attention. For the next phase of Maker's plan, a low profile was much more beneficial.

"Mission accomplished on that front," Maker said. Noting Erlen wandering farther into the ship's interior, he added, "I think someone wants a tour."

"You got it, el-tee," Wayne said with a grin.

## Chapter 6

The tour was a brief affair, with Wayne essentially pointing out the major sections of the ship — the bridge, living quarters, and so on — as well as some of the improvements that had been made. At its conclusion, Maker realized that it was almost time for him to brief the rest of their squad. With that in mind (and with Erlen and Jerry in tow), the two Marines headed to the secure ready room that had been made available for the use of their unit.

When they arrived, they found everyone else already present and gathered around a conference table. In addition to Adames, there were four other Marines in the room — two men and two women — who made up the remainder of Maker's contingent. Also in attendance were two civilians: a man named Bain Browing and a woman, Dr. Ariel Chantrey.

As usual, Maker fought to keep a frown off his face in the presence of Browing. The man irked him considerably, and with good reason: during their previous encounter with the Vacra, Browing had cut a deal with the insectoid aliens. Allegedly, he had only been following orders, but it still galled Maker to have to work with him. Orders were orders, however, and Browing had been assigned to assist his team.

While Erlen — followed by Jerry — padded over to a corner of the room, Wayne took a seat with his fellows, prompting Maker to turn his attention back to the task at hand.

"All right, let's get to it," Maker said, dismissing with any pleasantries. He tapped the controls on his p-comp and a hologram of a planet appeared — a green-white globe that spun lazily on its axis above the center of the conference table.

"This is Defalcator," he announced. "I won't mince words: it's a criminal planet. If you've got smuggled goods, illegal weapons, stolen cargo, or the like, it's the place to go."

"One of the places, anyway," Adames corrected.

"Right," Maker acknowledged with a nod.

"So this place is a major hub of illicit activity," said one of the female Marines, Sergeant Isis Diviana. She was an incredibly striking woman, with an almost exotic appearance, punctuated by an incredibly pale complexion that stood in stark contrast to her ebony eyes, onyx nails, and sable hair. The only flaw in her form was the fact that a disapproving scowl seemed to be permanently stamped on her features. Even with that, however, Maker could understand why most men would find her alluring — unless they knew how she'd dislocated the shoulder of one of the *Mantis* crewmen.

"I take it there's some connection to the Vacra here?" Diviana added.

"Yes," Maker said. "We've gotten word that a potential informant is located there — someone with intel we can use."

"Let me guess," interjected Browing. "This informant is one of Adames' contacts?"

"No," Maker said tersely. Browing's comment was a backhanded allusion to the fact that Adames came from a family of smugglers. Ironically, while the remark caused Maker to smolder internally on behalf of his friend, Adames himself only smiled and gave Browing a sardonic wink.

There followed a moment of tense silence, which threatened to stretch to the point of being uncomfortable until Dr. Chantrey asked, "So what's the plan, Lieutenant?"

The question brought Maker back to himself. "The pirate ship we commandeered — the *Raider*. We're going to use it to visit Defalcator without arousing suspicion."

"That would be prudent," said one of the male Marines, a shorter-than-average fellow named Cano Snick. However, anyone who made the mistake of underestimating him due to his stature was in for a rude surprise, as Snick was one of the best hand-to-hand combatants Maker had ever encountered. "The *Mantis* is far too conspicuous."

"That's putting it mildly," added Sergeant Luna Loyola, the other female Marine. "We're in a Space Navy vessel, which means we're the closest thing to terrestrial law enforcement for light years around, and nobody this far out in the Beyond wants anything to do with the law."

As always, Loyola was wearing goggles — tinted, circular lenses that covered her eyes. Or rather, the space where her eyes should have been. She'd actually lost her sight (and a good chunk of her face) in an explosion well before joining Maker's unit. They'd been able to reconstruct her features, but her body had rejected the new set of eyes that had been grown for her. Thus, she now relied upon a synthetic oculus in each eye socket — along with a bunch of hardware in her skull — in order to "see" by reading electromagnetic waves, much like a visual version of radar or sonar.

"I think I see where this is going," Browing announced to no one in particular. "The plan is to go in disguised as brigands of some sort, find this informant, and then wring whatever info we can about the Vacra out of him."

"In a nutshell," Maker said.

"So where's the *Mantis* while this charade is going on?" Browing asked. "Somewhere within hailing distance, I assume — in case we need help?"

Maker exchanged a knowing glance with Adames before responding with, "Not exactly."

"Well where, *exactly*, will the *Mantis* be?" Dr. Chantrey asked.

"I bet I can guess," said Wayne. "Captain Henry and crew will be headed back to Gaian Space."

"What?" Dr. Chantrey muttered, seemingly aghast at the notion. "Why?"

"The prisoners," Adames chimed in. "We can't keep carting them around forever."

"Not to mention the fact that the level of overcrowding in the brig is practically inhumane," said the final Marine — an imposing figure who stood well over seven feet in height, with muscles bulging over every inch of his frame.

"Well, not all of them are human," quipped Browing. "But if it makes you feel better, we could ask the captain to shoot enough of them out of an airlock to leave the remainder some elbow room."

A slight look of distaste came across the features of the big Marine. He was an augmented man — an Augman — a genetically-engineered super-soldier bred to unleash savage fury on mankind's enemies on the battlefield. However, there was an unanticipated flaw in his design, in the eugenic scheme of his entire species: Augmen refused to fight. They rejected violence in all its forms, and usually pursued occupations that promoted peace and harmony to some extent. In fact, the Augman in Maker's unit — whom Adames had given the moniker of "Fierce" — was actually a doctor. (He was also in a relationship with Loyola, although the two of them generally avoided any public displays of affection.)

"No one's jettisoning anybody," Maker stated adamantly in response to Browing's statement. "But the truth of the matter is that Fierce is right to a certain extent. The cells on this ship are stuffed to capacity, some of our guests are very unsavory, and the *Mantis* was never meant to serve as a maximum security prison."

"Not to mention the fact that those scumbags are sucking up resources," Diviana added. "Food, water, life support…"

"Is that true?" Dr. Chantrey asked.

"Yes, but before anyone panics, let me say we're a long way from starving to death, dying of thirst, or running out of air," Maker declared. "That said, Captain Henry prefers to feel that he's in charge of a Space Navy vessel rather than the warden of a penal colony. He wants our uninvited guests off his ship as soon as possible, and I don't blame him."

"But that basically means that we're going in without any support or back-up," Loyola noted.

"We shouldn't need any," Adames countered. "We're going in as smugglers. We land, get the info we need, and take off, with most of those on the planet none the wiser."

"Seems simple enough," Wayne said.

"I still don't like it," Browing said. "Just a handful of us and one small frigate."

"Well, it's not like we're going in blasting on all channels that we're there for a covert mission," Maker stressed. "But I'll tell you what. If you're so concerned about keeping your hide intact, you're more than welcome to stay on board the *Mantis* and hitch a ride back home with Henry and his crew."

Browing snorted derisively. "No thanks. I've got my orders, just like you, and right now my mandate is to stick with this squad until we locate the Vacra."

A crease formed in Maker's brow as he reflected on what he'd just heard. Browing's statement seemed to suggest that he had additional orders to follow *after* the Vacra were located, and Maker was sorely tempted to delve into those unstated implications. Before he could give voice to those thoughts, however, Loyola spoke up.

"So when do we leave?" she asked.

"In approximately twelve hours," Maker answered.

Maker spent a few more minutes going over the basics about Defalcator — slightly less than standard gravity, breathable air, and so on — before bringing the briefing to a close. He then dismissed his squad, who quickly filed out of the room, with a couple of them grumbling about the short notice before departure.

Maker smiled to himself. The comments about the lack of notice were somewhat exaggerated. His team had, on the whole, been aware for several days that something was in the works. Moreover, they were Marines, so in the ordinary course of things, they were generally ready to move out at the drop of a dime. In this instance, the twelve-hour notice was more for the benefit of their civilian companions — Browing and Dr.

26

Chantrey — who, Maker now noticed, had stayed back rather than leave with everyone else.

"One quick question," Browing said as the door slid shut behind the last departing member of Maker's squad. "Exactly what do you plan to do if this informant provides you with the location of the Vacra?"

"What do you mean?" Maker asked innocently.

"Don't be coy," Browing said. "Are you planning to take them on?"

Maker seemed to contemplate for a moment before responding. "Those are my orders."

"Actually," Dr. Chantrey interjected, "while your orders *were* to go *after* the Vacra, the implication was that you were only supposed to find them — seemingly just an extension of your original mission to locate them on Terminus. There was nothing about engaging them."

"That's subject to interpretation," Maker retorted. "As far as I'm concerned, it's open-ended, meaning it's left to my discretion."

"But you can't!" Browing insisted. "It would be suicide — even if you had the *Mantis* as your wingman. You remember what happened the last time we went head-to-head with them."

"Yes," Maker replied. "The Vacra lost a warship. I count that as a win."

Browing gave him a skeptical look. "And the fact that you almost got everyone on this ship killed?"

"If that ain't the pot calling the kettle black," Maker scoffed. "You're the one who made a pact with the devil. That bargain you made with the Vacra is what put us in the crosshairs."

Glaring at Maker, Browing opened his mouth with the clear intent to say something harsh, but Dr. Chantrey spoke up before he had a chance.

"That's enough," she firmly declared. "From both of you. People who outrank all of us put together have seemingly cleared everybody in this room of any wrongdoing in regards to the Vacra. So why don't we just act like everyone here has a clean slate instead of constantly trying to pin blame on each other?"

"Fine by me," Maker said after a moment. "It's your boyfriend who keeps hitting the rewind button."

"He's not my boyfriend!" Chantrey shot back almost reflexively.

Browing ignored the doctor's comments. "I wouldn't keep doing it if history didn't have a habit of repeating itself."

Maker struggled to keep the emotion from showing on his face, but he curled his fists into white-knuckled balls. Browing's statement was a pointed reference to mankind's first encounter with the Vacra, which only Maker and Erlen had survived.

"But I can hit the pause button on that if it makes things easier," Browing continued.

Maker just stared at him for a moment, fighting an urge to knock the man's teeth out. Then he let out a harsh breath and said, "Fair enough."

## Chapter 7

With a truce established (at least for the moment), Browing departed. Dr. Chantrey, however, stayed at Maker's request.

"I need to ask your professional opinion about something," he said when they were alone.

The doctor gave him an inquisitive glance. Her expertise was human behavior, as evidenced by advanced degrees in psychology, psychiatry, psychobiology, and cognitive science — to name a few. Although he was generally civil to her, she had no doubt that Maker was less than wild about her being assigned to his team, as she had initially been tasked with profiling him and predicting his behavior.

"Go on," Dr. Chantrey urged after a moment. Although he had made it clear that he didn't like being an object of study, Maker obviously respected her opinion, as this wasn't the first time he'd approached her in a professional capacity.

"Planck," Maker said flatly. "What's your assessment of him?"

The doctor's brow creased as she considered the question. Solomon Planck had been the lead scientist aboard a secret research vessel that had been conducting a wide range of experiments involving cutting-edge technology and weapons — many of which were forbidden by treaty, diplomacy, and law (not to mention plain decency and morality). The ship had somehow been raided by the Vacra, who not only made off with its cache of banned wares, but also took Planck prisoner. Ultimately, the man had spent four long years experiencing the Vacra's tender mercies until his recent rescue by Maker's squad.

"Physically," Dr. Chantrey finally said, "I'd say he's rebounded pretty well. He's still not where he needs to be — years of malnourishment and abuse can't be negated overnight — but he's getting there."

"I meant mentally," Maker clarified.

Chantrey nodded. "I know, but the condition of the physical body can affect one's mental state, so I started there."

"Okay, so his body's on the mend — got it. And his head?"

"Mentally, he's a complete wreck. I mean, he's still a brilliant man, but he's beset by an array of psychological disorders now: anxiety, depression, panic attacks, night terrors... The list goes on and on."

"But is he dangerous?"

"To himself or to others?"

"Both. Either." Maker seemed indifferent to the question. "Does it matter?"

"Maybe," Dr. Chantrey offered. "Why are you asking?"

Maker didn't immediately answer. Instead, a look of deep concentration crossed his face, as if he were weighing how best to respond.

"I get it," the doctor said after a few seconds. "You're thinking of taking him with us."

For a moment, Maker looked at her harshly, his expression making it understood that he didn't like her trying to analyze or discern his actions. But then his normal, impassive countenance reasserted its dominance.

"Planck's got more experience with the Vacra than the rest of humanity combined," Maker stated.

"That makes him an asset I can use. However, I don't want to have to worry about him trying to murder us all in our sleep."

Dr. Chantrey fought to keep a grin from her face. "In that case, I think I can put your mind somewhat at ease. In my professional opinion, despite his phobias and disorders, Planck's not currently a danger to himself or anyone else."

Maker frowned. "You said 'somewhat.'"

"Excuse me?"

"You said you can 'somewhat' put my mind at ease regarding Planck. That makes it a qualified answer. So what aren't you telling me?"

Dr. Chantrey was caught a little off guard by Maker's question, but admitted to herself that she shouldn't have been. Almost from the moment they'd met, Maker had shown himself to be far more astute than she'd initially given him credit for. He wasn't just some dumb Marine, and she should have known he'd pick up on her equivocation.

"I think that part of Planck's mental well-being — such as it is — remains rooted in the fact that he's no longer a prisoner of the Vacra anymore," she said. "He's out of harm's way."

"And if he comes with us?" Maker asked.

"There's a possibility that the notion of confronting his former captors will undermine the mental stability he's managed to achieve up to this point."

"But we've been hunting the Vacra for months," Maker scoffed. "It's an open secret on this ship. How will continuing that suddenly cause his fragile psyche to start fraying?"

"You have to consider the circumstances," the doctor insisted. "Right now, Planck's on a military warship, full of soldiers. If he goes with you…"

She trailed off, but Maker picked up on her train of thought. "If he goes with us, he's a lot more vulnerable."

"In essence."

Maker contemplated this in silence for a moment, then said, "I understand he might be reluctant, but the man's an indispensable resource for this mission."

"I get that. I'm just saying that it's probably a mistake to force him to go."

Maker was about to make a stern retort, when Dr. Chantrey's statement gave rise to a new line of thought.

"All right, Doctor," Maker said slyly. "We'll try it your way."

Chantrey's curiosity was piqued. "What are you going to do?"

"Not force him, as you said," Maker replied with a grin. "Now, if you'll excuse me."

"Of course — but one other thing before you go."

Now it was Maker's turn to be curious. "Yes?"

"I want to reiterate that Browing's *not* my boyfriend. We're not romantically involved, and never have been."

Maker took a moment to absorb this, then asked, "Is there a reason why you're stressing that fact to me?"

"Because you obviously wanted to know."

"I did?"

"Yes. That's why you inserted that comment into the conversation."

"It's just an expression. Why would I care about that?"

Chantrey crossed her arms and looked at him fixedly. "You tell me."

Maker simply stared back at her, then shook his head in derision.

"No comment, Doc, although I appreciate the pro bono analysis," he finally said. "Just keep putting those degrees to good use."

He then turned and left the room, with Erlen right behind him.

# EFFERUS

## Chapter 8

Maker stalked through the ship absentmindedly, without a clear destination in mind. Dr. Chantrey's final comments had aggravated him, to say the least. Sure, he'd admit she was easy on the eyes, but acknowledging that fact was a far cry from what she had been implying. His interest in her was strictly academic.

Those thoughts and similar notions about the doctor (and where she could shove her latest analysis) flitted back and forth through his brain for several minutes as he walked. Erlen, having accompanied him silently for the most part, suddenly let out a low rumble and swiped gently at Maker's ankle with a paw. Maker immediately came to a halt, wondering what the issue was. He glanced down at the Niotan, who gave him a blank stare in return for a moment, then let his eyes wander around their current environs. This caused Maker to look around as well, and for the first time he actually realized that he had been wandering aimlessly.

Or perhaps not walking *completely* at random. He was in an area that contained living quarters for some of the crew. More to the point, Erlen had caused him to stop right before the door of the suite that had been assigned to Solomon Planck.

Maker frowned. He had indeed wanted to talk to the man, but Dr. Chantrey's statements had seemingly distracted him to the extent that he hadn't been able to focus on anything else. Plainly speaking, he wasn't really prepared to have the conversation he needed to with Planck.

That said, his subconscious had apparently led him here, so maybe now was as good a time as any (not to mention the fact that time was of the essence). Mind made up, Maker pressed a button next to the door, sounding a chime within. A few seconds later, the door slid open, revealing Solomon Planck standing in the doorway.

The man facing Maker was thin — slender well beyond the point of what was healthy. However, it was obvious to Maker that he had put on weight since their first meeting. Also, his beard was now neatly trimmed, as was his hair. In addition, his skin had now taken on a more healthy tone as opposed to the deathly pallor it previously exhibited. However, he still had something of a haggard appearance, as if sleep were difficult to come by, and his eyes seem to dart about nervously, as if he were afraid something was going to come out of the walls and bite him. Still, on an overall basis, Maker had to admit that the man looked a lot better than he had when he had first been rescued from the Vacra.

"Lieutenant Maker," Planck said with a smile, seemingly pleased to see him. "Please, come in."

"Thanks," Maker replied as he stepped inside, followed by Erlen.

As the door slid shut, Planck gestured to a couple of chairs in the living room area. "Please, have a seat."

Maker sat in one of the indicated chairs and Erlen flopped down at his feet. Planck took a seat across from him.

"How have you been?" Maker asked.

Planck made a so-so gesture with his hand. "About as well as possible. I've improved in terms of being able to keep food down. I can sleep for several hours at a time now. But I'm still a bit jittery on occasion, and I probably wake up at least once a night thinking this is all a dream and I'm still the Vacra's prisoner. All in all, it's a vast improvement over when you first found me."

"Glad to hear it," Maker said sincerely.

There was silence for a moment, then Planck spoke up. "Well, while I don't doubt your genuine concern for my welfare, I'm sure this isn't a social call."

Maker nodded, appreciating the man's bluntness. "I'll try not to take up too much of your time."

Planck chuckled. "Time's all I have. Take as much of it as you need. It's not like I have any duties on this ship."

"Thanks," Maker said. "You already know about my mission to find the Vacra."

"Of course. You, your squad, and your mission are just about all the crew of the *Mantis* discusses."

"Well, we'll be breaking away soon — pursuing the Vacra in our own ship while the *Mantis* returns to Gaian Space."

"Let me guess. You're conscripting me as part of your team."

Maker shook his head. "No. I can't deny that you would be an asset — whether you know it or not, you're basically humanity's expert on the Vacra. However, I won't force you to become part of my mission."

"Thanks. But if you're not here to strong-arm me into coming with you, what is it that you want?"

"To pick your brain. We need as much info as you can give us if we're going to have any chance of success."

Planck looked confused for a moment. "But I've already spilled my guts on everything I know about the Vacra. I've given hours and hours of recorded statements, answered every question put to me about them. You weren't personally involved in my debriefing, but I'm certain you have access to the information I provided. In short, I don't know that any stone has been left unturned in that regard."

Maker leaned forward. "I'm not talking about the Vacra, per se."

"Oh?"

"I'm talking about what they took from you."

Suddenly Planck looked nervous, and his right hand began to shake slightly. "I can't talk about that."

"When the Vacra took you prisoner, they also confiscated everything on your ship," Maker continued. "A good chunk of that stuff is technology and weapons that most people have never even heard of, let alone seen. And now it's in the hands of the enemy."

Planck didn't say anything, but he had a look on his face that was reminiscent of a rabbit that had accidentally burrowed into a den of foxes. This was clearly a subject he wanted to avoid.

"I said I can't talk about that," he repeated. "Classified."

The statement was true to a certain extent. While Planck had willingly talked about the Vacra, he had been adamant about not discussing what had been on his ship. To put it plainly, no one on the *Mantis* had high enough clearance to hear what he had to say about the subject. About all he'd been willing to admit was that his ship had indeed been a sub rosa vessel — one on which a vast number of secret experiments and research had been performed.

"Look, I understand your reluctance to discuss this," Maker intoned sympathetically. "But everything from that ship is in the hands of the Vacra now. I need to know what my team is up against. I'm talking about good men and women who chose to disobey orders and rescue you rather than leave you a captive."

Planck stared at him for a moment. "Why is this so important to you? Going after the Vacra, that is."

Maker let out a harsh breath. "They ambushed my team — the one I commanded previously. They also attacked our ship. Only Erlen and I survived."

"I seem to recall that you blew up a Vacra ship yourself quite recently. I'd argue that the scales are somewhat even."

"They won't be even until Skullcap is dead."

"I'd wager he died when the Vacra ship exploded."

"You'd be wrong," Maker replied flatly. "One of their escape vessels jumped to hyperspace just before the ship blew up."

Of course, Maker had absolutely no proof that Skullcap had been on board the craft that got away, but it was something he knew deep in his soul.

"We're in a war," Maker went on, "only no one in authority seems to realize it yet. The Vacra haven't even gotten started with us."

Planck gave him a solemn stare. "That sounds like someone with a soldier's mentality."

"Maybe, but after you, I'm the next best authority on the Vacra. In fact, before we found out about you, I was the *only* authority."

"And you think we've got to fight back?"

"This wouldn't be the first time another species has tried to test us, and it won't be the last. I spent the first fifteen years of my military career fighting for humanity, to show other species that we weren't the little kid on the playground that they could bully. To make them treat us with respect."

"I don't know that the Vacra acknowledge the concept of respect in that sense."

"Then they'll learn to leave us alone — that we aren't worth the hassle of picking a fight with. That if they touch us they're going to get burned. That's why I'm here, why my team is here."

"And if you get them all killed?"

Maker let out a deep breath and reflected for a moment. "We can't cower in fear, no matter how much stronger our adversaries might appear to be. We've got to be willing to take the fight to them, even if the odds don't favor us. Otherwise, it's all for nothing. My years as a Marine, the work you did on that sub rosa ship. None of it will mean anything if we aren't willing to stand up for ourselves when it counts."

A weary, worried expression came over Planck's face. "I'm not sure I can give you what you want."

"What I want is for my people to have a fighting chance. For that, I need to know more about the Vacra's weapons and capabilities — specifically, what they got from your sub rosa ship."

Planck shook his head despondently. "I'm sorry. I really wish I could help you, but I just can't."

For a moment, Maker considered pressing his point, but one look at Planck's face — haggard and drawn — changed his mind. The man had simply been through too much as far as the Vacra were concerned.

"Okay," Maker muttered softly, nodding his head.

## Chapter 9

Maker stayed and chatted with Planck for a few more minutes, making small talk and reassuring the man that he held no ill will towards him. It was, in fact, a true statement. Planck had been through a hell of an ordeal, no doubt about that, and Maker didn't fault him for wanting nothing further to do with the Vacra. Still, Maker desperately needed what was in the man's head.

After he and Erlen left, his mind immediately began to play back the conversation he'd had with Planck, with Maker wondering what — if anything — he could have said differently to make Planck respond in a more positive fashion. However, he'd taken no more than a couple of steps before he heard someone speaking to him. He looked up to find Diviana in front of him.

"How'd it go?" she asked, sounding slightly impatient, at which point Maker realized that she was repeating her question. He had been so lost in thought that it hadn't really registered the first time. "With Planck," she added for clarity.

Maker frowned. "What do you mean?"

"You just left Planck's quarters. I assume you were in there asking him to join our little expedition."

"How'd you know…?" he began, then trailed off. "Wait, you sensed me in there, didn't you?"

"No," Diviana replied. "I saw you leave."

Maker laughed. His question had alluded to the fact that Diviana was psychic — telepathic to a certain extent. She couldn't read minds, but she could sense thoughts. (Diviana herself likened it to being able to hear people talk but without understanding what they were saying.)

"Well," Maker continued, "that still doesn't explain how you knew what I was doing in there."

"That's easy enough to explain," Diviana countered. "We're going up against an enemy that has us seriously outclassed, and we're desperately short in terms of intel. Basically, we need Planck's knowledge. So we're back to me asking how it went in there."

"It didn't. I mean, I didn't ask him directly."

"So what exactly did you do?"

"I made a small play to his ego by telling him that what he knows is essential, although that's actually true. And I also tried to sell it as a mixture of defending mankind and maybe getting a little payback."

"I take it that didn't go over so well."

"No," Maker muttered. "I was hoping to just get him talking about the stuff that had been on his ship, and then gently segue into the notion of him coming with us."

"And?"

"And nothing. The conversation never even got started because Planck considers his info classified." Maker then let out an exasperated sigh. "The most frustrating thing is that he's already spilled his guts to the Vacra — told them everything he knows about the cargo they took from that ship he was on. What the hell is wrong with telling us — his fellow human beings — the same thing?"

Diviana gave Maker a fixed stare that bordered on disapproval. "You didn't say that to him, did you?"

"No. I wanted to, but it would have seemed unsympathetic — almost cruel, considering what he's been through."

Diviana nodded. "Good. That means I can probably still fix this."

Maker frowned. "Huh? What do you mean?"

"I mean that I can convince Planck to come with us."

"I doubt that, but you're welcome to try."

"I'll do more than try," she said flatly, then sauntered over to the entrance to Planck's quarters.

"For future reference, though," she said, just before pressing the door chime, "never send a man to do a woman's job."

# EFFERUS

## Chapter 10

Aside from the obvious, Maker wasn't sure what Diviana thought she could do to change Planck's mind. However, he didn't waste a lot of time dwelling on it. He had enough to do getting ready to part ways with the *Mantis*.

Packing wasn't much of a chore. Aside from his customized battle armor and weapons, he had various iterations of his military uniform — fatigues, service dress, etcetera — and a few sets of civilian clothes. It took him no more than half an hour to pack it all up, along with toiletries and a few personal items. Once aboard the *Raider*, it took even less time to put everything away.

Shortly after Maker came on board, the rest of his crew began arriving. Like their leader, they all seemed to have adopted a minimalist approach when it came to attire, bringing little more than the essentials in terms of clothing. With respect to gear, however, they appeared — on the whole — to have packed more extensively.

Fierce, for instance, lugged aboard a large crate that apparently contained extra medical equipment. Wayne brought a steamer trunk that was reportedly full of various technological odds and ends that he could tinker with and use to build stuff. Loyola had more than an average number of gun cases, each of which presumably held a firearm of some sort. (Before being blinded, she had been an elite sniper. As far as Maker was concerned, she still was, and her uncanny marksmanship had saved his life during their prior mission.) Adames had several oversized, unmarked containers delivered to the cargo hold, while Diviana brought aboard two black carrying cases, contents unknown. The only person who packed somewhat modestly was Snick, who — aside from clothing — didn't appear to bring anything other than a cushioned mat for meditative purposes.

"I don't remember our people having this much crap on the last mission," Adames said to Maker later, after noting the amount of personal effects being brought onto the *Raider*.

"So says the man sticking oversized crates below deck," Maker shot back with a grin.

"Hey, the stuff *I'm* bringing on board is for the benefit of the entire squad."

"I'm sure every member of our team would say the same thing," Maker said half-jokingly, "but I see your point. However, you have to remember that our last mission was a short-term assignment. Not to mention the fact that at some point we expected to rendezvous with the *Mantis*, so there was no need to take everything."

Adames nodded in understanding. "Unlike this time around, when we don't know when we'll meet a law-abiding crew again."

"Correct."

"Still, with this much personal gear, you're allowing for a lot of individuality. You know, there's a reason the service makes us dress alike, march in formation, and so on."

"I know — it creates discipline, unity, etcetera. Allow people to do too much of their own thing, and they start thinking about what's best for them individually as opposed to what's best for the team."

"It's happened before."

"I know, but to be honest, I'm more concerned about us going too far in the other direction. That we become so focused on the group that all trace of individuality is wiped out. Like a hive of insects."

"Like the Vacra, you mean."

"Exactly."

"Well, if past experience is any indication, I don't think you have to worry about that with this crew. Nobody here is bending over backwards to fit any particular mold."

Maker laughed. "Does that include us as well?"

"*Especially* us," Adames replied with a grin.

Adames' humor was a welcome distraction and helped the time go by as Maker and his people readied the ship for departure. The vast majority of Maker's time — after getting his gear into his quarters on the *Raider* — was logistical: checking reports and stats to ensure that his crew had adequate supplies of everything they'd need, including rations, equipment, and (of course) weapons and ammo. After satisfying himself that everything was adequate for their needs, he signed off and digitally sent the final report to Captain Henry for approval.

It was an unnecessary action on his part. His mission parameters gave him authority to commandeer everything the *Mantis* had if he so desired. He didn't have to ask for permission or approval. However, doing so showed the proper deference for Henry's rank and years of service, and Maker had no doubt that the gesture would be appreciated. (Plus, Maker actually liked and respected Captain Henry.) Unsurprisingly, the captain's approval came back almost immediately.

Maker smiled to himself. They were essentially ready to depart, except for two minor points of concern.

*Speak of the devil*, Maker thought as he saw Browing and Dr. Chantrey making their way into the ship. He had halfway hoped that the pair had changed their minds about coming with them. This was really a military mission; he didn't fancy having a couple of civilians along, possibly slowing them down. (Or worse — if the fighting became hot and heavy — getting in the way.)

To be frank, however, he didn't think Dr. Chantrey would be much of a problem. She had an uncanny ability to blend in, a knack for making herself unobtrusive. More to the point, she got along well with just about everyone, for the most part. (In fact, prior to her recent faulty analysis of him, Maker probably would have been willing to admit that he actually liked her — platonically, of course).

Browing, on the other hand, was a different story altogether. The man had elevated being a pain in the rear into an art form (and that was without considering the fact that he'd previously made a deal with the Vacra). Boiled down to its essence, the main problem with dealing with Browing on a day-to-day basis seemed to stem from his expectation of preferential treatment. Simply put, he was used to being catered to.

Maker had gotten a taste of this firsthand when it came to cabin assignments aboard the *Raider*. Dr. Chantrey had been fine with sharing a room with the other two women in their group, but Browing had insisted on having private quarters.

"It's not a monstrously huge ship, so living space is at a premium," Maker had told him. "Wayne and Snick are sharing a room, as are the women. Fierce isn't even getting *that* — he'll be sleeping on a cot in the medical bay. You can be roomies with Adames. That way you'll be like everybody else."

46

"I don't see *you* sharing a room with anyone," Browing had retorted.

"Did you forget about Erlen? If you want to swap with me and share quarters with him, be my guest. But he snores, and also breathes out noxious fumes in his sleep."

Erlen, who had been at Maker's side at the time, had then made a coughing sound, blowing out a cloud of yellow-green vapor. The notion of sharing a room with the Niotan — which never had a great deal of appeal to begin with — was completely off the table at that point.

Ultimately, however, Maker had relented and allowed a room that had been intended for storage to be converted to living space for Browing. This concession was in large part due to needling from Adames, who had suggested it as not only an olive branch, but also a way to get Browing in their debt. (Left out of the discussion was the fact that it had the additional benefit of allowing Adames to remain the sole occupant of his own quarters.)

Watching Browing come aboard, Maker wondered if it had been a mistake to bend on the roommate issue. Browing didn't strike him as the type to view the indulgence of that request as a favor; he'd more likely envision it as something owed to him as a matter of right. In fact, it would probably just embolden the man in terms of asinine expectations.

Roughly thirty minutes later, Maker was not surprised to find his assessment confirmed when Browing came to him with a complaint. Maker was outside the ship at the time, performing a last-minute inspection. A soft growl from Erlen gave him notice that someone was approaching. When he saw who it was, Maker mentally sighed.

Browing, looking irritated, didn't waste any time on pleasantries. "I had a couple of special crates that were supposed to come on board. I'm told you wouldn't accept delivery."

"That's correct," Maker said with a nod. The items in question had been on one of the lists he'd previously reviewed, and he had indeed disallowed them being brought aboard as cargo.

"Might I ask why?"

"Because it was crap we didn't need — foodstuffs with special storage requirements, and cases of fruity wine."

Browing scowled. "The food consists of delicacies that have to be kept at select temperatures. The wine cases contain rare vintages that are hundreds of years old."

Getting angry, Maker fought to get his temper under control before responding. "Well, I'm sorry if it offends your palate, but you're going to have to eat what the rest of us poor folk will be dining on, which is military rations. If it's good enough for the Corps, it's good enough for you. Besides, I told you before that we've got limited space, and we've already gone above and beyond by giving you private accommodations. If you want that stuff on board, store it in your quarters. When the bullets start flying, I'm not telling my people that we didn't have room for more gear or ammo because you had to have caviar and a cask of Amontillado."

Browing leaned in close, plainly invading Maker's personal space and eliciting a low, rumbling growl from Erlen. On his part, Maker didn't flinch, but — without taking his eyes from Browing — he put a hand palm-out towards his alien companion, clearly communicating a basic message: *Don't interfere.* The Niotan immediately went silent.

Browing stared at Maker for a second, then hissed, "You think you know me *so* well."

"I don't have to know you, Browing. I know your type: career bureaucrats with more connections than skill and more ambition than common sense."

Browing gritted his teeth and, for a moment, appeared on the verge of moving the current dispute beyond the realm of mere words. Maker, not wanting to be caught off guard, was subtly shifting the position of his hands and feet, getting ready to defend against any attack his opponent might mount. However, before any fists started flying, a familiar voice cut through the air.

"Everything good out here, el-tee?"

Maker glanced over Browing's shoulder and saw Adames, as well as Dr. Chantrey. Each of them wore a look of concern that made it clear that they'd seen at least some part of the interaction between him and Browing.

"Everything's fine, Sergeant," Maker said in response to the NCO's question.

"It doesn't *look* fine," Chantrey stated as she and Adames both stepped closer. "What's going on with you two?"

"Just the usual," Maker replied. "King Browing's upset that we're not obeying the most recent royal decree."

Adames coughed softly to cover up a laugh that slipped out.

"It wasn't a decree," Browing countered. "What I sought was a courtesy, but I should have known that was too much to expect from *this* crew."

Maker gave him a stony look. "Well, I'm sorry that the current level of kowtowing doesn't meet your approval, but keeping you happy isn't part of our mission mandate."

"This isn't about my personal happiness," Browing declared, shaking his head.

"Good, because none of the decisions made regarding your requests were personal," Maker said. "They were made with the mission in mind, which is what this crew is focused on. I know that you think we're just one freak shy of a sideshow, but if you stopped focusing on yourself for two seconds you'd realize that we actually know what we're doing."

"Don't sell yourself short," Browing sneered. "I'm sure you have a full roster."

Maker frowned. "Huh?"

"Your sideshow roster," Browing said, using his chin to point in a direction over Maker's shoulder. "Seems to me that you have a full complement of freaks."

Still confused, Maker turned and looked behind him. His eyebrows went up in surprise when he saw who was approaching them, carrying a duffel bag: Solomon Planck.

## Chapter 11

Planck stopped a few feet from Maker, seemingly oblivious to the tension in the air.

"Uh, Lieutenant," Planck began, sounding a little nervous. "If, uh, it's at all possible, I think I'd like to come with you."

It took Maker only a moment to recover from his surprise.

"Of course," he said, smiling at Planck. "We'd love to have you."

"Are you sure?" Planck asked cautiously. "I mean, are you certain that you have enough room?"

"Absolutely," Maker assured him. "You may have to share a room with someone, but that's just about the norm on this ship."

As he made the last statement, Maker glanced at Browing, who was visibly turning red with anger. He plainly understood what Maker seemed to be implying: that Planck would be sharing *his* cabin.

"Sergeant Adames," Maker said a moment later.

Adames, taking his cue, stepped towards Planck. "You'll be bunking with me. Come on, I'll show you our quarters and give you a quick tour of your new home."

"Thanks," Planck said, then he and his new roommate headed inside.

"Is that wise?" Browing asked discreetly as the two men disappeared inside the ship.

"Huh?" Maker muttered, unprepared for the change in Browing's tone, as well as not fully understanding the question.

"Bringing Planck along. Is he stable enough for a mission like this?"

"That's a question for the good doctor," Maker said, gesturing towards Chantrey. "Why don't you ask her?"

He then walked away without waiting for a response, heading inside the *Raider*.

# EFFERUS

## Chapter 12

It only took Maker a few minutes to hunt down who he was looking for: Diviana. He found her in her quarters, along with Loyola, who excused herself (most likely to go spend time with Fierce) when it became clear that Maker was there to see her roommate.

"Okay," he said to Diviana after Loyola departed. "Planck. How'd you get him to join us?"

Diviana batted her eyes coyly. "I used my feminine wiles, of course."

Maker let out a short chuckle. "No, seriously."

His statement wasn't intended as a critique on Diviana's skills as a seductress. In fact, her ability to bewitch the opposite sex wasn't in question. The simple truth was that he thought her competent enough to achieve her aim in most instances (including this one) without resorting to those methods.

"It boiled down to two things that I discussed with him," Diviana replied, turning serious. "The first related to his time as a captive of the Vacra."

"What about it?"

"You have to understand, he's not a soldier. He's never been trained to endure the kinds of things that they did to him. He ended up telling them everything they wanted to know."

Maker nodded. Even hardened soldiers, in the hands of the enemy, had been known to give more information than the traditional response of name, rank, and serial number. (Oftentimes you had to give them *something*, if you wanted to have any hope of simply surviving.)

"However," she continued, "since being rescued, he's felt like something of a failure — like he let humanity down."

"He shouldn't. There's no shame in having buckled after what he went through."

"Yes, he buckled. So it's important to him now to show that he still has some resolve — that certain things are still important to him."

"I get it," Maker said with a nod. "That's why he won't discuss what was on his ship with anyone who lacks the proper clearance. He wants to show that the Vacra didn't break him completely."

"Exactly."

Maker took this in with a solemn nod. "You mentioned discussing two things with Planck. What was the second?"

"I simply told him that he belonged with us — that he fit in better with this crew than anywhere else."

"What do you mean?"

"It's no secret, el-tee, that we're a crew of misfits. And after what he's been through, conforming to societal norms is going to be a hell of an adjustment for Planck."

"But with us, no one will judge him if he's a bit...eccentric."

"Yes. And what's really important to him now seems to be finding his place in the great scheme of things — figuring out where he fits."

"And he told you all this?"

"Not per se. But it wasn't hard to get him to open up enough to figure out what the issue was."

"You should have been a therapist. Dr. Chantrey's been talking to him for weeks now and hasn't gotten anywhere near that much out of him."

"Your girlfriend's good at what she does, but has a tendency to be too clinical. She treats everyone as if they're a problem to be solved — a disease that has to be cured."

"She's not my girlfriend," Maker uttered a bit testily. "We're just colleagues."

"Yeah," Diviana said with a knowing smile. "Keep telling yourself that."

## Chapter 13

After leaving Diviana, Maker found himself somewhat distracted by the comments she had made. Even going through the final checklist for departure wasn't quite enough to make him forget what she had insinuated about his relationship with Dr. Chantrey. More to the point — and much like Chantrey's own statements — he wasn't quite able to figure out why it bothered him so much.

Thankfully, something happened to take his mind off the issue: a last-minute communication from the *Mantis* that Captain Henry was en route to personally see them off.

"More likely to personally *throw* us off," Adames commented when Maker passed the info to him a few moments later.

Nevertheless, the master sergeant wasted no time assembling their people and had them standing at attention outside the *Raider* when Henry showed up with several of his officers. (Maker, standing a few paces in front of his crew, struggled to keep from frowning when he saw that Kepler was among those with the captain.)

Standing somewhat apart from Maker and his team were Browing and Dr. Chantrey, who — as civilians — weren't expected to form up. Erlen was next to the doctor, growling in a barely audible but menacing way when Kepler came into view.

Maker brought his hand up sharply and saluted, and Captain Henry immediately returned the gesture.

"At ease," said the captain. He let his glance wander from Maker to the rest of his squad. "This will be quick. I just wanted to say that my crew and I are proud of the role we've played in supporting your mission. We wish you all the best of luck."

Captain Henry then gave a general "fall out" command, allowing those military members in the immediate area to move about freely. The captain himself then stepped towards Maker.

"Sir," Maker said as Henry drew near, "thank you for the well wishes. And for your hospitality. I know that you were never supposed to have us aboard the *Mantis* for this long — and that we've probably overstayed our welcome — but you've been a very gracious host."

"Thanks," Captain Henry intoned, nodding appreciatively. "Living in close quarters like this for an extended period is always a challenge, but let me assure you that you're far from the worst guests we've ever had."

A slight smile crept onto Maker's face. "Oh?"

"Yes. I remember once—"

The captain's anecdote was cut off as Browing approached, saying, "Excuse me, Captain Henry. I wanted to speak with you before we left and didn't know if I'd get another opportunity."

If the captain didn't like being cut off mid-sentence, he hid it well. Instead, he merely asked, "What can I do for you?"

"A couple of things, actually," Browing replied. "First, I have been expecting several messages to come in via your secure communications channel. I would greatly appreciate it if you would secure those in the ship's vault when they arrive. Next..."

Browing then proceeded to make a series of special requests — demands, really — which would have tested Maker's patience had he been in Henry's shoes. The captain, however, merely acquiesced with respect to each. It once again brought to mind the fact Browing apparently had very powerful connections in the military and government. It seemed odd, then, that he should be willing to risk life and limb traipsing about the Fringe with Maker's motley crew, but Maker didn't spend much time dwelling on it.

Instead, he took advantage of the opportunity to look around while Captain Henry was engaged with Browing. Much to his surprise, he saw an active amount of mingling between his people and the officers who had accompanied Henry. He saw a man that he recognized as the ship's doctor conversing with Fierce. Adames and Wayne were chatting with the chief engineer of the *Mantis*. Even Kepler was being sociable and was currently speaking to Dr. Chantrey, who still had Erlen by her side. Maker would have been hard-pressed to explain why, but the sight of the two of them talking actually irritated him.

"Well," Henry said, "I should be getting back."

The comment drew Maker's attention, and at that moment he realized that Browing had not only stopped monopolizing the captain's time, but had actually walked away.

"Ah…understood, sir," Maker droned with a nod. Out of the corner of his eye, he saw something that made him uneasy: Kepler suddenly pointing a finger sharply in Erlen's direction while seeming to utter some heated words.

"However," Captain Henry went on, "we'll be seeing you again at the rendezvous point."

Maker frowned for a moment, unsure of what the captain meant. Then he remembered: the *Mantis* and the *Raider* were slated to meet up again in a few weeks (depending on how much success his squad had in the interim in locating the Vacra). He had been so focused on watching Kepler that it had momentarily slipped his mind.

"Yes, sir," Maker acknowledged. Out of the corner of his eye, he noticed Erlen suddenly pounce forward and then cough in the direction of Kepler's hand, which still pointed a finger accusingly at the Niotan. Kepler drew his hand back rapidly, as though it just touched something molten hot.

"I'm still not wild about the rendezvous point being in the Beyond," Henry continued. "But if that's where we have to meet, so be it. However, I'd prefer to be stationary out there for as short a time as possible."

"Got it," Maker said. "We need to show up on time." Although he had responded to Captain Henry's statement, his attention was almost fully focused on Kepler, who had suddenly started scratching the hand that Erlen had coughed on. It started mildly at first, with Kepler gently rubbing his other hand across the back of the one that had been pointing at Maker's alien companion. Within seconds, however, it had turned from rubbing into a forceful back-and-forth action involving fingernails.

"Precisely," the captain stated. "Don't be late."

At that moment, Kepler let out an odd, slightly anguished moan, and then began vigorously scratching not just his hand but all over his body. His hands were everywhere, disheveling his uniform as they raked across his chest, back, scalp and more. He jerked about wildly, like a man walking barefoot on hot coals while covered with ravenous army ants.

Needless to say, his antics drew the attention of everyone present, including Captain Henry. As the ship's doctor rushed over to Kepler to render aid, the captain turned back to Maker.

There was a stern look of disapproval on Henry's face as he stated, "On second thought, take as much time as you'd like."

## Chapter 14

The trip to Defalcator was mostly uneventful. Maker and almost everyone else on the *Raider* spent their time in a small space that served as a briefing room, being coached by Adames on what to expect and how to act.

"This isn't just the Fringe in terms of mankind's expansion," Adames explained. He stood at the end of a rectangular table, with the rest of the crew sitting and facing him. "It's also the outer edge in terms of civilized behavior."

"So if I bump into someone, I shouldn't say 'Pardon me'?" Wayne asked, his robot Jerry next to him.

"If you bump into someone, you need to look at them like you want to stick a fish fork in their eye," Adames replied.

"Even if it's your fault?"

"*Especially* if it's your fault."

The master sergeant's instructions didn't just cover behavior, but also extended towards how to dress.

"Collectively, you lot are too clean-cut," he said. "Well-groomed appearances, clothes pressed and unsullied, shoes unscuffed…"

"Maybe we're a group that takes pride in their appearance," Browing suggested.

"When's the last time you heard of a genteel band of pirates?" Adames asked rhetorically. "Fortunately, somebody on this team thought ahead."

It turned out that one of the containers Adames had brought aboard held, among other things, a fair amount of raider garb — enough to outfit everyone on board. In almost no time at all — and at Adames' insistence — they had all changed into their new apparel and returned to the briefing room.

Or rather, most of them had changed. Browing, not quite liking the cut of the outfit he was given, had insisted on wearing one of his own coats as an outer garment.

"No problem," Adames announced before stepping to a beverage dispenser and punching in the code for a cold coffee. He then took the cup holding the liquid and, after taking a large gulp, intentionally flicked the rest in Browing's direction. The liquid immediately began to soak in, staining his coat.

"Hey!" Browing howled, coming to his feet. "What the hell are you doing?"

"Making you look the part," Adames said flatly. "We're supposed to be brigands, not bean-counters. No one's going to be admiring the cut of your jib, but they're going to notice if you don't fit in, and where we're going, a clean coat is more conspicuous than a dirty one.

"That goes for the rest of you, too," Adames said, glancing around at the others as Browing harrumphed and took his seat. "So don't take those clothes off. Sleep in them. Roll around on the floor in them. Go through dusty crawlspaces with them on."

"What about when we take a shower?" Wayne asked.

"Don't," Adames replied.

"Don't take them off?"

"No, don't shower," Adames corrected. "Again, we're trying to convince anyone we come across that we're authentic buccaneers. We don't care about being the sweetest-smelling rose in the garden."

"Like that's going to happen," Diviana said, which was followed by much snickering.

"We'll get to Defalcator in about a day," Adames said. "It won't hurt anybody here to join the unwashed masses for that period of time or to smell a little ripe by the time we arrive. In fact, for some of you, it may even add some character." He looked directly at Browing as he made his last statement. Browing merely glowered at him.

With that, Adames called an end to the briefing. Everyone stood up and filed out, except for Maker, who remained behind as expected.

"Good job," Maker said sincerely when they were alone.

"Thanks," said Adames. "Did I miss anything?"

Maker shook his head. "Not as far as I can tell. Then again, this is outside my wheelhouse."

It was a very true statement. Adames was the only member of their team who had any real experience with the type of environment they were about to enter on Defalcator. That being the case, Maker had wisely deferred to the master sergeant and was allowing him to call the shots for this part of the mission.

"There, ah, there is something else I wanted to ask," Maker stated. "It's kind of a personal question."

"Say no more," Adames announced, raising his hand palm outward. "I already know what you're going to ask."

"You do?" Maker asked in surprise.

"Of course. And my advice is to just stop before you go blind."

"Funny," Maker said sarcastically as Adames chuckled loudly at his own joke.

"Sorry, Gant. I couldn't resist. But go on — what's your question?"

"It has to do with Dr. Chantrey."

Adames sobered almost immediately. "Oh?"

Maker cleared his throat. "Have you gotten the impression that there's something between us — me and her?"

"You mean something romantic?"

"Yeah."

Adames shook his head. "No, I haven't."

Inwardly, Maker sighed in relief. It was satisfying to know that not everybody was seeing something he wasn't as far as Chantrey was concerned.

"However," Adames added, "you do seem to look more in her direction when she's around. And your features occasionally approach something like a smile when you look at her — or as close as a grouch like you can manage, anyway. And, as long as Browing isn't in close proximity, your demeanor isn't quite as rigid."

"Huh?" Maker muttered, caught off guard.

"Look, I'm not saying that you're going to be voted 'Most Congenial,' but your personality is a bit warmer in her presence."

Maker stared at him for a moment, then blurted out, "What are you trying to say?"

"I'm not saying anything — simply making observations."

"I don't get any of that. Seems to me that I argue with her more than anything."

Adames laughed. "Yeah. That would make it the first time in history two people have tried to mask a mutual attraction by bickering with each other."

"You know what? Forget I asked. Go back to figuring out how to deal with your grimy pirate buddies once we're planet-side."

"Relax, Gant," Adames, said, still chuckling. "With any luck, your love life will probably be the biggest snag we hit on this mission."

Shaking his head, Maker marched away, walking towards his cabin.

The next day, they arrived at Defalcator — and hit their first snag.

## Chapter 15

"They're not letting us land," Maker announced after hastily assembling everyone in the briefing room.

"What?" Wayne blurted, plainly surprised. "Why not?"

"We're a new crew, a group they haven't dealt with before," Adames replied. Along with Maker, he stood addressing the group while everyone else sat. "That being the case, Defalcator's regs say we can't land on the planet for our first visit."

Browing snorted in derision. "Are you kidding? A planet of lawless felons has rules and regulations?"

"Even criminals eventually figure out that every organization — no matter what side of the law it operates on — has to have structure of some sort," Adames retorted. "Rules, guidelines, what have you. Otherwise it would be complete chaos."

"So what do we do?" asked Loyola.

"We land here," Adames announced, tapping his p-comp. A hologram appeared in the air next to him: an immense metallic cylinder connected by elongated spokes to a massive, slowly-spinning wheel, all superimposed against a black field dotted with twinkling points of light.

"It's a space station," Adames continued, stating the obvious. "We dock there and then take a shuttle down to the planet."

"Oh," interjected Dr. Chantrey, seemingly unimpressed by what appeared to be a simple solution to their dilemma. "Then there's no real problem."

Maker, catching himself still watching Chantrey even after she'd finished speaking, hurriedly looked away, brow creased. Angry with himself, he almost didn't notice that Adames was speaking again.

"There's no problem getting *down* to the surface," the master sergeant clarified. "I'm more concerned with *leaving* it."

Planck frowned (as did almost everyone else in the room). "What do you mean?"

"What he means," said Maker, "is that we probably don't want to be down on Defalcator and have our only ride home sitting unattended in space."

"Exactly," Adames agreed. "It's one thing to have our ship parked on the surface with us and handy if we need to make a quick getaway. It's something else to have it docked in orbit and practically inaccessible."

"So basically," Dr. Chantrey concluded, "we can't take the *Raider* down to the planet, but we don't want to leave it in space."

Snick leaned forward in his seat. "An interesting dilemma. How do we resolve it?"

"Easy," Diviana declared, crossing her arms as if bored. "Not everyone goes down to the planet. Someone has to stay with the ship."

"Especially if you want a ship to come back *to*," Browing chimed in. "This is a planet of criminals, after all."

"He's right," Maker said, although it pained him to have to agree with Browing on anything. "We need someone on board at all times to make sure the *Raider* is not just available but also secure."

"So someone gets to stay behind," Loyola summed up.

"Several someones," Adames clarified. "We're not going to leave one person to hold down the fort alone."

"So who, specifically, is actually going down to the surface?" Fierce asked.

"We're still working on that," Maker answered.

"I volunteer to go," Browing chimed in almost immediately.

"That's nice of you," Maker said flatly, "but there's another wrinkle here to consider: they're also not letting us take any firearms."

There were several looks of consternation at this last statement.

"Again," Maker went on, "we're new, and apparently they want to minimize our ability to kick up dust if it turns out that we're troublemakers."

"Which, in essence, we are," Dr. Chantrey said. "After all, we'll be the closest thing to law enforcement on a world of desperados."

"True," Maker acknowledged, "but that's not our job. We have a very specific mission out here in the Fringe, and that's to find the Vacra — not to bring justice and order to a lawless frontier."

With that, he dismissed the group, promising to let them all know soon who would be going to the planet surface and who would be staying on the *Raider*.

# EFFERUS

## Chapter 16

In the end, Maker — with input from Adames — essentially split their group in two: Browing, Planck, Dr. Chantrey, Diviana, and Fierce were given the task of staying with the ship. Going down to the planet would be Maker, Adames, Wayne, Snick, and Loyola. (As usual, it was presumed that Erlen would accompany Maker. Similarly, Wayne had wanted to bring Jerry, but changed his mind when Adames mentioned that the little robot might get stolen for scrap.)

Unsurprisingly, Browing was not happy with the arrangements. Cornering Maker alone after learning who would remain on the *Raider*, he wasn't shy about making his feelings known.

"I was given a specific directive regarding this mission," Browing stated. "I'm to work with you until we find the Vacra."

"As if I could forget," Maker intoned irritably.

"Then you don't get to cut me out of the mission just because you don't like me."

Maker sighed in annoyance. "This isn't cutting you out, Browing, or being done so I can stick my thumb in your eye. We're about to enter a hostile environment; the odds against us are already bad enough, and I'm not raising them by taking untested and untrained civilians — specifically, you, Chantrey, or Planck — into an adverse situation."

"And we're somehow a worse bet than Loyola and Wayne? A blind sniper who won't be allowed to carry a gun and a still-wet-behind-the-ears recruit?"

"I've made my selections," Maker said in a tone of finality. "So either play ball or find another team."

Browing glared at him for a moment, then stalked away. Obviously fuming, he brushed rudely past Adames, who had just started approaching Maker to go over their final checklist.

"What was that about?" Adames asked.

"He's upset about being picked last for the team," Maker replied, then spent a moment giving more specifics about Browing's complaint.

"Do you think he has a point?" the NCO asked. "About Wayne, at least? I mean, the kid *is* pretty green."

Maker spent a moment contemplating. Wayne was the youngest and least-experienced member of their team. Thus, there was no doubt that the young Marine was somewhat untested, but he had managed to keep a cool head during the prior mission.

"He's a Marine under my command," Maker finally said. "I've got to get him trained — get him seasoned — or he'll not only be useless to me, but probably get himself killed. And it'll be my fault because I tried to protect him instead of prepare him."

Adames merely nodded in understanding, apparently agreeing with him.

# EFFERUS

## Chapter 17

They docked at the space station above Defalcator without issue, sliding into a berth as directed by the station's computer system. Maker and those going with him to the surface quickly disembarked, accompanied by Dr. Chantrey and Browing. They were met almost immediately by a contingent of seven armed guards, almost all of whom held rifles loosely in their hands.

One of the guards — an attractive blonde with a tattoo of a sunburst around her right eye — stepped forward.

"I'm Commander Dallen," she announced without preamble. "Which of you is in charge?"

"That would be me," Adames answered, giving her a glowing smile.

"This way," she said, then turned and began marching away, seemingly unimpressed by the NCO's attempt at charm.

Adames quickly fell into step beside her, followed by the others from the *Raider*. The remaining six guards took up positions around them: a pair to the left, a pair to the right, and a pair at the rear. Maker, walking directly behind Adames and with Erlen padding along beside him, didn't bother glancing back at their ship but knew that those remaining on board — Fierce, Diviana, and Planck — were watching.

Commander Dallen spoke as they walked, not taking her eyes off their route. "We don't have many rules here, but the ones we have we expect you to obey. In fact, you probably already know everything I'm about to say, but I'm going to tell you anyway so that there's no pleading ignorance if something untoward happens. Now, there are seven of you going down to the planet—"

"Five," Adames interjected. "Not counting our mascot." He nodded in Erlen's direction.

Dallen looked at him oddly, but didn't say anything or break stride. Adames allowed one corner of his mouth to slide up into a smile, as he knew what she must be thinking.

Although only five of them were going down to the planet, seven of their crew were currently present. It implied that Adames knew something of the space station's security protocols. In short, if things went sideways with Dallen's team for some reason, the group from the *Raider* wasn't going to be outnumbered; it would be man-to-man combat.

From the look she gave Adames, all of this must have flitted through Dallen's mind. A moment later, however, she turned her eyes back to their route and resumed speaking.

"As I was saying," she continued as they entered a long corridor, "we expect you and your people to comply with the rules. First and foremost, your ship stays docked at the station. When you leave, you fly along the flight path we direct until you reach open space and can activate your jump drive. Deviate from the designated route or try to jump early and we'll blast you to bits."

Adames nodded in understanding, which Dallen apparently noted with her peripheral vision and then went on. "No firearms. Guns of all types are strictly forbidden to you people on this excursion. Also, no explosives. In addition…"

The security commander continued speaking, laying out the strictures that would govern any planet-side visit as they tromped through the station, with Adames occasionally giving a nod or grunt of acknowledgment in response to something she said and Maker listening intently as he walked behind them. Needless to say, nothing that Dallen mentioned was new to them. However, she must have given the same speech a thousand times before, because she timed the end of it to perfectly coincide with arriving at what was apparently their destination: a modest-sized room at the end of a long passageway.

Erlen gave a soft growl as they crossed the threshold and entered, the sound intended as a heads-up to Maker. On his part, Maker gently scratched behind the Niotan's ears, indicating that he had gotten the message. At the same time, he glanced around the room.

The place was fairly nondescript: four white walls that came together in a square-shaped configuration. A line of computer equipment and monitors rested along one of them. Beyond that, however, the room was empty. The only other notable feature was a door set in the wall directly across from the one through which they had entered. Mentally, Maker marked it as the exit.

Dallen and her security team stepped towards the computer equipment.

"Over there," she said to no one in particular, indicating the wall opposite of where she and her team were standing. Maker and his people moved to obey without a word.

"Who are the two that are staying?" Dallen asked a moment later. Adames indicated Chantrey and Browing, and Dallen ordered them into a corner of the room. At the same time, two of the security detail moved into position to cover the two civilians. In fact, Maker couldn't help but notice that the entire security team from the space station now seemed to be gripping their weapons in a more business-like manner as Dallen turned her attention to the computer equipment and hit a few buttons on a nearby keyboard. She then glanced at one of the monitors and studied it as several lines of data suddenly appeared. After a few seconds, she spun back towards Maker's group.

"You," she said, indicating Wayne. "And you." This time she pointed to Adames.

Without being told, Wayne and Adames stepped forward. One of the guards went to Wayne and began to pat him down. A moment later, he removed a large Bowie knife from a sheath at the young Marine's waist. The guard handed the weapon to Dallen, who spent a moment examining it.

"Blades aren't on your list of restricted items," Adames volunteered.

"You're right," she agreed. "Blades aren't."

As she spoke, a gunsight suddenly sprang up from a hidden compartment at the top of the knife's handle while a trigger popped out beneath it. Clearly, Dallen had found the secret button that activated the knife-cum-gun. She handed the weapon to one of her subordinates and then stepped in front of Adames.

"Hands," Dallen said matter-of-factly.

In compliance, Adames raised his hands into the air. Dallen then pulled the waistband of his pants toward her and reached her hand down the front of his trousers.

"Not that I'm complaining," Adames said a moment later with a satisfied grin on his face, "but aren't you even going to buy me dinner first?"

Dallen ignored him, and a few seconds later she withdrew her hand. In it, she now held a small tubular object that Maker recognized as a modified firearm.

"Gee," Adames muttered in faux surprise. "How'd that get in there?"

As before, Dallen didn't say anything; she merely gave the weapon to one of the other guards and then looked over Maker's team, her eyes narrowing slightly as she stared at each of them in turn.

Maker kept his own face solemn. It was plainly evident that he and his people had been scanned as they entered the room — something that Erlen had picked up on. (In addition, the fact that security had decided to search the only two members of Maker's squad carrying firearms was also a dead giveaway.) However, it was a course of action that had been expected.

"They're going to scan and search us," Adames had said before they left the *Raider*. "We need to give them something to find."

Although there was a chance that trying to smuggle weapons down to Defalcator might get them banned before they ever set foot on the planet, Adames had felt it was worth the risk.

"It's what real brigands would do," he'd stated. "It'll look more suspicious if we don't even try."

And so, with Maker's blessing, Adames had given the gun-knife to Wayne and had tried to smuggle the smaller weapon (which was composed of a special metal and should have been concealed by body heat) in his pants. Neither stratagem had worked, but they hadn't really been expected to. Now, of course, everything depended on what Dallen decided to do.

The security commander continued eyeing them for a few seconds, then uttered in a loud voice, "This is Commander Dallen. Defalcator Three Echo."

"Passcode recognized, Commander," said a male voice that seemed to emanate from the ceiling — obviously an intercom system of some sort. "Your guests are cleared to take the shuttle planet-side."

"Acknowledged," the commander replied. At the same time, there was an audible click and the exit door slid open.

"Hey, Dallen," said the voice, now sounding less formal. "Come across anything interesting this time?"

Dallen's gaze went from the firearm she'd taken from Adames to the front of the NCO's pants, and then to his face. "Nothing to get excited about," she deadpanned.

## Chapter 18

After the search of Wayne and Adames, Maker's crew only had one other bump in the road with respect to getting to the planet surface: Dallen refused to allow Erlen to accompany them.

"Our sensors can't scan or classify this beast," the security commander said. "That being the case, it stays on the station. In fact, it's confined to your ship."

Erlen, seeming to understand that the conversation was about him (and not in a positive way), produced an angry rumbling in his throat. Aside from Dallen, all of the station security personnel suddenly had their weapons at the ready.

"It's okay," Maker quickly announced, raising his hands in an attempt to defuse the situation. "It's okay."

He knelt down next to the Niotan and, looking his alien companion in the eye, said, "Buddy, I'm going to need you to wait for me on the ship."

Erlen whined in a bit of a melancholy fashion. However, he didn't need words for Maker to understand the sentiment: the two had rarely been separated since Erlen was a newborn, and the Niotan didn't like that it was happening now.

Maker nodded his head. "I know, I know. But I'll be back as soon as possible."

Erlen stared at him for a moment, then leaned forward and licked the side of his face. Maker laughed, then stood and turned to Dallen.

"It's fine now," he assured the commander. "I'll just hand him off to my comrades" — he tilted his chin towards Browing and Chantrey — "and they'll take him back and confine him to our ship."

There was a moment of hesitation, and then Dallen — still looking worried — gave an almost imperceptible nod of her head. Her squad immediately lowered their weapons, and Maker (with Erlen in his wake) walked to over to the corner where Chantrey and Browing were standing.

"Can you look after him for me?" Maker asked Chantrey, who had undoubtedly heard most (if not all) of what he'd just said.

"Of course," she answered. Noting that Maker was patting the Niotan's head, she reached down to do the same thing, and took the opportunity to quickly but surreptitiously take Maker's hand and give it a gentle squeeze.

The action caught Maker unprepared, but he recovered quickly. Kneeling down again and with his back to the security guards, he moved his hand to the Niotan's nose and scratched it gently, saying, "Now be good, and don't give the doctor here any trouble."

In reply, Erlen made an odd noise, like a mixture of a cough and a growl and inconspicuously spat something into Maker's hand. Tearing a page from Adames' playbook, Maker covertly slid the object down the front of his pants as he rose and then walked back to join the rest of his squad that would be going planet-side.

"We good?" Adames asked him. Upon getting a nod in response, the NCO turned to Dallen. "Well?"

The security commander looked as though she were debating something internally for a second, then spoke to the two guards who had been covering Browing and Chantrey.

"Escort those two — and that animal — back to their ship," she commanded. "Assuming there are no issues, we'll send the confiscated weapons back to them later."

As the two guards moved to obey, Dallen motioned everyone towards the exit, which opened onto another passageway. Ultimately, the corridor terminated at an elevator, which went directly to the shuttle landing bay. Ten minutes after arriving there, Maker and his team were headed down to Defalcator.

# EFFERUS

## Chapter 19

The trip to the planet's surface was fairly brief. Inside the shuttle, conversation among Maker's team was dominated by Wayne, who spoke in bold and brazen terms of the things he anticipated doing at some of Defalcator's most notorious brothels, with the others occasionally interjecting humorous comments.

Of course, it was all manufactured dialogue, meant to provide additional support to their cover story should anyone be listening (which was probably the case). Like just about everything thus far, this had been something Adames had insisted on for authenticity.

"It's no different than Marines getting shore leave after a long deployment," Adames had said. "You'd expect them to be loud and boisterous. If we sit there silently like stone gargoyles, it won't seem natural."

Reflecting on that comment, Maker smiled as he listened not just to Wayne's anticipated escapades, but the exchanges between others around them. Including his own people, there were about thirty passengers on the shuttle, and from what he could catch of the other conversations, Adames had once again been right. Although he didn't need additional confirmation, it was further validation of his initial decision to have Adames on his team. The man was more than competent as an NCO, but on this particular mission he had already proven he was worth his weight in gold.

Maker's thoughts were interrupted by the sound of raised voices nearby. As often happened, two other groups of passengers had gotten into a heated exchange of words, and the situation had escalated to the point where a number of people were on their feet and weapons (specifically, blades) were being drawn. However, before any actual violence could commence, a voice resonated through the cabin.

"Sit down, all of you," came a terse command from the front of the shuttle. Maker looked and saw the co-pilot of the shuttle standing in the doorway of the cockpit with a raised gun in his hand. "Whatever issues you've got, save them until you've set foot on the ground. If you can't do that, then you can try resolving them on the other side of the airlock."

The co-pilot had a stern look on his face, and it was clear that he wasn't making an idle threat. The two groups of combatants all took their seats, but there was tension in the air for the remainder of the ride.

\*\*\*\*\*\*\*\*\*\*\*\*\*\*\*\*\*\*\*\*\*\*\*\*\*\*\*\*\*\*\*\*\*\*\*\*\*\*\*\*\*\*\*\*\*\*

After reaching the landing port on the planet's surface, the passengers quickly disembarked. To no one's great surprise, a fight broke out almost immediately between the two parties that had quarreled on the shuttle. Maker and his people quickly put some distance between themselves and the melee — particularly after they saw what appeared to be a security detail rushing to the area. A few minutes later, they were outside the port proper.

Looking around, Maker noted that they were close to — but not exactly in — the center of a large city. Tall towers stretched up into the sky, while hovercraft whizzed through the air. Not far away, winking neon signs advertised everything from hotels to restaurants to exotic encounters — all trying to get the attention of visitors leaving the landing port.

"What now?" Loyola asked, directing her question at Adames.

"Now I reach out to our contact and see when he's available to meet," the NCO replied. "I also need to look into getting us a hotel room and weapons."

"Weapons?" Snick repeated. "You mean guns? Isn't that a violation of the rules governing our visit?"

"Yes," Adames agreed, "but it's what a real band of smugglers would do under these circumstances. Besides, you don't want to spend too much time in a place like this without a gun within reach. It's just not a smart practice."

"That reminds me," Maker whispered to Loyola, getting her attention as Adames continued speaking. He reached into the front of his pants, causing Loyola to raise an eyebrow in curiosity (although the effect was muted by the lenses she wore). A second later, she grinned as she saw what he pulled out: a small firearm, which he held out to her.

"How...?" she began as she took the gun from him. "Where did you...?"

Maker chuckled. "Sleight of hand is one of my many secondary skills."

In truth (and unbeknownst to most of his crew), Erlen actually had a second stomach, which was excellent for smuggling — when necessary — because, as demonstrated at the space station, the Niotan couldn't be scanned. The plan had originally been to use Erlen to make sure they arrived on Defalcator with at least one gun. When Commander Dallen had tossed a monkey wrench into those plans, Erlen had coughed up the weapon into Maker's hands. Fortunately at the time, Maker had already been scanned for firearms, and apparently space station security didn't embrace the concept of continuous monitoring.

Giving the gun to Loyola at this juncture put his initial plan for the weapon back on track. She was unquestionably the best shot in their crew (no one else was even close), so putting it in her hands was the most sensible decision — despite the fact that he would undoubtedly feel more comfortable with a firearm of his own. That thought turned his mind back to what Adames had mentioned about trying to get them weapons, and he focused his attention on what the NCO was now saying.

"As to hotel rooms, it's important to realize that not all lodging is the same," Adames stated. "So, while there are rooms available nearby" — he motioned towards some of the neon signs — "we need to find something that suits our needs."

"So we've got some running around to do," Wayne summarized.

"Not *we*," Adames corrected. "*Me*. Our contact may get nervous if we show up in full force. Likewise with respect to anyone who might be willing to provide us with guns."

"And what do the rest of us do while you're off running errands?" Loyola asked.

Adames shrugged. "Whatever freebooters do when they have some down time. Go to a strip club, get in a bar fight, get drunk…"

"Got it," Maker said. "When and where do we meet back up?"

Adames glanced around for a moment, his eyes taking in the various venues around them.

"How about over there?" he said after a moment. He gestured towards a nearby bar that, according to an oversized billboard, was known as the Bandit's Cave. "Two hours from now."

"Sounds fine," Maker replied. "See you in two."

EFFERUS

## Chapter 20

The Bandit's Cave had an ambience that suited its name: dark, dank, and foreboding. The place was half-empty at the moment, so Maker and his squad found an empty, circular booth near a corner and sat.

Within a few minutes, a waitress came by to take their drink order. She was human, but obviously a gene-job of some sort, as she had four arms. While it suited her current occupation, Maker couldn't help but wonder what she had originally been designed for.

"What'll you have?" asked the waitress, interrupting Maker's thoughts.

"What do you suggest?" Maker shot back at her, noting that her features were actually quite comely.

The waitress winked at him. "Depends on what you're in the mood for, handsome."

Maker smiled. "Nothing too heavy or intense."

"So, something casual," the waitress intoned coyly. "That can be arranged."

She then began reciting a long list of available beverages that they could order. In the end, Maker chose a concoction that was imbued with lots of fruit flavor but light on alcohol content. In fact, he ordered the same drink for their entire table, intent on making sure his people stayed sharp for anything that might come later.

"I'll bring these out as soon as possible," the waitress said after he finished ordering. "And I'll be around if you want something more later." She then smiled coquettishly and walked away, heading towards a bar on the other side of the room.

"What was *that*?" asked Loyola when the waitress was out of earshot, looking pointedly at Maker.

"What was what?" he replied innocently.

"You and our waitress flirting with each other," she stated.

Maker's eyebrows went up in surprise. "You call that flirting?"

"Blatantly," Loyola declared without hesitation.

"Blatantly?" Maker repeated, then looked at the other two members of their group as if to solicit their opinions.

"It *was* rather open and notorious," Snick added.

Before Maker could comment on that last statement, Wayne chimed in.

"In defense of our leader's allegedly flirtatious behavior," the young Marine said, "it's probably worth noting that the waitress is a vamp — genetically engineered to flirt with and seduce people, usually for purposes of corporate espionage or the like. Having four arms allows her to stimulate multiple erogenous zones simul—"

"We get it," Maker interrupted, making it clear that Wayne didn't need to provide any explicit details.

"So what's she doing here?" Loyola asked.

"Probably using her charms to get men to buy drinks," Maker said.

"Well, don't worry — we won't tell Dr. Chantrey that your eye wandered a little bit," Loyola assured him, getting a snicker out of Wayne in the process.

"Let's just nurse these drinks as long as possible," Maker muttered, suddenly sobered by the comment about Chantrey.

\*\*\*\*\*\*\*\*\*\*\*\*\*\*\*\*\*\*\*\*\*\*\*\*\*\*\*\*\*\*\*\*\*\*\*\*\*\*\*\*\*\*\*\*\*\*

They had been at the Bandit's Cave for a little less than an hour and had just received their second round of drinks when Maker started to get the odd sensation of being watched. There were eyes on him; he was sure of it. It wasn't anything he could prove with empirical evidence — just an innate sense of being observed, an instinct honed by numerous encounters on the battlefield.

There were more patrons present than when they'd arrived, but the place was still noticeably below full capacity. Maker slowly but subtly began scanning the faces of those present, not quite sure what he was looking for, but —

*There!*

On the opposite side of the room, sitting on a stool at the bar, was a man wearing a brown duster. He was blatantly staring at Maker. However, as soon as their eyes met and it became clear that Maker was aware of the scrutiny he was being given, the man glanced away. A second later, however, the fellow looked back his way, and Maker saw some glint of recognition light in the man's eyes. More to the point, some sort of internal conflict must have resolved itself, because the fellow stood up and began walking towards Maker's table.

Standing up, he was a little shorter than Maker had anticipated. He was also younger — somewhere in his mid-twenties — with sandy hair. Finally, he walked with a slight limp.

The man's face was vaguely familiar, but Maker couldn't really place him. Somewhat wary, he tapped a forefinger on the table to get his companions' attention, then inconspicuously pointed at the man headed their way. Snick, who — along with Maker — was seated on the outside of their table, subtly shifted position, plainly readying himself to spring into action should anything untoward happen.

The fellow stopped when he was a few feet from their table. "Sergeant Maker?" he said, almost timidly.

Maker kept his face impassive, but mentally he let out a despondent sigh. It seemed his infamy as the sole survivor of the *Orpheus Moon* had reached even the Fringe. He couldn't think of any other reason why this man would know who he was.

"Sorry," Maker said after a moment. "I think you've got the wrong guy."

"You don't remember me?" the young man asked, acting as if Maker hadn't spoken. "E-2 Evan Gallico? You saved my life back on Pyrrhus V."

Maker frowned. He remembered Pyrrhus V — a hellish backwater that ended up being the site of a frenzied battle for reasons that were never made clear. (The best he'd been able to discern was that it had something to do with mineral rights.)

"My unit was pinned down and running out of ammo," Gallico continued. "We all thought we were dead meat until your squad swooped in and hauled our butts out of the fire."

Gallico's words tickled something at the back of Maker's brain, making half-forgotten memories stir.

"You lost an arm or something," Maker said, frowning in concentration.

"Leg," Gallico corrected, tapping his right thigh and smiling, plainly happy to be remembered. "Probably would have lost more than that if it weren't for you."

Gallico grabbed an empty chair from a nearby table and — without waiting for an invitation — placed it at Maker's table with the rear of it facing the booth and then sat down in it backwards.

"I was somewhat in shock from losing my leg," Gallico went on, "and then suddenly you were standing over me. I remember you telling me that I'd be okay, which sounded crazy with gunfire and explosions going on all around us. Then you slapped some cryo-film on me to put me in stasis, and the next thing I knew I was in the infirmary."

"So they gave you a new leg?" Wayne asked, jumping into the conversation.

"A cybernetic one," Gallico replied. "Pyrrhus V never had a great deal of reserves of any fashion, so they didn't really have the resources to supply me with a re-grown limb. By the time I reached a place where I could get one, I'd gotten used to it.

"Anyway," Gallico continued, turning back to Maker, "I never got to thank the Marine who saved my life, but I never forgot his face and I've always remembered his rank and the name tag on his uniform: Maker."

"I go by Baker now," Maker retorted almost immediately, feeling a little embarrassed.

"Of course," Gallico said, then lowered his eyes. "I, um… I heard about what happened to you. Being forced out of the service, I mean. That wasn't right."

Maker shrugged. "It's ancient history now."

"Still doesn't make it right," Gallico stressed again. "Anyway, what are you doing out here in the Fringe?"

"Trying to stay alive, like everyone else," Maker replied. "After practically a lifetime in the Marines, I really wasn't suited for civilian work, and I didn't really feel complete without a gun in my hand."

Although it was part of his cover story, Maker said the words with ease, mostly because they were true to a certain extent. Being a Marine was in his blood, something that would never be rooted out.

Gallico simply nodded at Maker's statement. "I understand. Oddly enough, a lot of ex-military end up on this side of the fence for the same reason."

"And you?" Loyola interjected.

"Physical therapy and rehab took longer than expected. By the time I was back on my feet, so to speak, my commitment was done and the military passed on letting me reenlist. I kind of drifted, looking for a place where I fit in, and somehow ended up he—"

A hardy clap on his shoulder cut off Gallico's words. He glanced up and over his shoulder to see who had interrupted him, then hastily looked back down at the tabletop, eyes darting about nervously.

"Gally, who're your friends?"

The speaker was a big, burly fellow with grizzled features, punctuated by a five o'clock shadow. He had dark hair that was just starting to go gray, but his bulky physique made it clear that it would be a mistake to consider him past his prime. Standing directly behind Gallico, he kept his two meaty hands parked solidly on the young man's shoulders, like a farmer preparing to wring a chicken's neck.

All in all, the new arrival gave off a dangerous vibe. In addition, he had roughly half-a-dozen companions with him, standing to his rear. Not to put too fine a point on it, Maker wasn't particularly wild about the odds at the moment; he cast a subtle glance at his squad.

From the look in his eyes, it was clear that Snick was ready for anything. She didn't have eyes that could be read, but Loyola gave a barely noticeable nod. Wayne, however, appeared to be in over his head, and the look on his face telegraphed the fact that he was still trying to read the situation. *Maybe he* was *too green for this type of mission…*

"I asked you a question, Gally," the big man said. Although there was a smile on his face, his tone made it clear that he didn't like having to repeat himself.

Gallico suddenly came to his feet, shrugging off the big man's hands and turning to face the newcomers.

"Nobody really, Rip," Gallico stressed. "Just somebody I thought I recognized from the Marines."

The big fellow — Rip — didn't say anything; he just kept staring at Gallico, who appeared to get more nervous as the seconds ticked by. (It probably didn't help that Rip let his hand rest on the butt of a gun that was tucked into the waist of his pants.)

Finally Gallico sighed, then waved a hand in Maker's direction. "This is Sergeant Maker — I mean, Baker. He served in the Corps."

"Maker?" Rip said, picking up on Gallico's Freudian slip. "*The* Maker? The one that you said saved your hide?"

Gallico, eyes downcast, muttered, "Yeah, that's him."

Rip turned his head towards Maker. "I gotta tell ya, the kid here must have told the story at least ten times to anybody who'd listen about what you did for him. It's sorta his claim to fame: there's a lot of people who were

91

killed by Maniac Maker, but not a lot who can say they were *saved* by him."

"Yeah," Maker said sarcastically. "I was batting a thousand until Gallico here actually pulled through."

Rip laughed. "That's funny. From the stories I've heard, I never gathered that you had much of a sense of humor. However, with a nickname like 'Madman Maker,' I did get the impression you'd be taller."

Maker's eyes narrowed. Twice now Rip had used unflattering appellations to address him. It implied something, which Maker decided to address head-on.

"I take it you had friends on the *Orpheus Moon*?" Maker asked.

"You mean that ship's crew you killed?" Rip responded, then shook his head. "Nah, I don't give a damn about a boatload of soldiers biting the dust." He placed a foot on the chair Gallico had vacated, and then leaned forward, resting his elbow on his knee. "But what I *do* care about is the fact that you're sitting at our table."

"Come on, Rip," Gallico said, sounding a bit anxious. "There's plenty of empty seats here, and you guys usually sit at the back."

Rip gave him an evil glare. "Well, maybe we like *this* table today."

The atmosphere was noticeably tense. Gallico gulped, looking unsure of himself. Before things could escalate, Maker spoke up.

"It's fine," he said. "We'll move."

Maker started to come to his feet, but he'd barely shifted his weight before Rip put up a hand, palm outward in his direction, indicating that he should stop.

"I'm afraid that's not good enough," Rip stated. "See, you've already tainted the booth and our mood just by sitting here. You can't wipe away that stain just by moving to another seat."

"Fine," Maker said. "We'll leave."

Rip shook his head. "And how will that look? People will say that the notorious Madman Maker sat in my booth, and then thumbed his nose at me by walking out without so much as a by-your-leave. I have a reputation to consider, after all."

Maker nodded solemnly. Now he understood: this fellow Rip was looking to bolster his own notoriety by besting the infamous Maniac Maker in some way. It put Maker in mind of the Wild West back on Old Earth, when people often tried to make a name for themselves by outdrawing famous (or infamous) gunslingers.

*Some things never change…*

Maker took one last stab at diplomacy. "Look, why don't my people and I just leave? Then you can tell everybody that you challenged us and we backed down."

"Not good enough," Rip replied. "You can always try to spin it and say it was a staring contest and I was the one who blinked first."

Maker looked Rip in the eye. "So there's no way we can leave here without things getting messy?"

Rip smiled. "Unfortunately, 'messy' is our motto to—"

His words were cut off as Snick, following an inconspicuous gesture from Maker, shot out a foot that kicked the chair out from under the big man. Rip lurched forward, off-balance. At the same time — almost faster than seemed possible — Snick slid out of the booth and, before Rip could recover, put a hand behind the larger man's neck and smashed his face down fiercely onto the edge of the table. He followed this up with a knee to the jaw that sent Rip sprawling.

For a moment, the large man lay on the floor, clearly dazed and moaning gently. Frankly speaking, considering the speed and force of Snick's attack, Maker was surprised that the man was even conscious: his nose looked like a squashed tomato, and blood was starting to drip from a corner of his mouth.

Maker looked towards Rip's companions, readying himself should they try anything. However, he seemed to be worrying for nothing; they were so transfixed by what had happened to their leader that none of them had moved. (Apparently they had rarely, if ever, seen their boss knocked on his keister.)

Catching movement with his peripheral vision, Maker turned back to Rip. Much to his amazement, the fellow seemed to be coming back around. The man's eyes seemed to focus, but his pupils were dilated to an incredible degree. Maker frowned, not liking what this indicated.

*Some kind of stim-chem*, Maker realized. *Internally and automatically injected.*

Maker could quote a laundry list of drugs and stimulants that could keep you conscious when you should pass out. Aside from giving him pupils the size of wagon wheels, whatever Rip was on probably had the additional benefit of deadening nerve endings so he couldn't feel pain, among other things. As if in confirmation of this, Rip suddenly propped himself up on one elbow, rolled his head to the side, and then spat out two teeth, along with a mass of blood and ensanguined phlegm.

Rip swiveled his head towards Snick, glowering and plainly furious. Snarling in anger, his hand shot toward the gun at his waist. Before he could reach it, however, a dainty foot in a high-heeled shoe came down on Rip's wrist, effectively pinning it to his stomach although it didn't break the skin.

It was the waitress. She stood there, holding a plasma pistol loosely in one hand and pointed towards the ground. In two of her other hands, she held a laser SMG; from the way she cradled it, Maker had no doubt that she knew how to use the sub-machine gun, which she kept pointed in the direction of Rip's crew. (Oddly enough, in her fourth hand she still held a tray of drinks.)

"You know the rules, Rip," said the waitress. "No gunplay in here. You can brawl all you want, but the day you shoot a firearm in the Cave will be your last."

Rip, acting almost as if he hadn't heard her, grunted and tried to go for his gun with his free hand. In response, the waitress pointed the plasma pistol directly at his face.

"You don't want to test me, Rip," she said menacingly. "Don't think that because we've had some good times in the past that I have a soft spot for a scumbag like you. I'm a vamp and genetically driven to engage in certain acts, but it doesn't mean I'm actually fond of the people I'm doing them with. I will blow your head clean off, mow down those deviants who lick your boots, and not spill a drink in the process."

Looking at the waitress now, Maker saw almost no resemblance to the coy woman who had flirted with him earlier. She clearly meant business, and apparently Rip realized it as well, because he hadn't moved from his position on the floor.

"So, do we understand each other?" the waitress asked the big man. For a moment, it wasn't clear that he'd heard her, but then he slowly nodded his head. "Good. I'm glad to see that whatever you're jacked up on hasn't interfered with your ability to understand simple sentences."

The waitress lowered her gun, at the same time lifting her foot from Rip's wrist.

"Carry on," she said as she turned and sashayed away, batting her eyes at Maker in the process.

Unsurprisingly, all other activity in the bar had come to a halt the moment Snick had sent Rip to the floor. Needless to say, all eyes were now on the waitress as she seemingly went back to her regular duties.

Rip, somehow breaking the spell the waitress had cast on the room, suddenly snapped his head towards his companions.

"What are you *bamdweeds* waiting on?!" He bellowed, then inclined his head in the direction of Maker's group. "Get 'em!"

A moment later, fists were flying everywhere.

## Chapter 21

"You do understand," Adames said in a bemused voice, "that when I said to get into a bar fight, I was being facetious. I didn't literally mean to get into a bar fight."

"Now you tell us," Maker replied in tongue-in-cheek fashion, getting chuckles from the rest of their team.

They were currently in a hotel room, which Adames had obtained while he was out. He had shown up at the rendezvous point earlier than expected — just a few minutes after Rip had ordered his people to attack Maker's squad — only to walk into a full-blown melee, with every patron of the bar involved. Although he had immediately thrown himself into the fray, the NCO had been mainly focused on getting his team members to stop brawling and leave. Now, half an hour later, they were clustered in the living area of a two-bedroom suite, licking their wounds.

"You're lucky you happened to be at the Cave," Adames said. "At some other place, I might have arrived to find you full of holes, but you picked a bar that doesn't allow gunplay."

"I take it that's unusual," Snick surmised, rubbing the back of his head where someone had smashed a bottle.

The NCO shrugged. "Depends. If customers think they're less likely to be gunned down, they might patronize a place more. So in that sense it's good for business and a lot of places have rules along those lines. On the flip side, some prefer an 'anything goes' environment."

"In other words," Wayne concluded, gingerly touching an eye that was starting to darken, "if someone asks you to meet them somewhere, the location can be seen as a barometer of their intent."

"That's probably a fair assessment," Adames acknowledged. "By the way, you did good back there."

"Yes — very impressive," Snick agreed with a nod. "And it was your first fight, correct?"

"If you don't count being tossed into a ring with a monster," Wayne muttered, referring to an encounter during their previous mission, when Maker had saved his life. "I guess all that training we did paid off."

"Indeed," Snick said, beaming at Wayne like a proud father. Maker had put Snick in charge of instructing the rest of their group in martial arts, and this had been the first real test of his "students." From the look on his face and his demeanor, it was safe to assume that they had all passed with flying colors.

"Still," Wayne replied, "it was a little harrowing. And that guy Rip that the el-tee took on — I don't think I've ever seen anyone that pumped up on drugs."

"Yeah," Loyola added, speaking through a split lip. "No offense, el-tee, but I was certain he was going to tear your head off. Somehow, though, you took him down without getting so much as a scratch."

"That's just my stupid Marine training," Maker countered. "Per the Corps manual, the only person allowed to tear your head off is your commanding officer — although most times they prefer to chew your rear off instead."

This brought another round of laughter from his troops, but inside Maker felt a twinge of guilt. All of his people had gotten injured in the altercation at the Cave.

Even Adames (who, as a Johnny-come-lately, had missed the worst of the fracas) had taken a fist to the jaw, which was slightly swollen now.

It wasn't as if Maker had somehow luckily dodged every kick, punch, or object thrown his way. In truth, Rip — whom Maker had taken on because he appeared to be the most dangerous combatant — had landed one or two solid shots to the body and face. However, Maker had barely felt the blows, and hadn't seemed to suffer any of the usual effects from being belted and jabbed multiple times: no bleeding, no bruising, no swelling.

That said, he didn't really notice his lack of trauma until they'd exited the Cave, at which point — upon seeing his companions' assorted injuries — he sensed something was amiss. More to the point, he immediately realized *why* he wasn't as black-and-blue as his subordinates: Erlen.

The Niotan was a living laboratory, a walking chemical plant with the ability to create just about any element, drug, or the like. Obviously, when he had licked Maker back on the space station, Erlen had put some kind of chemical or stimulant on his skin, which had then been absorbed into Maker's system. Whatever it was, it had apparently numbed Maker to almost all pain and probably ramped up his healing factor exponentially. In short, in his own way, Maker had probably been as jacked up as Rip — perhaps even more so.

Speaking of the big man, Maker reflected for a moment on their scuffle. It had been an odd dance, to say the least. Despite his blatantly greater size and strength, Rip hadn't been able to overpower Maker because of what the Niotan had done. On his part, despite being the more talented fighter, Maker hadn't been able to obtain the upper hand; every time he gained an advantage (such as landing a debilitating blow), Rip's auto-injected stims would kick in, giving the man fresh legs.

But the human body can only take so much stimulation of that sort, and Rip had probably received more chems within a shorter period than he'd ever experienced before. As a result, his eyes had suddenly fluttered as he was telegraphing a right hook he was about to throw at Maker, and then he'd simply keeled over. (And at that point, Adames had shown up, screaming at Maker and the others that they needed to leave.)

Thankfully, none of his people had been seriously injured during the ruckus at the Cave. More importantly, they had all taken stim shots since arriving at the hotel room. In essence, they would probably be as good as new within a few hours — certainly within a day. Nevertheless, Maker's conscience still ate at him over what had happened.

It wasn't the first time that Erlen's special abilities had given Maker an advantage; in fact, the Niotan's talents had saved his life on more than one occasion. However, there was still the fact that he'd never been at real risk of injury — even if that info had been unbeknownst to him — while his people had, and it bothered him. Basically, Maker felt that a leader should be willing to accept the same hazards and chance of harm as those under his command.

*Oh well, no use dwelling on it now.*

Maker turned to Adames. "How'd everything else go?"

"Well enough," Adames answered. "I reached out to our contact and he says he's got some information for us. Also, he knows a guy who can get us some guns."

"Great," Maker said. "Did our contact say when he could meet with us?"

Adames nodded. "Any time."

"Then let's go."

# EFFERUS

## Chapter 22

Half an hour later, Maker and Adames found themselves standing before an eight-by-twelve foot door made of reinforced steel. It was the entry to a spacious and windowless warehouse-style building — one of several such structures in the vicinity and apparently the base of operations for their contact, a man called Shoal.

Looking the building over, Maker couldn't help but note that the place was large enough to house a platoon. That was bad news for him and Adames, should the upcoming meeting become adversarial for some reason; the rest of their group was back in the hotel room.

According to Adames, Shoal had limited the number of visitors to two. It was a given that the NCO would have to be part of the team meeting their contact, and Maker — as the actual mission leader — naturally had to be included.

While Maker would have preferred keeping his group together, the real dilemma in splitting the team up had to do with resources — specifically, the gun he had passed to Loyola earlier. It was their only firearm at the moment, and it was a toss-up as to whether the wiser course of action was taking it with him and Adames to their powwow with Shoal, or leaving it with Loyola, Snick, and Wayne. (In retrospect, Maker wished he had taken the opportunity during the dustup at the Cave to relieve Rip of his weapon, but Adames had hustled them out so fast that he didn't have time.)

Weighing all the pros and cons, the three staying behind were probably in the safest position. The hotel Adames had chosen was one of the most secure on the

102

planet, as evidenced by the fact that the entry to their suite consisted of a renovated blast door, and all windows were made of tempered glass with special properties. On the other hand, he and Adames could very well be walking into a trap of some sort, and going into that situation without a firearm seemed like a very bad idea.

In the end, concern for his troops took priority and Maker decided to leave the weapon with the three staying in the hotel room, trusting that he and Adames — as seasoned Marines — would be able to handle any problems that might arise. (Plus, with Shoal allegedly having a line on some firearms for them, he and Adames would hopefully be able to pick up some firepower at their meeting.) However, the situation made him realize just how vulnerable they were. Thus, before leaving, he had ordered Wayne to go through their suite and find anything that could be used as a weapon.

An ominous creaking sound brought Maker back to himself as the huge metal door began to slide open horizontally along a track on the ground. Since they hadn't knocked and there didn't seem to be a doorbell, the implication — unsurprisingly — was that there were cameras of some sort outside. As the door retreated into a recessed area of the wall, it revealed a couple of people standing on the other side of the threshold.

It was two men, dressed similarly in some sort of guard uniform. After a moment, Maker realized that the two men were not only dressed the same but also looked alike. Twins.

They appeared to be young — roughly Wayne's age — with dark hair and handsome features. Unlike the young Marine, however, these two were well-muscled and looked like they had been around the block a few times and had "made their bones," so to speak.

For a moment, no one said anything as the two sets of men seemed to size each other up.

"Well," said one of the twins," "don't just—"

"—stand there," the other one chimed in. "It's getting dark out, and we don't have—"

"—all night," the first one finished.

The way that they spoke, finishing each other's sentences, was slightly distracting. However, Maker found himself fascinated by the fact that not only were their voices indistinguishable, but their timing was impeccable. If he'd had his eyes closed, he would have sworn that he'd only heard one person speaking.

*No one's* that *good*, he thought, as he and Adames stepped inside. *They must be telepathically linked or something.*

Once across the threshold, the door began to close behind them.

"Sorry, but we're going to—" began the first twin, whom Maker mentally dubbed Twin A.

"—have to search you," said Twin B as the door shut with a clang of metal-on-metal.

"Uh, we're going to skip that part of the show," Adames declared.

Twin A smiled. "I'm afraid that it's—"

"—mandatory viewing," Twin B finished. At the same time, Maker noticed that both men were suddenly holding laser pistols, although they had the good grace not to point them at their visitors.

Maker frowned. It was one thing to show up to parley without any type of firearm on your person. It was something else entirely to let others present *know* that you didn't have a gun on you.

"Don't you have a scanner for things like that?" Adames asked.

"It's on—" Twin B began.

"—the fritz," Twin A chimed in.

Maker crossed his arms defiantly. "Sorry to hear that. But as my friend said, we're not keen on having a pat-down at the moment."

"And it wasn't part of the deal," Adames added.

Twin A shook his head in mock sorrow. "Unfortunately, it's—"

"—non-negotiable," Twin B stated, as he and his sibling seemed to grip their weapons tighter.

"That's enough," said a rumbling voice from somewhere farther in the cavernous building. "Pier. Tier. Please bring our guests to the back."

Upon hearing their names, the twins — Pier and Tier — seemed to frown somewhat at being admonished. Nevertheless, they put their guns away; then, after indicating that Maker and Adames should follow, Twin A began walking away. The two Marines did as bid, with Twin B bringing up the rear.

They headed to the back of the building, passing a hodgepodge of materials, items, and goods as they passed through: hovercycles, artwork, alien artifacts, and more. Maker assumed it was all ill-gotten, if not outright stolen.

Shortly thereafter, they reached the rear of the building where something akin to an office was set up: an antique but well-used desk, a couple of timeworn executive chairs, some shelves full of bric-a-brac, and more. The most up-to-date item in sight was some sophisticated computer equipment which was not only state-of-the-art, but was probably better classified as advanced.

And standing in the middle of the office area was a Panthera — a human-feline hybrid.

"Welcome," said the Panthera in the same resonant tone Maker had heard earlier. "I'm Shoal."

"We know," Adames replied. "You and I spoke via vid earlier."

"So we did," Shoal acknowledged. "The introduction was more for your companion." He extended a hand towards Maker.

"A pleasure," Maker said, without deigning to take the proffered hand.

For a second, Shoal appeared angry and offended. Then, after glancing down at his hand, he broke out into laughter. He held up the hand, which had wicked-looking claws extending from each fingertip.

"My apologies," the Panthera muttered in a sincere tone as he retracted the claws. He extended his hand again and this time Maker took it, pressing it firmly as he looked Shoal over.

The Panthera had mostly human facial features, with the only cat-like characteristic being his nose and a few very fine whiskers on either side of it. The majority of his body was covered with short fur that was jet black in color. That, combined with the fact that he wasn't as large as some of the other Pantheras Maker had known, suggested that his crossbreed was probably a leopard or jaguar.

Shoal turned to the twins. "That'll be all."

"Are you—" began Twin A.

"— certain?" said Twin B.

Shoal nodded. "Yes. We have business to discuss."

The twins seemed to ponder this momentarily, then turned in a synchronized, seemingly choreographed, motion and began walking away.

Shoal let out a sigh after the twins were out of earshot. "You'll have to forgive the boys. They're extremely loyal, but sometimes it feels like they're smothering me."

"Not a problem," Adames assured him. "Although — if I were you — I'd find it eerie to have them constantly moving and speaking in sync like that. I've never seen twins that close."

"Clones," Shoal corrected.

Maker raised an eyebrow. "Excuse me?"

"They're clones," Shoal repeated. "Part of a unique batch that actually share a single consciousness."

*Well, that explains some things*, Maker thought.

"Needless to say, they were an expensive purchase," the Panthera added. "Especially when you have characteristics like unfaltering allegiance imprinted in their psyches. However, they're well worth the cost."

Adames cleared his throat. "As much as I'd love to debate the unique characteristics and lab-bred devotion of clones, we actually have other pressing matters we'd like to discuss. The Vacra?"

"Of course," Shoal said with a nod. "But first, my payment?"

Adames looked at Maker, who reached into a pocket and pulled out a thin, rectangular piece of metal. It was unremarkable in appearance, except for a tiny circular computer chip embedded in one end.

He tossed the piece of metal to the Panthera, who caught it out of the air before turning and inserting it into a slot on the computer equipment. A moment later, a darkened monitor came to life a few feet away, showing a hefty amount of data on the screen.

"Okay," Shoal said, staring at the monitor. "Your voucher here is good."

"Of course," said Adames.

"Hmmm," Shoal muttered, frowning at the screen. He turned to the two Marines. "The money's there, but there's some type of encryption — looks like an access code is necessary to initiate the transfer of funds."

"Do we look stupid?" Maker asked. "You haven't told us jack yet. You're not getting a cent until you give us the info that we came for. After we get it — and *verify* it — you'll get your money."

"Fine," Shoal said. "Come back tomorrow."

Maker blinked. "What?"

"I said come back tomorrow," the Panthera repeated. "First thing in the morning. I'll have the info for you then."

"What are you saying?" asked Adames with a frown. "That you don't have it right now?"

"That's *exactly* what I'm saying," Shoal answered. "Look, your insect buddies — the Vacra — come across as a paranoid lot. They don't stay in one place for long. So while they're getting supplies from some merchants on Defalcator, they haven't exactly planted their flag in any particular location."

"So they're here?" Maker asked, trying not to sound too excited. "Planet-side?"

Shoal made a vague gesture. "Not exactly. They have an intermediary here that they deal with. They give him their list of requirements, and then, after he gets all the stuff, they send him a rendezvous point."

"So you can tell us where they're going to be," Adames summed up.

"Yes, but I won't have the info until tomorrow," the Panthera admitted.

"Then why make us traipse over here?" Maker practically demanded. "You could have passed that along on the vid."

"Maybe I wanted to see who I was doing business with face-to-face," Shoal practically snarled, obviously starting to get worked up. "Maybe I wanted to make sure you had the cash. Or maybe I just wanted to have you scurry back and forth so you'd realize who actually needs who in this relationship."

Maker stared at the Panthera for a moment, feeling immensely frustrated. He had thought they were getting close to the Vacra, and to have their plans unexpectedly put on hold really grated on him.

"Fine," he finally said through clenched teeth. "In the morning." He turned and started heading back the way they'd come without another word.

"Hold up," Adames said to his back, causing Maker to stop and do an about-face.

It was at that moment, upon seeing the master sergeant still standing in close proximity to Shoal, that Maker realized with a start that he had probably overstepped his bounds. Adames was supposed to be the head honcho here, as he was in his element in this type of environment. In essentially dominating much of the conversation with Shoal and then storming off, he had probably sent an unintentional message about the true dynamics of the relationship between himself and the NCO.

"My friend's a bit of a hothead," Adames explained to Shoal. "He's not good at sitting idle — or keeping his own counsel."

"I understand," Shoal said in commiseration. "It's so hard to find good help."

Adames laughed, then asked, "So we'll see you in the morning. But in the meantime, about those firearms we talked about...?"

The Panthera nodded. "As I mentioned before, I know a guy. Tell me where you're staying, and I'll have him drop by."

"Thanks," said Adames, then gave the Panthera their hotel and room number.

## Chapter 23

Maker was still complaining when they got back to their hotel room.

"That was an absolutely colossal waste of time," he said as he and Adames entered the suite. "Come on, admit it."

Adames shook his head. "That would be like admitting that my contacts are all crap."

"Not *all* of them," Maker insisted. "Just this one."

The NCO laughed. "How about we reserve judgment until we see what he gives us in the morning."

The other three members of their troop were in the living room and immediately came to their feet when Maker and Adames entered.

"Well," Wayne asked. "How did it go?"

Maker gestured towards Adames, indicating that the master sergeant should brief them on what had happened. Needless to say, it took no more than a minute to bring Snick, Loyola, and Wayne up to speed.

"So in essence," said Snick when he'd finished, "there's nothing more to be done until morning."

"We may get an opportunity to pick up some guns," Adames said, "but not much more than that."

"Speaking of weapons," Loyola chimed in, "show them what you've come up with, Wayne."

The young Marine suddenly turned red, looking embarrassed.

"It isn't much," Wayne stated, "since there wasn't a lot to work with, but here's what we've got."

He walked over to a coffee table that sat in the center of the living room. On it were three palm-sized glass globes. Each seemed to be filled with an olio of odd fluids of varying colors.

"The hotel has an affectation for some old-style décor," Wayne continued. "Including light bulbs. So I" — he spent a moment searching for the right word — "*requisitioned* a few of them, then filled them with a blend of certain chemicals I was able to find."

Adames picked up one of the globes and made a twirling motion, causing the liquid inside to swirl around. "What do they do?"

Wayne gasped slightly. Reaching out, he gingerly took the bulb from the master sergeant, saying, "When the bulb is broken and the fluids inside are exposed to air, a chemical reaction occurs that is something akin to a Molotov cocktail combined with a grenade going off — if it works as intended."

"If?" Maker repeated, raising an eyebrow.

"Well, it's not like I could test them," Wayne said defensively.

"So there's no guarantee that they'll work," Maker surmised.

"Oh, they'll work," Wayne stated with conviction. "But for now, maybe it's best if I'm the one handling them."

He then gathered up the two remaining bulbs without waiting for a response, plainly concerned now that someone's carelessness might result in a regrettable accident. No one moved to stop him.

"How much you want to bet he blows himself up before morning?" Adames droned as Wayne took his creations to one of the bedrooms.

"Not gonna happen," Wayne said over his shoulder, making it obvious he was still within earshot and getting a chuckle from Adames.

"I hope not," Maker retorted. "The Marines are funding this mission, and I'd hate for the Corps to lose its deposit on this suite."

## Chapter 24

Roughly half an hour later, Maker and his squad were seated in the living room, discussing their plans for the following day. Piled up on the coffee table that they sat around was a small stack of opened — and devoured — MREs. The prepackaged "Meal, Ready to Eat" was a field ration and had been a military staple since Old Earth. Although the suite had come with its own food dispenser (and even a few ready-made meals in the refrigeration unit), Maker had insisted that they all eat a quick dinner from the supplies they had brought.

It was probably overkill on his part. Almost no one knew they were on Defalcator, and fewer still knew exactly *why* they were here or where they were staying. Thus, the odds of someone tampering with any food they got from the hotel was minute. Still, Maker wasn't one to take unnecessary chances; more to the point, he wanted to instill in his people the habit of being thorough.

By way of example, after Adames had brought them from the Cave to their hotel, Maker had assigned Wayne the task of going through the suite to make sure it wasn't bugged. In a similar vein, Loyola had been tasked with making sure the place was secure with respect to gunfire, despite Adames' assurances that it was probably the safest lodging on the planet. Ultimately, Wayne had given the place a thumb's-up from the standpoint of listening devices. Loyola, however, had qualified her response, saying that the suite was solidly protected for the most part, but still had some weak points. That said, she confirmed Adames' assessment that it was about as good as they were likely to get.

Now, as they sat there discussing strategy, Maker wondered if perhaps he was being too hardnosed. Maybe his desire to confront the Vacra was drifting into the realm of obsession, making him paranoid. He'd seen that happen before, witnessed good men — good soldiers — become so fixated on something that it clouded their better judgment. Whether it be winning a battle, obtaining a promotion, completing a mission, what have you, most soldiers (hell, most *people*, to be honest) had an Achilles' heel of this sort — something they'd risk almost anything and everything for. In Maker's case, he at least recognized that his preoccupation with the Vacra had the potential to become unhealthy, but thankfully, he didn't consider himself past that point yet.

A question from Loyola brought Maker out of his reverie.

"What are the odds that Shoal will crack the encryption on the credit voucher?" she asked. "If he does that, he'll have the money and there'll be no incentive for him to give us the info on the Vacra."

"Won't happen," Wayne assured her. "I double-checked the encryption myself and added a few additional safeguards. Maybe with some advanced cipher algorithms, cutting-edge decoding software, and other specialized equipment he could figure it out in a few years, but doing so by tomorrow morning is out of the question."

"Let's hope so," Maker added. "Otherwise the Marines will start docking your pay."

There were chuckles around the room at this; Maker had a penchant for making quips about the protection of Marine assets. In truth, however, Maker's mission parameters actually included access to almost unlimited funds. Moreover, for covert operations like this, any use of capital was structured to be untraceable in terms of identifying the origin of the money. In short, Maker was in the type of position that would have made skimming an incredible temptation for many people, but it was a notion that had barely entered his mind. Maker's sole focus was the Vacra. In fact, their hotel room was probably the only time Maker had authorized spending more than absolutely necessary, as the suite — while not opulent — was far larger than standard and included a kitchen, dining area, and a small meeting room.

"Anyway," Adames said, bringing Maker back to the conversation at hand, "assuming Shoal comes through, we'll—"

The NCO's words were cut off as a musical chime sounded, indicating that someone was at their door.

All five Marines immediately came to their feet. Adames stepped over to a wall where an intercom and monitor were installed. He tapped a button, and an image appeared: a trio of men — apparently standing outside their door.

"Yes?" Adames asked.

A clean-shaven man with a queue hairstyle — apparently the leader — spoke up. "Shoal sent us."

Adames gave a terse nod, then hit a button that disconnected the intercom, causing the screen to go dark.

"It's the arms dealers," he said to no one in particular. He pressed another button on the intercom, causing a slight buzzing to sound throughout the room. At the same time, the door to their suite slid open. A moment later, their visitors stepped into the living room.

In addition to the leader (who appeared to be around Maker's age), there was another fellow in roughly the same age bracket with spiky hair that was dyed in black-and-white stripes like a zebra. The last guy was a little younger than his companions, with dark wavy hair and strikingly good looks.

The three newcomers fanned out as they entered, with the leader in the center. All of them wore sidearms in a rather conspicuous manner, with the spiky-haired fellow also carrying a large, locked gun case. Finally, while not soaking wet, a notable amount of water was dripping off each of them.

The man with the queue reached behind his head and grabbed his ponytail. "You'll have to forgive us," he said as he twisted his braided hair, causing a stream of water to go gushing down to the floor. "It's really starting to come down out there. We'll be lucky if we don't get any hail."

Maker glanced towards a set of glass doors that led out to a balcony. Although it was dark out, it did indeed appear that there was a downpour outside. He couldn't tell if there was any hail or not.

"Shoal said he knew a *guy*," Adames stressed, looking at the leader and ignoring the man's comments, as well as the puddle of water he had just wrung from his hair. "Singular."

"Yeah, right," retorted the man with the queue sarcastically as he flipped his ponytail back behind him. "I'm going to show up all by myself to conduct an illegal arms deal with an unknown number of people whom I've never dealt with before."

"An 'illegal' arms deal?" Adames repeated mockingly. "On Defalcator?"

The guy with the queue smiled. "Call it 'unauthorized' then." He turned to the third member of his group. "Malo, check it out."

Without a word, Malo whipped out a rectangular device about the size of his hand, which Maker recognized as a scanner. Malo spun in a swift but unhurried circle, staring at the scanner as he did so.

After a moment, he looked up. "It's clear, Joss," he said to the man with the queue. "No other bio-signs."

In response, Joss pointed at Maker and Snick, saying, "You and you. Out." He jerked a thumb towards the door.

Much like Adames at the space station, it was clear that Joss didn't like the idea of conducting a deal when he was outnumbered.

"Not him," Adames objected, pointing to Maker. "He's my bursar. You want to get paid, he stays."

Joss frowned, then uttered in an annoyed tone, "Fine." He then pointed at Wayne. "You. Take the bursar's place and get on the other side of the door."

Wayne and Snick hesitated for only a moment, then — after a curt nod from Adames — quickly exited the apartment.

After they were gone, Joss turned to his compatriot with the black-and-white hair. "Okay, Streak."

Streak stepped lithely over to the coffee table. Reaching down with one hand, he grabbed one side of it and tilted the table up, causing everything on the surface (mostly the empty MRE packages) to slide unceremoniously to the floor. He then let the table drop back down with a thump before swinging the gun case he still held up and letting it drop onto the tabletop with a heavy thud.

Maker noticed that the gun case, now lying flat on the table, had a square glass plate on top. Streak placed his right hand on the plate, which began to light up with symbols. After a moment, Streak's authority was obviously recognized, because the locks on the case popped open. Streak opened the case and took a step back. Inside, to no one's great surprise, were guns, sitting in molded foam.

On one side of the case were four handguns — pulse pistols, from what Maker could tell. On the other side was what appeared to be a plasma rifle, although it was currently broken down into four components.

"Now that you've seen the merch, let's talk price," Joss said, as Streak began to close the case. "It'll cost—"

"Slow down, Junior," Adames interrupted. "We're not interested in buying a pig in a poke. How about you let us inspect the goods?"

Joss frowned for a moment, as if insulted that anyone would insinuate that he was dishonest. Then he shrugged and gestured for Streak to leave the case open.

Adames nodded at Loyola, who stepped forward and began examining the weapons, starting with the pistols. No one said anything as she went through the process of inspecting each firearm before placing it back in its proper place. She did the same thing with the rifle, calmly but quickly assembling the weapon and then methodically breaking it down again.

Although interested, Maker only halfway paid attention to what Loyola was doing. He was keeping his eyes focused primarily on their visitors. They hadn't done anything particularly out of the ordinary yet, but something about them left him ill at ease — especially Malo, who stood just a few feet away from him. Something about the way the young man stood, his body language radiating bottled-up tension, put Maker on edge.

Loyola was just putting the final rifle component back into the case when Maker heard the distinct sound of gunfire and people shouting nearby. He instinctively turned his head in the direction the sounds were coming from — the hallway outside their door, where Snick and Wayne presumably were. Almost immediately, he realized that he had made a terrible error in judgment. He jerked his head back towards Malo just as the young man's sidearm was clearing the holster and coming up in his right hand. At the same time, with his peripheral vision, he noted frantic movement coming from where Loyola and Adames were standing, but he couldn't spare a glance to see what exactly was going on.

Instinct and training took over. Maker quickly slid in Malo's direction, but at an angle, slanting towards the right side of the young man's body. This took him out of the line of fire and put him to the side of Malo's gun hand. Next, he spun and grabbed the wrist of the hand holding the weapon, then twisted violently.

As expected, Malo dropped the gun. But, in an astonishing display of dexterity, he bent down and caught it in his free hand as it fell and attempted to aim it at Maker.

Still gripping his opponent's wrist, Maker twisted again and stepped to Malo's rear. In doing so, he brought his adversary's arm up behind his back just as the younger man fired the gun. Being jerked about by Maker's treatment of his arm caused Malo's shot to go wild; nevertheless, it was followed by a grunt of pain from nearby.

Maker took a moment to glance in the direction the shot had gone, and was rewarded with the sight of Loyola shooting Streak in the face with the gun he'd given her earlier. He didn't immediately see Adames or Joss, although he did see Loyola follow her shot by going down to the floor. He couldn't tell if she were hurt in some way or not, but it didn't look like it. Regardless, that was all he had time to observe, because the next second he was unexpectedly flying backwards.

Still gripping Malo's arm, Maker found himself headed rearward with unexpected haste, his feet barely touching the floor. He slammed into a wall with concussive force, then slid to the floor in a daze.

With his arm no longer held by Maker, Malo seemed to glide forward and turn around simultaneously with a grace that made it seem like he was floating rather than walking. Smiling, he raised his gun, aiming it at Maker at point-blank range.

Before he could fire, a noise like a muffled explosion sounded from the hallway outside the suite. The entire room shook for a second, as if caught in a quake of some sort, and for a moment the lights flashed on and off haphazardly.

The flickering lights seemed to briefly distract Malo, and Maker took advantage of the situation by flinging himself to the side. (And not a moment too soon, as Malo fired and punched a hole in the wall right where Maker had been positioned a moment before.)

"Move, el-tee!" he heard someone shout.

Reacting intuitively to what was obviously a command, Maker scrambled madly along the floor on his hands and knees, seeking cover behind whatever was at hand: end tables, an ottoman, and so on. He heard gunfire going on around him, and somewhere in the back of his mind, he realized that, with the lights now back on steadily, Malo should have had ample opportunity to blow his head off. Nevertheless, he somehow made it safely to a small washroom and scurried inside. He took a moment to catch his breath, then peeked out. He immediately saw two things that were noteworthy.

First of all, the reason Malo had seemed to float earlier was because he actually *was* floating. Or rather, he was gliding through the air on one side of the room, his feet never touching floor.

*Some kind of anti-grav boots*, Maker realized.

The other thing he noticed was that Malo was trading gunfire with Loyola, who was currently in the kitchen area. It only took Maker a second to understand that it was Loyola who had both ordered him to move earlier and enabled him to make it to the safety of his current position. She had laid down cover fire, allowing him to reach the washroom unscathed.

As he watched, Loyola fired off two shots, both of which found their mark, striking Malo in the chest area. Malo merely grunted slightly, and Maker realized that the arms dealer was wearing some type of body armor. More to the point, the gun he'd given Loyola was essentially small-caliber. Even at full power, it probably wouldn't cause much damage to a decent set of body armor (which Malo appeared to have). In short, the only way Loyola was likely to bring Malo down with her current weapon was with a headshot.

Unfortunately, Malo wasn't cooperating. He was constantly bobbing, weaving, twisting, turning…even going upside-down occasionally. Just watching him, Maker had to admit that he'd seen few people who had ever mastered anti-grav boots so well. Malo was practically in a class by himself.

Loyola fired off another shot and was once again rewarded with a direct — but ineffective — hit. On his part, Malo didn't really return much gunfire. It was almost as if he were playing with Loyola. And then the truth dawned on Maker: Malo wasn't so much toying with her as he was getting her to expend ammo. Assuming she was firing at full power in an attempt to penetrate Malo's armor, she'd run out soon. Then they'd be dead in the water.

Maker scanned the immediate area, looking for something — anything — that could even the odds. On the floor of the living room was Streak's body, as well as the coffee table, which had been overturned. Other pieces of furniture had been banged around as well, giving the place a general appearance of disarray.

It was plainly obvious what had happened: at the same time that Malo had pulled his weapon on Maker, his compatriots had attempted to engage with Loyola and Adames. It hadn't worked out well for Streak, nor for Joss, whose legs Maker now observed jutting out from behind a divan. And that's when he saw it — the gun case that Streak had been carrying earlier.

It had obviously been knocked to the floor when the coffee table was tipped over. Of more interest to Maker, however, was the fact that the case was still open and one of the handguns had fallen out.

Maker didn't even think about what he did next. Dashing out of the bathroom, he dove for the gun. Getting a hand on the weapon, he rolled forward and came up with it in his hand, firing.

Malo was still expertly ducking and dodging, but Maker managed to land a shot to the shoulder that elicited a painful "Ooomph!" from the man and also spun him slightly around. The guns from the case were quite obviously of a different caliber than the one Loyola held, both literally and figuratively. That fact was not lost on Malo; coming to the realization that Maker now represented a credible threat, he suddenly had his gun up.

Maker went low as the arms dealer fired. It was a further testament to Malo's skill that his shots came close to hitting their mark even as he continued oscillating back and forth. Maker ultimately sought cover behind the overturned coffee table, which lay on its side.

The next few seconds saw a barrage of gunfire come from Malo. He fired almost nonstop, alternating between Maker and Loyola as his targets. (Apparently it was one thing to be facing a single opponent armed with what was essentially a peashooter thanks to his armor. It was quite another to be going toe-to-toe with *two* combatants — at least one of whom had a decent weapon.)

As before, the arms merchant stayed constantly on the move thanks to his anti-grav capabilities. Thus, although he got off a few shots from behind cover, Maker had little luck actually finding his mark. That said, Malo wouldn't be able to continue his dodgeball act forever; sooner or later he'd get tired, slow down, make a mistake...

Apparently Malo realized the same thing, because he suddenly changed tactics. Keeping up the gunplay, he made a beeline for the glass doors that led to the balcony. At the same time, Maker heard the slight scrape of metal on metal and noticed a subtle change in the acoustics of the room.

Peeking around the table, he saw that the door to their suite was now open and that Wayne had furtively stuck his head into the room. Said head was hastily withdrawn a second later as shots from the area of the balcony peppered the door.

Turning back to Malo, Maker saw the fellow pressing a button on a control panel near the balcony doors, which immediately began to open. However, before Malo could go out, something went sailing over his head and out onto the balcony.

At the same time, someone shouted, "Hit the deck!"

Maker complied, going flat on the floor as the room shook once again from another muffled explosion, this time coming from the direction of the balcony. Despite having his eyes tightly closed, he still sensed a bright flash and felt a wave of oppressive (but not painful) heat wash over him.

Opening his eyes, Maker quickly sat up, placing his back to the overturned coffee table. There were spots before his eyes, and he blinked several times to try to clear his vision. At the same time, he heard some kind of wailing, like a siren of some sort. After a moment, however, he properly categorized the sound — or rather, *sounds*: a mixture of the wind howling from the storm outside and someone screaming in pain.

Maker looked towards the balcony, where the sounds were coming from. As his vision returned to normal, he saw Malo there, although he was difficult to recognize. His hair was almost completely gone, with only small, seared tufts scattered here and there across his head. Although the man's scalp was highly visible, it consisted mostly of charred flesh. Finally, his eyebrows and eyelashes had been singed off, giving him an unnatural look that was exacerbated by the fact that one ear appeared to be missing in its entirety.

Surprisingly, Malo was still floating. (Truth be told, considering his physical appearance, it was the only way Maker had actually recognized him.) And, although his head had clearly been unprotected and his clothing was aflame in various spots, his body appeared to be largely unharmed below the neck thanks to the armor he wore.

The balcony itself was scorched and smoldering in certain spots. Oddly enough, the glass doors had held, once again giving credence to Adames' claims regarding the safety and security of their hotel. (The blast of heat he'd previously felt had obviously come in through the open doorway.) That said, there was a small crater in the balcony floor, which Maker automatically understood to be ground zero for the blast that had occurred. Moreover, reflecting back on what had happened, Maker also recognized the origin of the explosion — the item that had arced over Malo's head and out onto the balcony earlier: one of Wayne's Molotov bulbs.

Movement near him drew Maker's attention; on reflex, he looked in that direction, simultaneously bringing his gun up. He let out a ragged breath when he saw that it was Loyola, ignoring him as she pulled something out of the gun case. Behind her he noted Adames, walking with an obvious limp.

Suddenly Loyola stood and began walking quickly towards the balcony, her hands seeming to juggle some odd objects at the same time. With a start, Maker grasped the fact that what she held were the rifle components, and Loyola was hastily assembling the weapon on the fly.

Outside, Malo had stopped screaming and had floated out towards the edge of the balcony, where the downpour had started to put out the remaining flames covering him. His head snapped in the direction of the doorway just as Loyola reached it and began bringing her weapon to bear.

Malo growled in anger as he brought up his own gun. At the same time, he began his evasive maneuvering again, an obvious attempt to avoid being hit. In fact, he floated up over the edge of the balcony and out into open air.

Loyola bent her knees as Malo began firing, then leaped forward. Tucking her head, she rolled as she hit the ground, then came up in a firing position and squeezed the trigger once.

Her shot took Malo in the right bicep. The injured arm immediately went limp and he dropped his gun. Also dropped at that juncture were all efforts by the arms merchant to showcase his talent at avoiding gunfire. Rather than the previous bob-and-weave technique, he simply zoomed straight up.

Not wasting a moment, Loyola dashed to the end of the balcony. She did a one-eighty turn and then leaned out backwards over its edge. With rain cascading down onto her face, she aimed up with the rifle. The barrel waffled from side to side for a moment, as if Loyola were tracking something that was moving somewhat erratically, and then she fired.

Loyola straightened up and began casually walking back towards the balcony doors, holding the rifle loosely in one hand. Placing her free hand to her forehead, she wiped up and then back, pressing her hand firmly to get as much water as possible out of her hair. Behind her, a man-shaped object — aflame in certain spots despite the rain — went plummeting past the balcony towards the ground.

"So what's our next move?" she asked nonchalantly as she stepped back inside.

## Chapter 25

Their next move, physically, was to another room four floors above their original suite. This was the result of Adames — in an attempt to account for certain contingencies — having booked a second room under a different name earlier.

"It's like having a safe house," the NCO had previously remarked. "A place to retreat and get your bearings if things go off-track."

Bearing in mind what had happened with the arms merchants, things had definitely gone off the beaten path, as evidenced by the havoc wreaked on their suite. That said, Maker wasn't too worried that the local sheriff — or whatever might pass for law enforcement on this rock — would start poking around in an effort to figure out what had happened. This was Defalcator, after all. People shooting up rooms was probably the rule rather than the exception.

However, the hotel had to be owned by someone, and considering where they were, that owner was probably a criminal or criminal organization. Moreover, having their property damaged or destroyed was likely to get said criminal's attention. In short, it may not be the local law, but *somebody* was likely to launch an investigation, and Maker preferred to be elsewhere when they showed up. Thus, he and his team had quickly gathered together their belongings in anticipation of vacating their original room.

In addition to their own gear, they had also done a quick search of the bodies of Joss and Streak. The latter, of course, had been shot by Loyola; the former had met a similar fate at the hands of Adames. Basically, at the same time that Malo had drawn on Maker, his companions had tried to take down the other two Marines.

Needless to say, the gun sellers had clearly misjudged their marks. As Maker learned later, Adames had had almost no trouble taking Joss' firearm and shooting him with his own weapon, while Streak discovered to his dismay that Loyola was actually armed. The only hiccup was that Malo's initial shot when Maker was twisting his arm had actually struck Adames in the leg and caused him to collapse. It wasn't life-threatening, but Loyola had quickly rendered aid (which is apparently what Maker was observing when he'd seen her go to the floor) and dragged the NCO to the kitchen to get him out of any line of fire.

Looting the two corpses yielded very little booty, including a few low-value credit vouchers, a communicator, and a couple of mid-level p-comps. Nevertheless, after having Wayne make sure none of it was traceable, Maker took it all with them. They also confiscated the gun case and its contents, as well as Streak's gun (which was still in his hand), and the one Adames had taken from Joss, which the master sergeant had dropped after being shot.

All in all, they were ready to depart within three minutes after Loyola stepped back inside from the balcony. Armed with the rifle, Loyola automatically took point as they left the suite, followed by Snick, who was helping Adames walk. Maker and Wayne brought up the rear.

As they left, Maker spared one last look at their suite. Gutted by gunfire, charred and burned in spots, and with furniture tossed about in helter-skelter fashion, it was almost impossible to reconcile the place before him with the room he'd been in perhaps ten minutes before, joking with his squad. It was practically surreal how quickly it had all changed.

Noting the scrutiny his commander was giving the room, Wayne also looked at the suite and then made a tsking sound. "Sorry el-tee, but the Corps can kiss that deposit goodbye."

# EFFERUS

## Chapter 26

A few minutes after leaving their original room, Maker's team was in their "safe house," for lack of a better term. They managed to make it there without incident, the only notable event being the fact that they passed several bodies in the hallway outside their initial suite. Pressed for time, Maker hadn't bothered to plunder those corpses.

Once in their new digs, Loyola and Wayne automatically assumed their respective tasks of checking the suite's security and confirming that the place wasn't bugged. During that time, Maker and Snick set about treating Adames' wound. Thankfully, the injury was far less severe than it could have been. They patched him up and gave him something for the pain, but full treatment would have to wait until the NCO could see an actual physician.

Around the time the two men finished doctoring on the master sergeant, Loyola and Wayne returned, reporting essentially what they had with respect to the first suite: the place was fairly — but not perfectly — secure, and no listening devices were present. Now feeling a little less anxious, Maker relaxed a little, and it was at this point that he learned what had transpired with his other teammates while he had been grappling with Malo.

He had been in the suite with Loyola and Adames, so he was practically able to extrapolate the sequence of events that had occurred in regards to them. With respect to Snick and Wayne, however, he'd needed them to essentially brief him on what had happened, although it was fairly straightforward.

Basically, after leaving the suite, Snick and Wayne had tried to stay near the door in case they were needed. They had only been there a minute or so when they heard voices and saw a group of four men approaching from the far end of the hall. Seconds later, the newcomers opened fire.

Snick had then kicked open the door of a nearby broom closet and the two Marines had taken shelter inside. However, their assailants quickly began closing in on their position. When he sensed that their attackers were close, Wayne had taken a calculated risk by opening the closet door, tossing one of his Molotov bulbs toward the men shooting at them, and then slamming the door shut again. The resulting explosion had seemed to shake the building, as well as put their attackers out of commission. After giving the flames a little time to die down, Snick and Wayne had raced back into the suite, where they had found the rest of their group engaged in a shootout with Malo.

"Well," Loyola said after Snick and Wayne had finished the tale of their misadventures, "at least you escaped unscathed."

"We should all have been so lucky," Adames added, grimacing as he shifted the position of his injured leg in the chair where he was sitting.

"So what did we do?" Wayne asked. "Why did they come after us?"

Maker shrugged. "Easy marks, I suppose. They knew we had few, if any, guns — that was the whole reason we were dealing with them in the first place."

"So robbing us was easier than actually making a deal," Snick surmised.

"And more profitable," Adames chimed in. "Ripping off newcomers is probably a cottage industry around here. I'm just glad they didn't catch us with our guard down."

"By the way," Maker said, turning to Wayne, "good job on the makeshift weapons."

Wayne gave a short nod of acknowledgment. "Thanks, although I'm surprised that last guy was still mobile after we firebombed the balcony."

"He was wearing armor," Loyola pointed out. "It not only protected him to a large extent, but probably injected painkillers and other meds after he was injured."

"That would explain why he stopped screaming like a banshee," Wayne suggested, "and didn't seem to mind that his head got toasted like a marshmallow."

Maker nodded in agreement. "I guess—"

His words were cut off as a weird chiming began to sound. A moment later, everyone had a gun in their hand, looking around warily. Maker frowned as he suddenly realized where the sound was coming from: the communicator they had taken from Joss' corpse. It was sitting on a poseur table near the door, along with the other items that they had taken from the bodies in their previous quarters.

Maker stepped over to the table and retrieved the communicator. He contemplated for a moment, then turned it on.

There was a brief period of silence, then a voice said, "Joss? Are you there?"

Maker's brow creased in concern. The voice he was hearing was distorted, altered by a modifier of some sort. In short, the speaker was probably afraid of being overheard…or didn't want anyone knowing who he was.

"Joss!" the voice went on. "Is it taken care of?"

No one spoke, but the implications were disturbing. Although the phrase "taken care of" could relate to almost anything, based on the timing of the call it quite possibly (and probably) referred to Maker's squad. It suggested that Joss and his companions hadn't simply tried to take advantage of an opportune situation. It indicated that Maker's group had been specifically targeted.

"Joss?" the voice inquired again. Then the communicator suddenly went dead.

"Well, that's not good," Adames intoned, verbally reaching the same conclusion that Maker had mentally.

"That could be considered an understatement," Snick added.

"So what do we do?" asked Wayne.

That turned out to be the question of the day, and the group spent the next half hour debating the issue, considering everything from staying put to finding a new base of operations to simply abandoning the current mission. Maker gave everyone a chance to offer input, but — as the ranking officer — it was ultimately his decision.

"Here's what we're going to do," he finally said. "Nothing. Nobody knows where we are at the moment, so we hunker down. In the morning, Adames and I will get the info from Shoal regarding the Vacra and then we'll plot our next move."

"In that case," Adames interjected, struggling to his feet, "I'm going to find a bed to stretch out on and convalesce for the next eight hours."

"Roger that," Maker droned as Adames began limping away.

Suddenly Adames came to a halt. "Whoa," he muttered softly.

"What is it?" Snick asked.

"I just saw a weird flash of lightning," Adames replied. "Looked like it sort of rippled across the balcony's glass doors."

"It is coming down pretty hard," Maker admitted, glancing toward the doors in question. Then, hearing a distinct pattering against the glass, he added, "Sounds like we might also be getting some of that hail Joss mentioned earlier."

The others all glanced casually at the balcony doors as he spoke. A moment later, Loyola drew in a sharp breath and jumped to her feet, still holding the rifle. If she'd had eyes, Maker imagined they would have widened considerably. As it was, he saw her eyebrows shoot up in what he interpreted as shock or surprise.

"Down!" she screamed as she turned and leaped at Adames, her weight bearing the two of them to the floor.

Heeding Loyola's instruction, Maker and the other two Marines also dove for cover, with Maker leaping behind the sofa (and tipping it over onto its back in the process). At the same time, the glass in the balcony door shattered and came raining down like a waterfall. In conjunction with that, a neat row of holes appeared in the wall directly behind the area where Adames had been standing a moment before, as if an invisible man had gone wild with an equally invisible rivet gun.

*Bullet holes*, Maker realized as Snick and Wayne, scrambling along the floor, joined him behind the sofa.

Looking towards Loyola and Adames, Maker saw the two of them — still entangled — rolling along the floor like a pair of lovers who'd forgotten to disrobe before getting intimate. A moment later, they were behind a loveseat that faced the balcony, at which point they disengaged.

"Sniper!" Loyola yelled, lying flat on her back with her head resting against the bottom of the loveseat. "In the building directly across from us!"

She had to shout to be heard over the storm, which was now coming into their suite. Maker nodded in understanding, and somewhere in the back of his mind he noted, ironically, that this was almost the exact situation they'd found themselves in a short time before in their previous room. It would have been comical had the situation not been so serious.

Maker took a deep breath, then risked a glance around the edge of the sofa. A moment later, he jerked his head back, having noticed three things.

First of all, it was pitch black outside and the rain was still coming down in torrents. Visibility was so poor that he couldn't even see the building across from them, although he knew one was there because he'd seen it earlier.

Next, he noticed that not all of the glass had fallen out of the balcony doors; roughly the bottom two feet of it was still intact.

Finally, he'd heard an ominous tapping noise sounding in triplicate. At the same time, he witnessed some of the remaining glass in the door — in direct line of sight with his eye — begin to splinter, as if someone was tapping at it with a hammer. It didn't take a genius to figure out that, in the second or so he'd spent glancing out from behind his cover, the sniper had drawn a bead on him and fired three times.

*He's good*, Maker thought, at the same time thanking his lucky stars for the portion of glass that was still in the door because it had probably saved his life.

"That was stupid!" Loyola growled, not mincing words. "You're lucky he didn't blow your head off! That's a pro over there!"

"Yeah," Maker agreed. "And he's got us pinned down. We're going to have to run for it." He pointed with his chin towards the door leading to the hallway outside their room.

Loyola shook her head. "We'll never make it. He's got a high-intensity laser gun that will burn a hole through you like you're a snowflake. He's alternating that with a high-powered sniper rifle."

"He's using two guns?" Wayne asked.

"The glass in the windows and balcony doors is part of the security features," Loyola answered. "It dissipates light from lasers — disperses it harmlessly. That's probably what Adames saw earlier. He thought it was lightning of some sort, but it was actually someone taking a potshot at him."

As she spoke, Loyola pulled a small plastic packet from a pocket. Tearing it open with her teeth, she began smearing the contents — a dark, viscous fluid — over the barrel of the rifle she had gotten from Joss' case.

"The glass is also bulletproof to a certain extent," Loyola continued, "but not impenetrable. Our friend across the way is using the sniper rifle to shatter it."

As if on cue, the pattering sound began again on the remaining glass in the balcony door. Despite the circumstances, Maker found himself once again impressed by Loyola's knowledge of firearms.

"Once all the glass is gone," Loyola went on, "he can use the laser to carve up this room like a turkey, and us along with it. Or use the sniper rifle to ventilate everything in sight."

"But if there's still glass left, what's the problem with making a run for it?" Wayne asked.

"There's not enough left to give adequate cover," Maker responded, already knowing the answer. "There's barely enough left to shield us now."

Wayne gulped. "Can't we just turn off the lights in here? Wouldn't that help?"

"It's a sure bet he has infrared tech that will allow him to pinpoint us by body heat," Adames said. "Killing the lights will just tip him off that we're about to try something."

"So we appear to be out of options," Snick surmised.

"Not completely out," Loyola countered. "Just give me a second. I'll get this guy."

With that, Loyola — still lying on her back — lifted the rifle up and then gently and unobtrusively slid it forward until the end of the barrel was resting on the top part of the loveseat's back. Thus the gun, like the loveseat, now faced the direction where the sniper was located. Moreover, with the barrel covered with the dark fluid from the packet, there would be no telltale glare from the weapon. (And if Loyola were as thorough as Maker suspected, the liquid would also mask any heat from any previous firing of the rifle.)

The sound of the sniper's rounds continued. It was more than a little disconcerting to realize that every shot weakened the glass a little more...brought them a little closer to being drilled full of holes. Maker tuned it out as best he could by focusing on Loyola.

What she was attempting would be an awkward shot, to say the least. Lying on her back, she was essentially going to be shooting at a target behind her, and having to do so using her thumb rather than her forefinger because of the position of the trigger. And if that wasn't difficult enough, Maker had no clue how she expected to see what she was shooting at.

In answer to his unasked question, Maker saw Loyola swivel the rifle slightly, as if lining up her sights. Instead of looking at the weapon, however, her attention seemed focused on something on the wall she faced. Following the direction of her gaze (or — considering Loyola's visual impairment — the place where she seemed to be looking), Maker saw a painting hanging on the wall.

It was a mid-sized "still life" composition showing various fruits and vegetables in a bowl. Encased in a metallic frame, it was colorful art that seemed to suit the room, but Maker didn't think there was anything particularly compelling about it. (He certainly couldn't understand why Loyola would be so interested in it.) Looking closely, he could even see his reflection in the frame. It was a little distorted (his forehead was oversized), but he could make out...

Like a bolt from the blue, Maker suddenly realized what Loyola was looking at: she was using the reflection in the painting's frame to aim. Frankly speaking, it was probably only a hair better than simply shooting blind.

The sound of glass splintering and cracking highlighted the fact that they were almost out of time. At that moment, Loyola stopped swiveling the gun, held her breath, and then squeezed the trigger just as the last pieces of glass cracked and fell out of the balcony door.

## Chapter 27

It was a phenomenal shot, by any measure. Truth be told, Maker wasn't even sure Loyola had hit her target until — mere seconds after squeezing the trigger — she stood up, thereby indicating that the threat had been eliminated. The others quickly followed her lead and came to their feet.

They made ready to depart even faster this time than they had from their previous suite. Their position had obviously been compromised in some way. (Not to mention the fact that — as before — someone was likely to come around soon to investigate.) That said, and despite the fact that everyone was ready to walk out the door in about a minute, Maker called things to a halt. It didn't take long to sum up what he was thinking.

"I trust everyone on our team," he said, "but somehow that sniper knew exactly where to find us."

"So what are you saying, el-tee?" asked Wayne.

"He's saying that someone either told that guy where we were," Adames explained, "or he had some way to track us."

Wayne shook his head. "It can't be either of those. None of us would sell out the team, and I checked all our gear before we left the *Raider* and again after we checked into the hotel, in case somebody tried to pull a fast one after that fight at the Cave. It's all clean."

Maker scratched his temple as Wayne's words brought something to mind. "*Our* gear may be clean, but what about stuff that *isn't* ours?"

Wayne frowned. "Huh?"

Maker nodded his head towards the gun case that had originally belonged to Joss, which Snick was carrying at the moment.

"Oh, damn," Wayne muttered.

\*\*\*\*\*\*\*\*\*\*\*\*\*\*\*\*\*\*\*\*\*\*\*\*\*\*\*\*\*\*\*\*\*\*\*\*\*\*\*\*\*\*\*\*\*\*\*\*\*

It took Wayne practically no time to confirm that the gun case was indeed outfitted with a tracking device (albeit one with a limited range).

"I'm sorry, el-tee," Wayne apologized. "I didn't even think about that case. I was more focused on the suite and bugs that would let people listen in."

"It's nothing to beat yourself up over," Maker assured him. "All of us should have realized that gun case probably had a tracker. It would have let Joss and his people track down their goods if anyone ever ripped them off."

"Anyway, we're taking the guns and leaving the case," Adames added, tucking a gun into his waistband near the small of his back. "Problem solved — not to mention the fact that everyone is actually packing some firepower now."

"So where to?" Loyola asked as everyone began heading towards the door. "Do we have another safe house out there somewhere?"

"Unfortunately, no," Adames admitted. "I didn't really think we'd even need the one."

"We're just going to have to play it by ear," Maker declared. "Now let's move."

Seconds later, they were in the hallway outside the suite, hustling toward the elevator. As they moved, Maker tried to get his head around the problem of where exactly they were headed to, but it was a difficult task considering that they didn't know who was after them or why.

*Let's just take this in baby steps,* he finally decided. *First, get to the elevator. Then, get to the lobby. Next —*

He found his thoughts cut off by the sound of a soft chime. This was followed by the elevator, which was about ten feet away from them, opening up. Three men — plainly ruffians, to be honest — stepped out as the elevator doors slid open.

Maker's team had come to a halt as soon as they heard the elevator ding. Similarly, the trio who had just stepped into the hallway suddenly stopped in their tracks. The tension in the air was immediate and concrete, and for a moment, both parties just stared at one another, each sizing the other up.

Without warning, Snick — who was closest to the three men — let loose with something akin to a battle cry and charged. At his shout, the trio all froze momentarily, and it was all the time Snick needed to reach them.

The men had exited the elevator in a triangular pattern, with one in the vanguard walking in the center of the hallway and the other two positioned behind him to the right and left. Snick reached the one in front first, just as the man was raising his left hand (which, unsurprisingly, held a gun). But before he could fire, Snick was inside his guard.

Catching his opponent's gun hand at the wrist, Snick lifted the arm up and then spun so that his back was to his adversary. He then brought the arm down hard across his shoulder. There was an audible crack accompanied by a sharp cry of pain, but the sound was cut off almost immediately as Snick slammed an elbow into the man's solar plexus. The force of the blow knocked the man backwards into the fellow who was to his rear left and they both went down, entangled.

Snick spun toward the man who had been at the rear right (and who now had a gun aimed in his direction). He immediately went low, dropping beneath the weapon's line of fire, and then, in one continuous motion, he kicked out at the fellow's leg, connecting solidly with the medial joint line. The man grunted in pain as his leg wrenched to the side and he went down to one knee.

The kick not only took the fellow's leg out, but also jerked his body to the side. As a result, he was no longer even facing in Snick's direction, let alone aiming at him. Snick took advantage of the situation, landing a vicious kick to the side of the man's head and smashing it into the wall. The fellow slumped to the ground, unconscious.

Before his last opponent even hit the floor, Snick was on his feet again, stepping towards the other two men, who were still on the floor. The guy who had been in the vanguard was out cold, with one arm twisted at a very odd angle. The other man was struggling to get out from under his companion, who had landed on top of him. Snick kicked the last man in the jaw; the fellow's head jerked to the side, and he stopped moving.

Snick looked back at his companions, smiling; for a moment, they all stared at him in silence. From the time he had first screamed and charged to the moment he knocked out the third man, about seven seconds had passed.

"You do know we have guns, right?" Loyola asked jokingly. Her tone made it clear, however, that she was impressed.

"A firefight between us and them would probably have resulted in casualties," Snick said as the rest of the team began walking towards him. "On both sides."

"So you thought it better to rush them barehanded," Adames commented skeptically. "And maybe get yourself killed."

Snick seemed to contemplate for a moment before responding. "My charge was intended to draw their attention to me, and was successful in that regard. More importantly, however, is this: firearms tend to imbue people with a false sense of superiority. A man with a gun will tend to underestimate an opponent who appears unarmed. It's an inherent flaw that the proper individual can use to his advantage."

"Well, I'd say you fully exploited it," Maker said. "Of course, it raises the question of why you even attacked these guys, since — other than getting into a staring contest with us — they hadn't actually done anything."

In response, Snick reached down and into the trouser pocket of the man whose jaw he had kicked. He pulled out a little square of white plastic and squeezed one corner of it between his thumb and forefinger. Above the card, a small holographic image of a face appeared. It was Maker.

"I glimpsed the hologram from this image card for a brief second as these three stepped off the elevator," Snick explained. "Apparently I was the only one of us at the proper angle and able to see it before it was turned off."

Everyone stood there silently for a moment. The fact that these guys had an image of Maker implied a lot of things about their current situation — all of them bad.

Maker reached for the image card and Snick handed it to him. He searched it for other info but there was nothing else on it other than the pic of his face.

"Well, Snick," Wayne said, "it's nice to know you didn't take out some innocent hotel guests."

"Speaking of which," Loyola intoned, "doesn't anybody find it odd that none of the other guests have stuck their head out the door to see what's going on — even after we firebombed our first suite?"

Adames chortled. "That's not likely. The quickest way to get your head blown off on a place like Defalcator is to stick your nose where it doesn't belong. People mind their own business here."

"Let's keep moving," Maker interjected suddenly, tucking the card into his own pocket. "We need to—"

Maker suddenly went quiet as Snick unexpectedly held up a hand in a "stop" gesture. He tilted his head slightly to the side as if listening for something, then put a finger to his lips to indicate silence. As the others began bringing their weapons up, Snick tiptoed quickly but quietly to a door across from the elevator that led to a stairwell.

Without warning, Snick yanked open the door. His hands shot out quickly two times and were followed by harsh grunts of pain from someone on the other side of the threshold. He then reached out with both hands and yanked hard, pulling whoever was in the stairwell towards him. Turning and twisting, Snick threw the person over his hip, slamming them violently to the floor, facedown. All of the air went out of the person's body in a whooshing sound that was almost cartoonish.

Maker, Loyola, Wayne, and Adames immediately had their weapons pointed at the newcomer, who appeared to be a young man. It was a wordless statement of their intentions should the guy try anything, but they needn't have bothered; being manhandled by Snick had clearly taken all the fight out of him. Gasping, the person rolled over, finally letting everyone get a peek at his face.

Maker blinked in surprise. "Gallico?"

The young man nodded, still trying to get his breath. Maker made a calculated decision, then put away his gun and reached out to help the young man up.

"Thanks," Gallico said after getting to his feet, still sounding a little winded.

"What are you doing here?" Maker practically demanded.

"Looking for you," Gallico answered.

"Why?" Maker asked.

Gallico hesitated for a moment, as if carefully choosing his words. "There's a bounty out on you. A big one."

"And you thought you'd collect, right?" Adames chimed in somewhat angrily.

"No!" Gallico blurted defensively. "I owe the sarge. I came to warn him — warn all of you."

"How'd you even know where to find us?" Loyola asked.

Gallico gestured towards Adames. "I overheard that one mention where you'd be staying as you were leaving the Cave, plus you're carrying a tracking device. I figured I'd let you know about the reward being offered for you."

"Well, at this juncture we are well aware of the tracker *and* the fact that people are after us," Maker stated. "We just don't know why."

Gallico shook his head. "Sorry, I haven't got a clue about that. I just know there's a huge price on your head."

"Well, we can figure out the 'why' later," Maker said. "Right now we need a place where we can retreat and regroup."

"Sure, sure," Gallico muttered, nodding in understanding. "I know a place. But we need to sneak out of here first. With the price tag you guys are sporting, you won't be able to just walk out through the lobby. Every hood on the planet will be on the lookout for you in hopes of earning a major payday."

"Nice to be wanted," Maker said. He stared at Gallico for a moment, trying to figure out if he could trust him. The young man could be lying to them, trying to lure them into a trap by pretending to offer aid. However, he wasn't giving off a treacherous vibe — at least not one that Maker could pick up on. He looked towards Adames to get his assessment; the NCO merely shrugged.

"All right," Maker declared firmly. "I'm trusting you. Not just with my life, but the lives of my people. Understand?"

Gallico nodded solemnly. "I won't let you down, Sarge." He turned and quickly began heading back to the stairwell, motioning for Maker's squad to follow him.

"By the way," Gallico added, "how long do you think you'll need to hide out for?"

"Just until morning," Maker replied. "Then we'll meet with Shoal and find some way off this rock."

"Shoal?!" Gallico practically barked, turning to Maker with a stunned expression.

"You know him?" Adames asked.

"Yeah," Gallico replied, still looking incredulous. "He's the one who put the bounty out on you."

## Chapter 28

Shoal was sitting at a desk in the office area of his warehouse, busy trying to crack the encryption on the credit voucher he'd gotten earlier, when one of the clones stuck his head around the corner.

"They're here," the clone said.

Shoal nodded without looking up. "Bring them in, Pier."

Of course, he knew which "twin" he was addressing, even without laying eyes on him. Normal humans found it practically impossible to tell clones apart in most instances, but Shoal — being a hybrid — had a special tool: his nose. He had a highly developed sense of smell that was so sensitive that he could even tell clones apart.

The sound of footsteps reached his ears before anyone actually came into sight. He put the voucher aside, stood, and stepped around to the front of his desk. A moment later, he was greeted by the sight of the clones flanking a group of six individuals. There were three men who seemed to have their hands bound behind their backs. This trio appeared to be guarded by two men to their left and right (one on each side) as well as a woman to the rear, all of whom carried firearms.

Shoal recognized two of the bound captives: the two men who had come to see him earlier (and who had provided the voucher that had been frustrating him). The one who had initially made contact with him now walked with an obvious limp, and Shoal's nose — picking up traces of blood — told him that the man had been injured. The other fellow, the one who had raised a stink about Shoal wasting his time, glared at Shoal like he

151

wanted to murder him. The third person bound was a slender young man that Shoal hadn't seen before, but there didn't seem to be anything noteworthy about him.

"Welcome back," Shoal said, focusing his attention on the first two captives.

"Thanks," said the one who'd been giving Shoal the stink-eye. "I don't suppose you've got that information on the Vacra?"

Shoal laughed. "Not exactly. You'll find out where they're going to be, but you won't like the circumstances."

Understanding dawned in the man's eyes. "You're handing us over to them."

"Yes and no," Shoal said. "They want *you*" — Shoal nodded to the man he'd been speaking with, who was undoubtedly the leader of the captives — "but not your friends."

"And why is that?"

"Apparently you have something they want, and they're willing to pay top dollar to get it."

The man's eyebrows furrowed, as if in thought. Then he let out a sigh. "So when and where will it happen?"

Shoal shrugged. "No idea. I wasn't kidding when I called your Vacra friends paranoid. They play their cards close to the vest."

"So you just wait around until you hear from them?"

"No. I've sent word to them that you're in my custody. They should responding any time now with a rendezvous point." Shoal glanced down at his wrist, which sported a wearable p-comp. "Unfortunately, no word yet, so you're my guests for a while."

The captive leader was silent for a moment, then said, "If I go to the Vacra, what happens to my friends?" He nodded at the other two bound men.

"Lots of trades and industries have a shortage of labor," Shoal replied. "Slave pits. Gladiatorial arenas. We'll find something that's a good fit." The Panthera laughed, obviously amused by his own wit.

"But why go through all this?" the man asked. "You had two of us here earlier, and without any firearms. Why not just take us then?"

"I thought about it," Shoal admitted. "But I have people coming here to do business all the time. It wouldn't do for word to start spreading that meeting with me on my own turf could be hazardous to one's health. I have my reputation to consider, after all."

Shoal chuckled again, but his statements were only partially genuine. In truth, he actually *had* planned to capture the two men earlier just as had been suggested. However, his nose had told him not to.

In brief, the captive leader didn't quite smell the way a human being should. He wasn't a gene-job or a lab product — of that the Panthera was certain. However, there was a scent about him that Shoal couldn't place, explain, or even accurately describe. It was as though the man had been exposed to something incredibly exotic and as a result had become infused with an aspect that defied categorization. Bearing that in mind, trying to capture him would have meant dealing with the unknown, and Shoal hadn't gotten this far in life by taking unnecessary risks. Thus, despite his original intent, Shoal had been wary of taking on the two men and had decided to outsource the job.

"I guess that explains why you sent others to do your dirty work," the man said.

"Huh?" Shoal muttered, wondering if he'd somehow been speaking aloud.

"Your vaunted reputation," the man repeated. "That's why you had Joss try to jump us first. That was you who called on his communicator, trying to see if he'd gotten the job done."

Shoal took a slight bow. "Guilty as charged. Unfortunately, when it became obvious that Joss had failed, I had to go to Plan B."

"Which was putting out a reward for us."

"Yes, but I also put out the word that you had to be taken alive," Shoal assured him. "*You*, that is. Anyone with you was fair game."

"Apparently that message got garbled. A sniper almost took my head off."

The Panthera sighed wearily. "What do you want me to do? I even provided a holopic so that nothing like that would happen. I guess to some of these guys every bounty is 'Dead or Alive.'"

All of a sudden, Shoal frowned. With a suspicious gleam in his eye, he turned to the three people who had been guarding the bound captives. "And speaking of bounties…"

There was silence for a moment, and then one of the male bounty hunters — a young man who seemed somewhat nervous — spoke up. "Y-yes?"

"There's a sizeable reward for these folks you brought in," Shoal responded. "I'm surprised you haven't asked for it yet instead of just listening to us jabber."

"We're patient," the young bounty hunter replied, as if that explained everything.

"Patient," Shoal repeated, saying the word as if he'd never heard it before. "Interesting. What's your name, by the way?"

"Gallico."

"Well, Gallico, if you captured these three you must be good at what you do," Shoal surmised. "Confident. Competent."

"Of course," Gallico said, smiling a little nervously.

"Riddle me this, then, Gallico," the Panthera said, raising his hand and extending his claws. "If you're so cool and capable, why do you stink of fear?"

# EFFERUS

## Chapter 29

It had certainly been a bold plan: have Maker, Adames, and Wayne pretend to be captives whom Gallico, Snick, and Loyola would take to Shoal for the bounty. Once inside the Panthera's warehouse, they could hopefully get some of the answers they were hoping for.

Initially, they had simply intended to break in and overpower Shoal and the clones once they were inside. Snick, however, had suggested something more subtle.

"If he thinks he has prisoners who are bound and helpless," Snick had said, "he may be more inclined to part with information. And if he isn't, we can always revert to the original plan."

Once a course of action had been decided, the only real question was whether they could truly trust Gallico. However, the young man had been true to his word, guiding them out of their hotel unseen through little-used passageways that were actually reserved for hotel staff. (Apparently Gallico had worked there for a short time.) He had then smuggled them into his own apartment — a small efficiency in a run-down tenement — where they had come up with their fake-prisoner stratagem.

Once in Shoal's place, Snick's suggestion had proved itself worthwhile almost immediately, as the Panthera was apparently a talker. They had gotten far more info in a shorter period of time than they would have otherwise. However, they hadn't really discussed what the three bounty collectors would do while Maker was engaging Shoal in conversation. Their idleness — and blatant lack of interest in collecting the bounty — had ultimately aroused the Panthera's suspicion.

Now, with Shoal essentially threatening Gallico, their plan was clearly about to come apart.

*It was fun while it lasted*, Maker thought, then yelled, "Now!"

Maker's shout came on the heels of Shoal stating that Gallico reeked of fear. Of course, neither his hands, nor those of Adames and Wayne — the other two "captives" — had actually been truly bound, and they all reached for their weapons. In fact, aside from Shoal, everyone in both parties immediately brought their guns up into firing position. Oddly enough, however, no one fired a shot.

Silence reigned for a moment as the two parties kept their weapons aimed at one another. Glancing around, Maker saw that Loyola and Wayne had their guns trained on one of the clones; Adames and Snick were covering the other, while he and Gallico were aiming at Shoal. It wasn't hard to see who had the advantage.

"Give it up," Maker said after a few seconds. "Drop your weapons."

"Now why would we do that?" Shoal asked almost rhetorically.

"This isn't exactly a Mexican standoff," Maker replied. "We've got you outnumbered two-to-one."

The Panthera smiled and subtly tapped a button on his p-comp. "Look again. I think you've miscounted."

As he spoke, Maker caught the distinct sound of gears whirring, machinery in motion. To his surprise, a half-dozen panels unexpectedly sprang open in the walls around them. In each of the recessed spaces now visible, a turret gun slid out.

"I think all of *you* should drop *your* weapons," Shoal sneered. Eyeing Gallico, he added, "Especially you, boy. I gutted the last man who pointed a gun at me with *this* hand."

The Panthera held up his hand, claws extended, for effect. Gallico gulped, but kept his weapon pointed at Shoal.

"Let me put this another way," Shoal said. "Those turrets have auto-targeting systems that key in on biometrics. Unless I shut them down, in about a minute they're going to gun down anyone they don't read as either me or the clones. Now drop your weapons."

Maker hesitated only a moment, then tossed his gun to the floor. The rest of his squad immediately did the same.

"Now see how easy that was," Shoal said. He motioned for Maker's team to step back, away from the weapons they had just tossed to the floor, and they complied.

"So what exactly did you think?" the Panthera went on. "That I just let armed parties come in here willy-nilly, without any kind of back-up or contingency plan? As you can see now, there was a reason I didn't bother to take any weapons from your fake bounty hunters or even search any of you."

As Shoal spoke, his words hit Maker in the gut. In actuality, Maker had indeed found it a little odd that no one had checked their restraints or searched them when he, Adames, and Wayne were pretending to be captives. He had simply thought they were catching a few breaks, which seemed overdue considering everything that had happened to them of late. In hindsight, he should have realized that an oversight like that meant there were other tactics being employed.

Motion from the turrets drew Maker's attention, and he watched as they all withdrew back into the walls. Apparently Shoal had deactivated them; he certainly didn't need them now that Maker and his people had been disarmed.

Shoal turned towards Gallico, and let out something like an angry growl. "Now, I warned you what would come from pointing a gun at me." He then raised a hand, extending his claws as he advanced on the young man.

"Wait!" Maker shouted. "I pointed a gun at you, too. Plus, Gallico was only following orders. If you want to punish someone for aiming a muzzle in your direction, punish *me*."

Shoal seemed to take a moment to contemplate.

"Yes," said one of the clones. "Do—"

"—it," chimed in the other. "Gut them—"

"—both," finished the first.

Shoal shook his head. "As much as I'd like to, the Vacra want this one" — he nodded towards Maker — "alive. Plus, I'm going to need him to give me the encryption code for that credit voucher." He jerked his head back towards Gallico. "You, however, I'm going to teach a lesson to."

The Panthera leaped at Gallico, swiping at the young man's mid-section. Shoal was incredibly fast, his reflexes literally cat-like. Much to everyone's amazement, however, Gallico managed to raise a leg up and into the path of the eviscerating blow.

There was a sound like a side of raw beef being slammed onto a countertop, followed by a literal roar of pain. Shoal, standing on somewhat wobbly legs, was cradling the hand he'd used to attack Gallico. From what

Maker could see, it looked as though someone had smashed the hand with a sledgehammer. It wouldn't have shocked him if every bone in it was broken.

Almost immediately, Maker grasped what had happened. The leg that Gallico had lifted to block Shoal's had was his cybernetic limb. Hitting it had probably been like punching the side of a building.

Before anyone could react, Gallico suddenly extended his leg, kicking Shoal in the shin. There was a stomach-turning crunch as the Panthera's leg bent backwards with the bone sticking out. Off-balance, Shoal went face-first down to the floor and didn't move. Gallico immediately placed the foot of his cybernetic leg on the back of Shoal's head.

"Back off!" Gallico shouted to the clones, who were swinging their guns toward him. "Back off or I'll squash his head like a grape!"

The clones froze. A silent exchange seemed to take place between them (which was probably what literally happened), and then they turned over their weapons — one giving his gun to Snick and the other handing his over to Adames.

It struck Maker as odd that the two would surrender so easily. Then he recalled that they were bred to be completely loyal to Shoal. They probably had some kind of ingrained mental block that prevented them from taking any action that might put their owner/benefactor in danger. Thus, even though they'd probably had the upper hand when they were armed, the mere possibility that the Panthera might get killed (or simply hurt) was enough to force their submission.

Snick and Adames kept the clones covered while Wayne began an impromptu inspection of Shoal's warehouse. However, it was unlikely that Tier and Pier would try anything as long as Gallico had his foot on their boss' neck, and Gallico didn't move.

After a few minutes, Wayne came across what they needed: a small storage closet with an external lock. After confirming that the room contained nothing that could readily be made into weapons, they locked the clones inside. (It wasn't necessary to tell them what would happen to Shoal if they tried anything.)

At the sound of the lock engaging, Maker suddenly relaxed, feeling an immense amount of tension leaving his body. In all honesty, he hadn't realized how wound up he'd been, but it shouldn't have been unexpected. He — and presumably every other member of his squad — had been on edge for hours. In fact, he could sense a more tranquil mood coming from everyone as they recovered their weapons and then reconvened around a still-unconscious Shoal, whose blood was starting to pool around his mangled leg. Unsurprisingly, no one felt a lot of sympathy for him.

"So what now, Lieutenant?" asked Loyola.

"Lieutenant?" Gallico repeated as Maker bent down and removed the p-comp from Shoal's arm.

"I may have understated my current relationship with the military," Maker said, rising. Gallico merely nodded in response, accepting the statement at face value. "Anyway, I'd say that we have what we came for" — he held up Shoal's p-comp in his hand — "so we can skedaddle."

Adames tilted his head towards Shoal, saying, "What about him?"

Maker shrugged. "Tie him up and toss him in a closet, I guess. Then we hustle to the landing port and take the first shuttle back to the space station."

"I wouldn't advise taking the shuttle if I were you," Gallico warned unexpectedly.

"Why not?" asked Wayne.

"Shoal didn't actually pay up, so the bounty on you hasn't been collected," Gallico answered. "It's still active. Plus, it won't take a lot of snooping around to figure out that you weren't allowed to land on the planet, so it's a given that you'll have to take the shuttle back."

"And there will be a lot of scumbags hanging out at the spaceport looking for a payday," Adames surmised.

Silence reigned for a moment as this fact sank in.

Maker sighed. "Well, I guess the solution is obvious: we need to commandeer a ship."

## Chapter 30

For the first time in what felt like forever, Maker and his team seemed to catch a lucky break: Shoal actually had a ship. It was on the premises, in fact — kept in another part of the warehouse that served as a hangar. It was Gallico who made them aware of this fact.

"I've actually been hired once or twice to unload stuff from it, along with a bunch of other guys," Gallico had said. "Basically day laborer stuff, but I know where the ship is kept."

With that, he had shuffled off with Adames to show the NCO where the vessel was located, while Loyola and Snick tied Shoal's arms behind his back. After ensuring that he was securely bound, they lifted him onto a nearby table and — per Maker's orders — went about tending to his wounds.

The Panthera was still unconscious and looked terribly pale; in addition, his hand and leg were disturbing to look at and his clothes were soaked with blood.

"Tell me again why we're saving the guy who wanted to sell us into slavery," Loyola said as she applied a coagulant to stop Shoal's bleeding.

Snick shrugged. "Common decency, I suppose."

"No," Maker stated, shaking his head. "It just suddenly occurred to me that we may need to pick his brain to see if he knows anything else about the Vacra."

He turned to Wayne and handed him the Panthera's p-comp. "Here — take this. The Vacra are going to attempt to contact Shoal on it, and we need to be ready when they do."

Wayne gave him a nod of acknowledgment as he reached out and took the p-comp. A moment later, he was busy tapping on the device's controls, trying to extract whatever information he could from it. Maker watched for a moment before stepping away to pursue a task of his own.

It took Maker only a few minutes of pecking around to find what he was looking for: the credit voucher that he'd previously given Shoal. Smiling, he put the voucher in his pocket. In light of everything that had happened since he'd last held it, he'd almost prefer to chop off his arm than leave it with the treacherous Panthera — even if Shoal couldn't crack the encryption on it.

With that thought, he rejoined the rest of the squad, noting that Gallico and Adames had returned, with the latter practically beaming.

"Green light on the ship," the master sergeant said. "We're good to go."

Five minutes later, Maker's squad — along with Gallico and Shoal — was in the air.

## Chapter 31

The flight up to the space station was worry-free for the most part. That said, Loyola — who was piloting — had initially zoomed away from the surface at a speed that was almost terrifying. Sitting in the co-pilot's seat next to her, Adames had screamed at her to take it down a notch.

"Sorry," Loyola muttered sheepishly as she slowed the ship's acceleration, "but the lieutenant said to step on it."

"That I did," Maker admitted. He had indeed told her to get them up to the station as fast as possible. "But seeing as there's a price on our heads, I should have tempered that order by saying to get us there as fast as *reasonably* possible."

"Got it," Loyola said with a nod. "Don't draw unnecessary attention."

"Good idea," Adames said. "And now that we're no longer approaching at ramming speed, the station is also less likely to blast us out of the sky."

Loyola's cheeks turned red at this, but it was clear that she recognized the comment as merely good-natured ribbing — especially after Adames gave her a friendly wink. The NCO then got on the comm with the space station and began obtaining permission for them to dock.

Maker spent the time in transit trying to get information from Shoal. The Panthera had not yet regained consciousness when they took off and was cuffed to a chair at present. Frankly speaking, in his current condition, Shoal was unlikely to pose a threat to anyone, but Maker saw no need to take chances. Thus, he once again checked that the restraints were secure before administering a stimulant to the Panthera. Thirty seconds later, Shoal was conscious and alert (and still in quite a bit of pain).

It took all of five minutes to figure out that Shoal knew practically nothing more than he'd already revealed: he'd sent word to the Vacra that Maker had been captured, and was awaiting instructions on where to meet them. (Needless to say, the entire thing had been a set-up from the start. The Vacra had known Maker was looking for them, and had used Shoal to bait a trap.) About the only additional piece of information the Panthera had to offer was something Maker had already surmised: although the Vacra wanted *him*, Maker (and were willingly to pay a hefty sum to get their hands on him), his capture wasn't truly their endgame.

"They're after some weird animal," Shoal hissed painfully between clenched teeth. "Some freakish alien thing, or maybe some kind of hybrid... All I know is that I've never seen anything quite like it, but the Vacra think you can lead them to it."

Maker tapped his p-comp, causing a hologram of Erlen to appear.

"Is this what they're after?" he asked.

Shoal stared at the image for a moment, then nodded. "Yeah, that looks like it."

Frowning as the hologram vanished, Maker went back to grilling the Panthera, but the fellow really didn't know much else. (He did, however, provide one additional nugget by identifying a hologram of Skullcap as one of the Vacra he'd had contact with.) Somewhat disgusted, Maker then injected Shoal with a sedative, once again rendering him unconscious.

# EFFERUS

He spent the remainder of the flight brooding over the information (or lack thereof) he'd gotten from the Panthera.

## Chapter 32

Their luck continued to hold, as Maker's crew had no trouble docking or getting through the station to their own vessel. Gallico went with them, while they left a still-unconscious Shoal bound and restrained aboard his own ship.

The reunion at the *Raider* was short and sweet, consisting mostly of those who had been planet-side rushing aboard as fast as possible. Not unexpectedly, Erlen rose up onto his hind legs and practically bounded into Maker's arms the second he stepped inside.

"Yeah," Maker said as the Niotan nuzzled his neck. "Missed you, too."

Upon reflection, Maker realized that his phrasing might sound odd. They'd been gone, what — maybe half a day? But the truth of the matter was that he and Erlen had rarely been separated since the Niotan was entrusted to him. Tack that on to everything they'd been through on Defalcator, and it felt like he'd been gone a lot longer.

As Erlen flopped back down to the floor, Maker began barking orders, telling everyone to prepare for immediate departure. No one had to be told twice — especially those who had gone down to the surface with him. Maker was certain that they, like him, were anxious to put Defalcator as far behind them as possible. However, his thoughts on the subject were interrupted by the approach of Browing and Dr. Chantrey.

"So, how'd it go?" the doctor asked when she and Browing drew close.

"I'll tell you later," Maker replied, subconsciously eyeing Shoal's p-comp, which he had retrieved from

Wayne once they were aboard the *Raider*. "Right now, we need to put some space between us and this planet."

Browing let out a grunt of disdain. "In other words, you've done your usual bang-up job of spreading joy and making friends. Who'd you shoot this time?"

"You should be more concerned with who I'm going to shoot next," Maker stated flatly, eyes narrowing. "Any other questions?"

"Yeah," Browing said, then hooked a thumb towards Gallico, who had taken a seat in order to stay out of the way. "Who's that?"

Maker smiled. "Someone I spread joy to and made friends with."

Browing exhaled sharply, but before he could say anything, Dr. Chantrey chimed in.

"I think what Bain meant to ask," she said, "is what's he doing here?"

Maker sighed, then glanced at Gallico, who was definitely out of earshot. "Look, he's someone I met in the Marines a few years back, and he helped us out of a scrape down on the surface. In fact, we probably wouldn't be here without him."

"Gratitude aside, he can't come with us," Browing declared. "He's not cleared for this mission."

Maker frowned. He hated to admit it, but Browing had a point. Although this wasn't a typical assignment by any measure, it clearly wasn't appropriate to have unauthorized personnel accompany them.

Maker glanced at Gallico. In the short time that they'd spent together, he felt that he'd gotten to know the young man. Maybe not thoroughly or completely, but enough to realize that Gallico wasn't the kind of person who belonged on a planet like Defalcator.

Of course, it had never been explicitly stated that Gallico would come with them. Events had simply unfolded in such a way (and with such swiftness), that having him with their team felt natural. But now with the issue plainly before him, Maker understood that dragging the former Marine along with them was simply out of the question.

Maker let out a heavy sigh and nodded in acquiescence. "All right. I'll tell him."

However, before he even began walking in Gallico's direction, he heard someone calling him.

"El-tee," said Diviana from the pilot's seat. "You might want to take a look at this."

Brow crinkling, Maker hurried over to her, followed by Chantrey and Browing.

"What is it?" Maker asked.

"This," Diviana replied, tapping a monitor in front of her.

Maker stared at the screen, which depicted an odd scene. Dozens of spaceships, of various makes, models, and designs, were gathered in a distinctly confined area of space. They appeared to be sitting almost motionlessly, as if waiting for someone to give a signal for them to move. As he watched, more ships moved to join those already present.

"What is this?" Browing asked, staring at the monitor.

"It's an area outside the space station," Diviana answered. "Just inside the range for a hyperspace jump."

Maker frowned, thinking about what this meant. Whenever a ship made a hyperspace jump, it actually shifted a certain area around it — known as the jump field — into hyperspace. The jump field usually didn't extend beyond a ship's exterior, but anything that got too close could accidentally get torn apart, with pieces of it being dragged into hyperspace.

To avoid anything like this happening, most space stations had rules requiring ships to be a particular distance away before activating their jump engines. If a station detected hyperspace engines being fired up too soon, the ship in question would probably find itself getting blasted to pieces. (In fact, he suddenly recalled Commander Dallen warning them of that outcome if they tried to jump before permitted to do so.)

Bearing all this in mind while looking at the growing congregation of ships, Maker started to get a bad feeling.

"This is live?" Browing asked.

"Yes," said Diviana. "That's an image from one of the station cameras — they'll let you hook into their system for a nominal fee — but this is happening all around the station."

"They're all just sitting there," Dr. Chantrey observed.

Diviana nodded. "Looks like they're waiting on something."

"Yeah, Browing agreed, "but what?"

There was silence for a moment, then Maker responded.

"Us," he said simply. "They're waiting on us."

# EFFERUS

## Chapter 33

Browing was absolutely livid.

"There's a bounty on our heads and you didn't tell us?!" he practically screamed.

"Technically, the bounty's only on *my* head," Maker countered.

Browing glowered at him. "And the rest of us are just what — collateral damage? You should have told us."

Maker didn't immediately say anything. They were currently in the *Raider*'s briefing room, and everyone was present — including Gallico. Upon figuring out what the ships outside the station were doing, he had immediately called everyone together and made them aware of the events on Defalcator, including the bounty. It was a revelation that had immediately set Browing off, and he had not been shy about expressing his opinion. Of course, Browing's anger was nothing Maker would lose sleep over, but he didn't want any of his people — basically, those he'd left at the space station — to be in the dark about this stuff.

Maker sighed. "First of all, everyone who went planet-side with me knew. Next, we've been on board for maybe ten minutes, so forgive me if I focused on getting us away from here first and then briefing the issue, as opposed to doing the reverse."

There was silence for a moment, then Diviana said, "It's fine, Lieutenant. It was the right call."

The rest of the Marines either murmured in agreement or nodded, giving Maker a strong showing of moral support. Browing, not to be outdone and still on his high horse, was about to say something when Dr. Chantrey spoke up.

"It's a moot point at this juncture," she declared, "since, with all those ships out there, we aren't going anywhere."

"So, just to make sure I understand," Planck chimed in, "all those ships out there are waiting to pounce on us, essentially with the hope of capturing Lieutenant Maker?"

"More or less," Maker replied. "They're inside jump range, so we'll run into them before we get far enough to go to hyperspace."

"And if we try to jump before that," Fierce added, "the station will vaporize us."

Planck frowned slightly, as if trying to work out a math problem in his head. "But if they want him so badly, why didn't they just capture him when all of you were moving through the station from that other ship to the *Raider*?"

To everyone's surprise, it was Gallico who joined the conversation at this point, saying, "It's the rules of the space station. They don't allow anything that might damage the facility — especially violent altercations. Anything like that will cost you the privilege of landing at either the station or on the planet, and this far out in the Fringe, you need access to every resource you can get. Basically, no one's willing to risk getting cut off."

"But how do they even know we're here?" Loyola asked.

Maker shrugged. "Probably just playing the odds. As Gallico said previously, it wouldn't take much effort to figure out that we have a ship docked at this station. And since we haven't been captured yet, it's a sure bet that we'll be trying to leave the area as soon as possible."

"And how can they be certain that we haven't left yet?" asked Browing.

This time the answer came from Adames, who muttered, "Bribes, most likely. All they have to do is grease the right palm — someone in the control tower, maybe — and they'll have an inside line on when our ship leaves."

"So maybe we just need to take off without talking to the control tower," Wayne suggested. "Why do we need their permission, anyway?"

"Because they'll blast any ship that doesn't get it," Adames declared. "They can't have this station be a free-for-all, with everyone coming and going whenever they like in haphazard fashion. It's too dangerous. There have to be controls in place."

"Plus," Gallico added, "if someone really has been bribed, this ship is probably being monitored to some extent so they'll know when you leave."

"Well, we have to do *something*," Browing interjected. "We can't just sit here forever."

"Yeah," Loyola agreed. "It would be great if we could send all those ships on a wild-goose chase."

"Hmmm," Maker muttered, drumming his fingers. "Maybe we can."

## Chapter 34

It didn't take Maker long to outline his idea. Amazingly, although there were obviously a few kinks to work out, it was met with less skepticism than he'd anticipated — even from Browing.

"It's not entirely risk-free," Browing said, "but it has merit. And it's not like we have a lot of options."

Maker almost had trouble hiding his surprise. That was high praise coming from Browing — particularly in light of the fact that the two of them were constantly butting heads.

"The technical aspects are going to be a little tricky, though," Adames noted, bringing Maker back to the conversation at hand.

"I'll take care of those," Wayne said, his robot Jerry next to him. "I can rig something together in, say, twenty minutes?"

"Ten would be better," Maker quipped.

"Yes, sir," Wayne said with a grin. Maker knew solely from the look on the younger Marine's face that Wayne was relishing the thought of the challenge he was being given.

With nothing further to discuss, Maker dismissed the meeting, although he asked Gallico to stay for a moment. He caught an inquisitive look from Dr. Chantrey as she was leaving and understood immediately that she was offering her help. Maker gave an almost imperceptible shake of the head. This wasn't the first time he had to give bad news to another soldier (which was how he thought of Gallico).

"Listen," Maker began when they were alone, "you've literally been a life-saver for us, and we appreciate everything you've done, but—"

"But I can't go with you," Gallico interjected.

Maker nodded. "Yeah. I'm sorry."

"No need to apologize," Gallico assured him. "I figured this was how things would shake out."

"Oh? How'd you reach that conclusion?"

"Well, you practically admitted that you were still in the Corps. Add to that the fact that you're pretending to be buccaneers, and it's pretty obvious that you're on a covert mission of some sort. That being the case, you can't go around picking up strays."

Maker sighed and clapped Gallico on the shoulder. "You're a good man. If it were strictly up to me…"

"I know," Gallico said as Maker trailed off, looking forlorn. "It's just that, I'm at a point in my life — a *place* in my life — where things aren't so great, and I don't even know how I got here. I guess I saw leaving with you guys as a way to maybe get back on track."

"I understand," Maker intoned sincerely. "But just because you can't go with us, it doesn't mean you have to stay *here*."

Gallico frowned. "What do you mean?"

Maker pulled out the credit voucher he'd initially given to Shoal.

"Take this," he insisted, pressing the voucher into Gallico's hand. "There's more than enough on there for a man to start fresh somewhere — anywhere he wants, in fact."

He then told Gallico the encryption code, as well as how much money was on the voucher. The younger man's eyes bulged in awe at the figure.

"Why are you doing this?" he asked.

"Because I know what it's like to need a second chance," Maker replied. "To yearn for an opportunity to hit the reset button."

"But this amount of money — it's not like a couple of credits tossed into a panhandler's hat on the street. Isn't someone going to take notice that it's gone?"

"Not really. It's what I was going to pay Shoal, had he played straight with us, so the money was going to change hands regardless."

"Wow," Gallico muttered, still plainly impressed. "This is way more than I ever could have anticipated. I mean, I didn't do it for money, but... I mean..." He struggled for words for a moment, then let out a deep breath and said, "I just wish there was something more I could do."

"Actually, there is," Maker said, eyes narrowing as a new idea occurred to him.

## Chapter 35

Ripper Rage (who preferred the simple appellation "Rip") was a man on a mission. Sitting in the captain's chair aboard his spaceship, the *Oceanic Khan*, he was poised for the biggest payday of his criminal career — and all he had to do to collect was a little bit of bounty hunting.

Truth be told, however, Rip had both personal and professional reasons for wanting this particular reward. On the professional side, he was mostly a smuggler by trade, with income from those endeavors occasionally supplemented by a little piracy on the side. In short, collecting bounties wasn't one of his usual sidelines, but for the amount of money being offered in this instance, he'd be crazy not to at least try.

With respect to the situation being personal, Rip knew — or at least had run into — the primary individual the bounty was being offered for: Madman Maker. Reflecting back on their altercation at the Cave, he absentmindedly ran his tongue over the spot in his gums where his two teeth had been knocked out. Maker hadn't actually done that — it was one of his underlings — but as Maker was clearly the leader, Rip had no problem with holding him liable.

More specifically, it was the actual one-on-one he'd had with Maker that really stoked Rip's ire at the moment. He'd never been in a fight like that before. With most opponents (at least those who weren't augmented in some way), his internally injected stim-chems did the bulk of the work. With the right ones, Rip could count on adrenaline flooding his system so he'd be stronger than an

178

adversary, having his nerves numbed so he couldn't feel pain, and so on.

All of this was the result of skills developed in his prior occupation. Before turning to a life of crime, he had been a pharmacist (and a damned good one at that), working in the field of drug development. By the time he switched to his current line of work, Rip knew how to fashion the most potent stimulants imaginable with the least amount of side effects.

Needless to say, this gave him a significant edge over the majority of opponents in hand-to-hand combat. But with Maker, the plan had backfired. Although Rip landed solid shots — hits that would have taken most men down — Maker had just kept coming. In addition, Maker's own blows had packed quite a punch, forcing Rip's body to continue injecting stimulants and such until he basically overdosed and passed out.

When he came to later, an elemental truth dawned on Rip about the fight with Maker — something that had eluded him while they were actually trading punches: Maker was on something. He *had* to be. There was no other explanation for the way the fight had gone.

But whatever it was, it didn't manifest the way other drugs did — especially considering how powerful it must have been to allow Maker to go toe-to-toe with Rip. Basically, Maker should have been exhibiting textbook indicators of robust stimulant use, but there had been no telltale signs that Rip had detected: no dilated pupils, no lack of coordination, no delayed reaction time.

The thought of getting his hands on such a drug damn near made Rip's mouth water. First and foremost, he could use it to supplant the chemical cocktail he currently used, which he now thought of as an inferior product. In addition, Maker's drug would be worth a fortune; there was nothing else like it as far as he knew, either from legitimate pharmaceutical companies or on the black market. What he could get for such a drug would dwarf the bounty being offered — which was admittedly quite sizeable. (Of course, Rip would have to find a way to produce a watered-down version to peddle to others — can't have anybody else competing on the same level as the Ripper!)

But before any of those pipe dreams could become reality, Ripper had to actually get his hands on Maker. And at the moment, he had competition for the privilege.

His ship currently sat not too far from Defalcator's space station, but it was merely one of scores of vessels doing the same. And of course, they were all eyeing the same prize: Maker (although Rip was probably one of the few who knew their quarry by name, since the bounty offer had only included an image of the man for identification purposes). Seeing so many rivals actually frustrated Rip, because he'd actually had a head start to a certain extent.

In truth, because of the drug he was interested in, Rip had already been hunting for Maker when news of the bounty began circulating. He'd started his search almost as soon as he regained consciousness following the bar fight. It hadn't taken much time or effort — just a little bit of cash and some deductive reasoning — to garner some solid leads. For instance, he'd never laid eyes on Maker or any of his companions (other than Gally) before their run-in at the Cave, so he started with the simple premise that they were new arrivals. Crossing the right palm with silver at the landing port had confirmed this theory (or rather, verified that a group fitting the description of Maker's party had taken a shuttle down from the space station).

Around that time, the bounty offer had gone out, including an image of Maker that appeared to have been taken in something akin to a warehouse. Additional info had also included the tracking cipher for a homing beacon of some sort that Maker was believed to have on him. However, the beacon was a low-level device with a limited range; you'd need to be within a block or so of it in order to pick up a signal.

Still, to the average yokel on Defalcator, collecting the bounty probably looked like easy pickings. Rip, on the other hand, had been a bit more circumspect — for several reasons.

First of all, having already tangled with them, he knew that Maker's team was a rugged bunch. Next, it seemed peculiar that the person offering the bounty, Shoal, could have tracked Maker via the homing beacon but had chosen not to do so, opting instead to offer a reward for his capture.

Rip knew Shoal, and recognized the Panthera as a tough customer in his own right. The fact that Shoal wasn't willing to go after the target himself in this instance meant something. To Rip, it implied that Maker's team wasn't just formidable, but extremely dangerous as well. In short, capturing Maker and collecting on the reward was going to be an onerous task.

Moreover, the size of the bounty was sure to attract a lot of the trigger-happy crowd, who would have no qualms about blasting one another to bits considering the amount of money involved. Finally, running all over the planet hoping to get within a block of the homing beacon really didn't appeal to Rip. Thus, he had devised another plan.

In addition to being a daunting foe physically, Rip surmised that Maker was also smart. (He *had* to be if he were the creator of the miracle drug — as Rip thought of it — and at the moment there were no other candidates.) It wouldn't take Maker long to find out about the bounty, and at that point anyone with half a brain would start trying to put some distance between himself and Defalcator. That being the case, Maker would need to get back to the space station asap, which probably wouldn't present that much of a challenge, in all honesty.

Bearing all that in mind, Rip had eschewed hunting Maker planet-side, electing instead to pursue the man in space. With that agenda, he and his people had headed for their ship *tout de suite* and taken off.

Had it been allowed, he would have tried to seize Maker on the space station. But that kind of thing was against the rules, and he couldn't risk getting banned. This far out in space, planets like Defalcator were your lifeblood — especially considering his line of work. Therefore, he'd had to settle for a plan that involved attacking Maker's vessel once it left the station, which had resulted in Rip and his people waiting in their current position for the past few hours.

Unfortunately, this particular strategy wasn't exceptionally original or unique, and Rip's ship was soon joined by numerus others. On a side note, he wondered if those aboard the other vessels had — like himself — made a few well-placed bribes at the station to ensure that they received word when Maker's ship was leaving. Regardless, there was bound to be a massive dogfight at some point after Maker's ship slipped away from its berth.

A snap of fingers drew Rip back to the present. It was Coram, the fellow Rip had assigned to manning the comm and one of about half-a-dozen people on the bridge.

"It's our man on the inside," Coram said, putting a finger to the comm unit in his ear.

"About time," Rip muttered impatiently.

"He says they're departing," Coram went on. "He's relaying the signal from their transponder so we can track them."

As Coram spoke, a monitor set in a nearby wall blazed to life. Displayed on the screen was an intricate schematic that Rip recognized as the space station. Slowly moving through the diagram was a modest, pulsing white light.

"Calculate their exit point and bring it up on screen," Rip ordered.

A moment later, a second screen — placed next to the first — suddenly switched on as well. Rather than a graph, however, this one showed a live feed of the space station — specifically, an open bay that led to one of the docking areas.

Rip watched both screens, his gaze swiveling back and forth between them. The pulsing light was, of course, Maker's ship, and it traveled at a leisurely pace through the space station. In a minute or two, it would reach the bay entrance, where he'd actually be able to see it on the second monitor.

Unexpectedly, a noise like a siren began to boom throughout the *Khan*. Letting out a groan of frustration, Rip reached towards a control panel built into the armrest of his chair and tapped a button; the siren ended. Moodily, he looked towards the first monitor and saw several red blips moving in the direction of the white light. These were other ships, plainly getting in position to go after Maker — and the bounty — the second his vessel moved a respectable distance from the space station. The siren had been a collision alert, a warning that another craft had passed within close proximity to the *Khan* (although, in space, "close" was a relative term that might mean anything from a thousand feet to a mile).

The fact that other ships were in motion indicated that they probably had the same info that Rip did regarding Maker's movements. In other words, his "man on the inside" was everybody's inside man, and had probably sold the same information and access dozens of times over.

*Honor among thieves*, Rip thought, then gave the order for his own ship to move forward. Almost all of the other vessels started closing in as well.

To someone observing it from afar, it probably looked like an oddly synchronized dance: scores of spaceships that had previously been motionless suddenly and almost simultaneously converging on a single area of the space station. Watching it on the first monitor, all of the red blips advancing towards a particular rallying point put Rip in mind of a rosebud slowly closing, its petals pulling in snugly against one another.

Without warning, the white light that represented Maker's ship seemed to surge forward on the screen, as if given an abrupt boost in speed. As Rip watched, it continued accelerating, and a moment later he saw it come rocketing out of the space station's bay on the second monitor.

"After them!" Rip barked. "Now!"

A moment later, he felt the change of momentum as the speed of his own ship increased. And just like that, the chase was on.

The *Khan*'s proximity warning sounded again, letting Rip know that other vessels were getting unreasonably close to his own as they also went in pursuit of Maker. Again he killed the siren — this time indefinitely. (There were going to be other ships in the nearby vicinity for at least the next few minutes, and he didn't need that particular alarm distracting him.) He then set the *Khan*'s exterior cameras to track his quarry, with the feed coming through on the second monitor.

Maker's craft seemed to be traveling at a pretty good clip, although its movements were a little sporadic — like whoever was at the controls had the shakes or something. As Rip had anticipated, Maker was trying to get far enough away to activate his jump engines. Unfortunately, there was nowhere to run. There were simply too many ships between him and the distance he needed to reach in order to jump to hyperspace. The trick, however, was going to consist of actually bringing Maker to heel.

Apparently someone had an idea of how to do this, because one of the other pursuers fired on Maker's ship, causing Rip to draw in a sharp breath through clenched teeth. He had been expecting this, but the actual act caused a bit of concern.

*Careful! We want to catch him — not kill him, you idiot!* Rip thought. *There's no reward if he's dead!*

Rip's fears proved to be unfounded, however, when the shot — from an energy weapon of some sort — seemed to dissipate before actually hitting its target.

185

This was a clear indication that Maker, as expected, had his shields up. (Plus, the vessel that had shot at him most likely hadn't fired at full power. As Rip had observed, anyone wanting the bounty needed Maker alive.)

As Rip watched, other ships also began firing on Maker, but one at a time and in carefully controlled bursts. It was obvious what the game plan was: to disable Maker's shields, then fire a disruptor of some kind to take the ship's engines and other systems offline. At that juncture, they'd board in overwhelming numbers and take Maker prisoner. It was a tactic often employed by pirates, leaving no doubt in Rip's mind as to the primary occupation of many of those around him.

Maker's ship, plainly outmatched and outgunned by sheer numbers, seemed focused on simply fleeing rather than returning fire on anyone. It led all of the ships on a merry chase for several minutes, but there was no doubt as to what the outcome would be. As if he needed proof, the *Khan*'s scanners were keyed in on their quarry and showed the effectiveness of Maker's shields continuing to diminish with every hit they took: thirty-six percent strength…thirty-two percent…twenty-seven percent...

They were coming down to the wire. Soon, Maker's shields would fail, and that's when the real fight would begin, with all of the bounty hunter ships — which had been cooperating up until now in pursuit of a common goal — turning on one another. Each of them wanted the reward for Maker's capture, and splitting it was absolutely out of the question.

Rip had been preparing for the eventual dogfight. During the pursuit of Maker's ship, he hadn't wasted any time or ammo firing on the craft. Instead, he had devoted most of his attention to the other vessels involved in the chase, cataloging their weapons and trying to figure out which of them represented the greatest threat. Now, as Maker's shield percentage entered the teens, he thought he had a workable plan of action: basically, he'd let these other idiots vaporize each other and then swoop in at the end, mop the floor with whoever was left, and claim his prize.

With that in mind, Rip had slowed their speed until the *Khan* was at the rear of those chasing Maker. Per his order, they were now surreptitiously backing out of the crowd of ships altogether, trying to put some distance between their vessel and the upcoming melee.

"Rip, there's something weird," Coram suddenly announced. "The transponder signal... I'm losing it."

"Huh?" Rip uttered, confused. "Don't worry about it. We've got a visual on the target. He's not going anywhere."

"Maybe not," Coram went on, "but the transponder signal just moved."

Rip frowned. "Moved? What do you mean *moved?*" He glanced at the screen showing Maker's ship, which was on the verge of having its remaining shields demolished. "Moved where?"

"Behind us. It's coming from another craft back by the space station, but moving away at a high rate of speed."

"What?!" Rip roared. He looked at the first monitor, and saw that the white light indicating Maker's ship had indeed jumped from the vessel they'd been chasing to another craft. And from all indications, that new ship was getting farther away by the second.

"Turn us around!" Rip practically screamed.

He wasn't sure how, but Maker had pulled a fast one — sent all of those hoping to capture him on a snipe hunt. As the *Khan* swiftly reversed direction, Rip saw other ships around him doing the same. (Apparently they, too, had become aware of the hoax.)

However, it was too late. Maker (and Rip had no doubt that's who it was) had too much of a head start. They'd never catch him, nor would any of the other bounty hunters. Thus, all Rip could do was watch, frustrated and vexed, as Maker's ship reached jump range and then made the leap to hyperspace.

# EFFERUS

## Chapter 36

As the *Raider* exited hyperspace, Maker (who was piloting) let out a sigh of relief. They had actually been out of danger before even reaching jump range, but he'd found himself undeniably tense from the moment they left the space station, even though it was his plan that they had been implementing.

It was Loyola's comment about a wild-goose chase that had given him the idea: give all those waiting ships something else to chase after (preferably, another craft). Fortunately, they actually had another vessel at their disposal — Shoal's.

That alone, however, wasn't enough. Sending out a decoy wasn't going to fool anybody as long as the *Raider* could be identified by its transponder signal, and Maker had no doubt it would be used to track them the second they departed. Wayne, however, had been confident that he could rig something together that would solve the problem.

In the end, Wayne had actually constructed two devices: a mechanism that would cause Shoal's ship to mirror the *Raider*'s transponder signal (and vice versa), and an instrument that would allow the Panthera's vessel to be remotely piloted.

With respect to the second item, Wayne had simply said, "We need it, unless we plan on leaving someone behind."

Of course, there had been no guarantee that any of Wayne's constructs would work as intended. Bearing that in mind, someone had suggested that they simply switch vessels, but Maker had rejected the idea out of hand. Not only was it impractical to move everything to the Panthera's ship, but he had no idea of the other craft's full offensive and defensive capabilities. The *Raider*, on the other hand, had been specifically outfitted for their mission.

In addition, merely switching transponders would likewise have been inefficacious. Not only would it have taken an inordinate amount of time, but at some point they intended to rendezvous with the *Mantis* again, and the right transponder would assure that they were recognized as friendlies instead of met with a barrage of gunfire.

In short, Maker's plan — despite its inherent flaws — had seemingly been their most sensible option. Maker had increased the odds of success slightly by recruiting Gallico to go back to Shoal's ship and — after paying for the privilege — get permission to move it to a berth next to the *Raider*.

"It'll be less conspicuous," Maker had insisted, "if it's two ships next to each other swapping transponder signals than two on opposite sides of the station."

Afterwards, Wayne had spent a few minutes quickly installing his devices on Shoal's ship (whose owner was still aboard, bound and unconscious). Following this, Maker and his team had said their goodbyes to Gallico, and then put the plan into motion.

Much to everyone's surprise, it went off without a hitch for the most part. The mirror-link between the transponders (as Wayne referred to it) worked beautifully, with each ship broadcasting the other's signal. And, after getting permission to depart, the remote piloting also operated as intended. That said, there were two related issues that required more than a little attention to detail.

First of all, the remote piloting wasn't quite as responsive as one would have hoped. Thus, the movements of Shoal's ship were a little irregular as Wayne operated the controls. In addition, Wayne had warned them that the mirror-link was only effective within a certain range, and if the distance between the two crafts became too great it would cease to function properly. That had actually happened, but by the time it occurred, Maker and his people were well on their way to safety and shortly thereafter made the jump to hyperspace.

Now that they were out of danger, Maker noticed that he wasn't the only one displaying a sense of relief. The rest of the crew — particularly those who had been on Defalcator with him — had apparently been pretty wound up as well. Like so many of their recent escapades, the ruse with the second spaceship seemed to have succeeded based on little more than luck and sheer strength of will. His crew was tough, but too many episodes like that would eventually take their toll.

They had dropped out of hyperspace in a region of space known to them. In fact, it was the place where they were supposed to meet back up with the *Mantis* in a few weeks. Maker had selected it as their current location because it would serve as a safe haven — no one should be able to track them here.

"All right," he said, speaking to no one in particular, "we're in a secure location and we've earned some down time, so let's take it. Fierce" — the augmented man's eyebrows went up on hearing his name called — "I need you to check out everybody who went planet-side with me, starting with Adames."

"I'm fine," the NCO almost snapped.

"You got shot," Maker reminded him, "and have yet to be treated by a real physician."

Adames grumbled something unintelligible, but allowed Fierce to begin guiding him to the sickbay.

"The rest of you," Maker continued, "Marines, that is, you've got watch duty for the next eight hours. Regular two-hour intervals, unless you're being seen by Fierce. When you're not on watch or getting checked out, try to get some sleep. That's all."

There was a unanimous chorus of "Yes, sir," after which Maker's subordinates began acting in compliance with his orders, with Diviana taking the first watch. Maker himself was about to head to his cabin when he noticed Browing approaching.

*What now?* Maker thought, rolling his eyes mentally.

"What about the rest of us?" Browing asked. "The non-military. What can *we* do?"

Maker was caught a bit off guard. He was so accustomed to dealing with what he interpreted as demands from Browing (as well as his skeptical view of how Maker was conducting the mission) that hearing him say something that wasn't self-serving was almost a shock. (Even Erlen, who essentially hadn't left Maker's side since he returned, let out a startled grunt.)

"Well, uh," Maker stammered, "I suppose you can uh, run diagnostics on all the systems and check inventory levels — especially rations and ammo."

It was essentially busywork, and Maker felt certain Browing would object to it. He was almost shocked when the man merely nodded and said, "No problem."

Thinking that wonders would never cease, he and Erlen headed to their quarters. Once there, he headed to the bedroom, where he tossed his p-comp onto the nightstand, along with Shoal's. He then set the alarm to wake him in four hours and practically collapsed onto the bed, while Erlen curled up on the floor. He was asleep in less than thirty seconds.

## Chapter 37

Maker came awake with the distinct impression that he was being watched. Currently lying in bed on his side, he could feel eyes on his back, practically boring into him. However, he didn't get the sense of danger that usually accompanies a threat — no feeling of dread or uneasiness. (Plus, Erlen would have been applying claw and fang to any type of menace before it even got close to Maker.)

Convinced that he was in no danger, Maker rolled over to find Dr. Chantrey sitting in a chair, staring at him.

She smiled. "Look who's finally awake."

Maker gave her a small grin in return, then sat up and stretched.

"What are you doing here?" he asked, sliding over to the edge of the bed so that he was directly across from her. Looking around, he saw Erlen still asleep on the floor.

"Just checking in on you."

Maker shook his head. "No — I mean, how'd you get in? The door was locked."

"As ship physician, Fierce has the authority to override all cabin locks."

"That's only in the event of an emergency," Maker noted. Then his eyes widened at the implications. "Wait a minute. Did something hap—"

"Calm down. Nothing's happened," Chantrey assured him. "I just convinced him to let me check on you, like I said."

"Oh," Maker said, somewhat chagrinned. "So how long have you been here?"

"About twenty minutes."

"Twenty minutes?" Maker repeated. "What if someone gets the wrong idea?"

A mischievous look came across Chantrey's face. "You assume that there's a wrong idea for them to get."

Maker simply looked at her a moment, uncertain of how to respond. Then he chuckled. "You're funny, Doc. For a second there, I thought you were serious."

"And if I was?"

Maker gave her a solemn stare. She seemed sincere, and her question had caught him flatfooted.

All of a sudden, Chantrey slid forward and took one of his hands between both of hers.

"I know how you feel about me, Gant," she said.

Hearing her call him something other than his surname caused Maker to feel an unexpected fluttering inside him — plus, she spoke softly and in a tone that seemed almost hypnotic.

"It's my job to know things like that," she continued, "even if you don't know yourself."

"No," he muttered, shaking his head and trying unsuccessfully to withdraw his hand from hers (although it was clearly a half-hearted attempt). "You're wrong. I mean, I don—"

His words were cut off as Chantrey suddenly leaned in and kissed him. He resisted only for a moment, and then he returned the kiss hungrily, feverishly. Her lips were soft and seductive, a whirlpool drawing him into its depths with an allure that was inescapable. At the same time, he felt something within him — some wall of defiance — crumble into dust, and with its disappearance a certain truth he'd been avoiding about his feelings for Chantrey became evident.

When they separated a few moments later, Maker found that Chantrey had moved from her chair to his lap. He hadn't even noticed when it happened. She gently caressed his cheek as they sat there, foreheads touching and eyes closed.

"And I thought you didn't like me," Chantrey said breathily.

"So did I," Maker countered, causing them both to snicker.

"Sorry if I was a bit forward, but I got tired of waiting for you to make the first move — even though I dropped enough hints."

"Consider the hints picked up," Maker declared. "But we obviously need to talk."

"Hmmm," she mumbled. "We're here alone, in your bedroom. I wouldn't have put talking at the top of the to-do list."

"But we're *not* alone," Maker reminded her. He opened his eyes and tilted his head toward the end of the bed. As expected, Erlen was sitting on the floor there, now awake and watching them.

Chantrey, who had followed Maker's gaze to the Niotan, turned back to him and murmured, "Any chance you could send him out for a bit? Then you could spend a little time showing me exactly how much you don't like me."

"Time!" Maker suddenly shouted, his eyes going wide. He jumped to his feet, practically shoving Chantrey from his lap and onto the bed as he did so. "What time is it? How long have I been asleep?"

"Uh, about nine hours," Chantrey replied, ignoring the way Maker had unceremoniously dumped her on the bed.

"Nine hours!" he nearly shrieked. "I set the alarm for four!"

"I know," Chantrey said, getting to her feet. "Fierce initially let me in to check on you hours ago. I turned the alarm off then."

"Why would you do that?" Maker demanded, clearly getting angry.

"Because you needed it! You and the rest of the team who went planet-side were practically running on fumes when you got back here."

"So you just decided all on your own to shut off my alarm."

"No, Fierce did. In his medical opinion, you all needed a full eight hours of rest. However, being on watch duty meant that the others would get no more than six hours each. And if your people were only getting six hours, we knew you'd give yourself less, so we made a command decision."

Maker drew in a deep breath, then let it out slowly.

"Look," he said, trying to keep his voice even. "I know you meant well, but you may have compromised us to a certain extent."

Chantrey frowned. "What do you mean?"

"With the Vacra."

"The Vacra? I thought we were still waiting to hear from them."

Maker grabbed Shoal's p-comp from the nightstand and said, "We've *already* heard from them."

# EFFERUS

## Chapter 38

Within fifteen minutes, everyone was assembled in the briefing room. Not one to mince words, Maker immediately began bringing them up to speed.

"We've received word from the Vacra," he stated simply.

"When?" asked Diviana.

"Shortly after those of us who went planet-side came back to the *Raider*," Maker responded.

A look of annoyance settled on Browing's face. "Any particular reason you're only telling us now?"

"Just the fleet of bounty hunters that was waiting on us outside the space station," Maker quipped. "I thought it was better to focus on one issue at a time, and news about the Vacra would have been a distraction."

"But getting a lead on the Vacra was the whole reason we went to Defalcator," Browing stated. "It would have been nice to know the mission was a success."

"Frankly speaking, I thought that was a given," Maker said. "We almost got killed a dozen times over on Defalcator for that information. There was no way I was leaving without it."

That wasn't exactly true; however, he liked the way it sounded. In all honesty, had the Vacra not made contact before they fled the space station, he simply would have gotten his people to safety and then started his search for them anew.

"What does the message say?" asked Snick, cutting to the heart of the matter.

"Just what Shoal told us it would be," Maker answered. "Coordinates to a rendezvous point."

"And you plan to meet them?" asked Planck, looking nervous. He was plainly reflecting on his time as the Vacra's prisoner.

"The information we received is useless if we don't," Maker said bluntly.

"So what exactly is the plan?" asked Browing.

"They think they're getting me as a prisoner," Maker explained. "With any luck, we can convince some of them to come aboard to scoop me up, but we'll take them into custody instead."

Specifically, he was hoping he could get Skullcap to come aboard. That would be the ideal scenario, but Maker didn't kid himself that it was likely to happen. He didn't think Skullcap took risks of that nature.

"Do you think we're ready?" Chantrey asked.

Maker found himself fighting an urge to smile as he answered her. "As ready as possible under the circumstances."

Browing gave him an odd look. "What exactly does that mean?"

"It means our people are well-rested and alert, for starters," Maker said. "It's part of the reason I didn't mention the Vacra making contact after we jumped here. I wanted our team getting some R-and-R, not getting wound up because another confrontation was imminent. In addition, we've had diagnostics run and all systems are functioning properly."

"Sounds like we're in good shape, el-tee," Wayne chimed in. "So why does it seem like you're worried about something?"

Maker sighed. "I had actually hoped to wake up almost six hours ago and start giving this briefing. I also wanted to have a few dry runs in terms of how this meeting with the Vacra would go. Finally, I don't trust them, so I wanted to get to the rendezvous spot early if possible and scope it out."

"When are we due to meet them?" asked Diviana.

"Roughly two hours," Maker said. "So about all we have time to do is get there and make sure it isn't an ambush."

"And if it is?" asked Fierce.

"Then we'll probably find out what if feels like to be vaporized," Maker declared flatly.

# EFFERUS

## Chapter 39

To everyone's great relief, it wasn't an ambush. Dropping out of hyperspace at the rendezvous point about an hour early, they were happy to discover that no one was lying in wait for them. In fact, their long-range scans picked up no other spaceships in the vicinity.

Trying to get their bearings, they quickly found out that they were in a solar system well out beyond the Fringe that consisted of a single star which was orbited by a solitary, apparently lifeless, planet. The only other item of note was a massive volume of a gaseous, blue-white substance that floated across an immense area of space.

Watching it on one of the *Raider*'s monitors, Maker quickly concluded that it wasn't a nebula (although extensive, it was nowhere near big enough) or any other type of dust or gas he'd encountered in space before. In truth, he had to admit he'd never seen anything quite like it, but all of his instincts told him that they should keep their distance.

Wayne, who was in charge of the scanners and related equipment, suddenly called out to Maker, saying, "Lieutenant, you need to see this."

The view on the monitor shifted, going from displaying a region of outer space to what appeared to be a dry, arid area of land.

"What are we looking at?" Maker asked. He seemed to have posed his question on behalf of himself and the remaining crewmembers present, which included everyone except Planck. The scientist had seemed agitated over the idea of being around his former captors again and had become increasingly distraught as they got closer to the time of the rendezvous. Ultimately he had retreated to the room he shared with Adames and hadn't been seen since.

As to Maker's question, he was clearly referring not so much to the landscape being shown on the monitor as to what populated it: a vast array of spaceships.

"This is the surface of the planet in this system," Wayne stated. "It seems to be some sort of spaceship graveyard. There are warships, passenger ships, battle cruisers, space yachts... All kinds of ships down there, and not all of them of human design."

"What happened to them?" asked Chantrey.

Adames shrugged. "Who knows? Maybe they were derelicts that got caught in the planet's gravitational pull. Maybe someone uses this planet as a scrapyard for old vessels. Maybe—"

Adames' hypothesizing was cut off by a sharp gasp from Diviana, who was frowning but had an intense expression on her face.

"There's something alive in there," she said.

"What, in one of those ships?" asked Wayne.

Diviana shook her head, closing her eyes. "No. The cloud."

Wayne frowned, but Maker — picking up on Diviana's meaning — said, "Switch back to the image of that weird gas."

Wayne did as commanded, and the scene on the monitor once again showed the blue-white gas in space.

"Long-range scanners detect no life signs," Wayne stated, looking at the instruments before him.

"The scanners are wrong," Diviana declared matter-of-factly. "There's something in there. I can sense its thoughts. Not human, but definitely thoughts."

As if in support of her statement, Erlen left his usual place at Maker's side and came over to stand next to Diviana, growling softly and rubbing himself against her leg. However, she had a faraway look in her eyes and didn't seem to notice the Niotan.

"Wayne," Maker said, "fire a probe into that cloud."

Wayne nodded, and then spent a few moments tapping on a keyboard in front of him.

"Done," he announced a few seconds later. "Probe is en route."

"How long before it reaches the cloud?" Maker asked.

"About thirty seconds," Wayne replied.

Maker merely nodded in response, and then silence reigned on the *Raider* as everyone gathered around Wayne and waited with bated breath while the probe made its journey. Subjectively, it felt a lot longer to Maker — a lot closer to thirty minutes than thirty seconds — before the probe reached its destination.

"Contact in five," Wayne proclaimed, breaking what seemed like a spell. "Four... Three... Two... One..."

An odd look suddenly came over Wayne's face, and a moment later, he began adjusting the probe controls. After a few seconds of this, Maker's patience began to grow thin.

"Wayne, report," he ordered.

"Uh, we seem to have lost the probe," Wayne said.

Maker's features took on a look of incomprehension. "What do you mean, 'lost'?"

"Just what I said," Wayne answered, frowning. "As soon as it entered the cloud. I thought maybe we just lost the signal or there was some interference, but it's just...gone."

Maker rubbed his chin for a second, pondering. They weren't here on some scientific expedition, so — while the cloud was a curious anomaly — figuring out the mystery it represented wasn't a priority for them. On the other hand, they were on an unfamiliar battlefield. The Vacra had picked this place to meet, so they must believe it conferred some advantage to them. That being the case, Maker really needed to get the lay of the land.

Decision made, he said, "Fire another probe."

Wayne acknowledged the order with a curt "Yes, sir," and a few moments later, a second probe left the *Raider*.

The wait this time didn't seem nearly as long, and before he knew it, Maker was hearing Wayne counting down as before.

"Probe Two about to initiate contact," Wayne declared, "in five...four...three...two..."

An almost inhuman wail suddenly sounded from behind those assembled. Turning, Maker saw Planck standing to the rear, looking pale as a ghost and visibly trembling, with his eyes bulging in abject terror.

"Efferus!" Planck screamed at an almost ear-splitting level. "Efferus! Efferus!"

## Chapter 40

Planck continued screaming the word "Efferus" over and over — even after Maker had Fierce drag him down to the medical bay.

"Get him out of here," Maker ordered the Augman. "Give him something to calm him down."

As Fierce moved to obey, Maker shook his head in disgust. They were getting close to the meeting with the Vacra. The last thing he needed was some maniac screaming bloody murder in the background while he tried to entice them to come aboard the *Raider*.

"Dr. Chantrey," he said, getting her attention. "I need you to go with Fierce and help with Planck. See if you can figure out what pulled the pin out of his grenade."

Chantrey simply nodded and left.

Maker turned back to Wayne. "What's the story on the second probe?" he asked.

"Right," Wayne said, shifting his attention to his instruments after Maker's comment put him back on point. "Uh, we lost it, just like before. As soon as it entered the cloud, apparently."

Maker frowned, not quite sure what to make of what he was hearing. He glanced at Diviana.

"Are you still getting the sense that something's alive in that cloud?" he asked.

"Most definitely," she replied.

Maker looked at Erlen, who let out a grunt of affirmation.

"I know you only sense thoughts," Maker acknowledged, speaking to Diviana, "but is there anything else you can tell us about what's in there?"

Diviana's brow wrinkled as she concentrated for a moment. "No. I just know it's alive and…different."

"Different how?"

"I'm not sure, but it's not like anything — human or alien — I've come across before."

Maker nodded, deliberating for a moment, then said, "Okay, we don't know exactly what that cloud is, what it did to our probes, or what kind of life-form is in there. That being the case, we don't go anywhere near it."

As expected, no one voiced disagreement or dissent over this decision. Still, Maker had to admit that it — the cloud — was an interesting enigma, and it piqued his curiosity. At the end of the day, however, it was just another mystery of the universe that would probably never be explained.

He went back to getting his people and ship ready for the upcoming encounter with the Vacra, but was still thinking about the cloud in the back of his mind when Chantrey returned from the medical bay a few minutes later saying that Planck wanted to talk to him.

## Chapter 41

"How is he?" Maker asked as he, Chantrey, and Erlen headed to sickbay.

"Same as he's been since you rescued him — a complete mess," Chantrey replied. "But he's lucid at the moment — recovered enough from this last episode to converse with."

"Did he say what it was about?"

"I didn't get the full story, but it's better if you hear it from him yourself, anyway," Chantrey said as they reached the sickbay doors. "One other thing. Fierce had to give him something to calm him down — a sedative of some sort — so he may seem a little out of it."

"It's Planck," Maker noted. "When isn't he a little out of it?"

Chantrey giggled slightly at that, a sound that Maker found enchanting.

"Listen," he said. "About earlier, in my room…"

"It can wait," she said, cutting him off before he had a chance to say anything more. "Let's deal with the Vacra first."

Maker nodded in agreement and then went inside, followed by Chantrey and Erlen. It was the first time Maker been in the medical bay since Fierce had come aboard, and he took a moment to look around.

The place wasn't particularly large — maybe two hundred square feet in size. Both side walls contained built-in cabinets and shelves, which currently appeared to house various types of medicines as well as medical apparatus of all kinds, from forceps to trauma shears. Also set in one of the walls were two doors which led to a washroom and storage room, respectively. A couple of carts containing various equipment served as mobile medical units. Finally, there was an examination table in the center of the room, as well as three in-patient beds along the back wall — the center of which was occupied by Planck.

Maker began heading towards Planck, but had only taken a few steps before he was intercepted by Fierce. In all honesty, Maker hadn't even noticed him before, which was odd considering the Augman's size.

"I know you have some questions," Fierce began, "but I'm going to have to ask that you not distress my patient."

"Your patient just distressed our entire crew with his squalling," Maker said. "If I *do* upset him, it'll be karma."

Fierce didn't say anything; he merely gave Maker an expectant look. At the same time, Chantrey laid a hand on his forearm and gave it a gentle squeeze. Maker glanced at her, noting that the expression on her face showed that she agreed with the Augman.

Maker let out an acquiescent sigh. "Fine. I'll be gentle."

Fierce gave him a short nod, then stepped out of his path. Shaking his head, Maker walked swiftly towards Planck, with the others following in his wake. Already sitting up, Planck began to speak before Maker could say a word.

"Lieutenant, please allow me to apologize for the scene I caused earlier," he said in a flat, emotionless voice. "I wasn't prepared to see what was on the monitor at the time, and my emotions got the better of me."

"What exactly did you see?" Maker asked.

# EFFERUS

"Efferus," Planck replied, as if that single word explained everything.

## Chapter 42

"I'm afraid I don't understand," Maker said, frowning. "What does that even mean?"

"It's a little difficult without context," Planck replied. "If you'll allow me to expound?"

"Please do," Maker virtually insisted.

Planck nodded, then took a moment to compose himself before speaking.

"Back when I was a prisoner of the Vacra," he began, "we spent a period of time in this region of space. They were interested in that white cloud that's out there." An apprehensive look suddenly came onto Planck's face. "We aren't close to it, are we?"

Maker shook his head. "No, we've been keeping our distance."

Planck seemed to relax. "Good. Don't go anywhere near it."

"Why not?" Maker asked.

"Because it devours anything it comes into contact with. Metal, minerals, flesh, bone. Anything that touches it is just…gone. The Vacra did all kinds of experiments with it, but always with the same result. Man or machine, living or dead, it all got absorbed or something."

"What did the Vacra want with it?" Dr. Chantrey chimed in.

Planck gave her an incredulous look. "Can't you guess?"

"I can," Maker announced. "They were trying to weaponize it — turn it into something they could use in battle."

"Exactly," Planck agreed. "But you can't make a weapon out of something you can't contain or control, and they never managed to do so. Whatever came into contact with that cloud simply ceased to exist. The Vacra had a name for it, but I called it 'Efferus.'"

"What exactly does that mean?" Maker asked.

"It's an ancient word from an Old Earth language," Planck explained. "It means fierce, cruel or savage, which seemed a good description, in my opinion — especially considering everything I've seen it do."

Chantrey tilted her head slightly, intrigued. "What do you mean?"

Planck wiped his face with a slightly trembling hand, then took a deep breath. "At one point, the Vacra decided to send a ship into Efferus. They're an insectoid culture, with very little focus on the individual. It's the group — the hive — that matters most, so there wasn't a great deal of concern about personal safety. Thus, with shields powered to the max, they went in."

Planck paused, a faraway look in his eyes. At the same time, his fists clenched in white-knuckled anxiety.

"What happened?" Maker prompted, trying to get Planck to focus. It seemed to work, as the man blinked a few times and then seemed to come back to himself.

"Almost immediately, the shields started collapsing," Planck said. "They were down to fifty percent in less than a minute. Thankfully, it was only slated to be a short trip — just in and out — so the ship was already exiting Efferus at that juncture. It made it about halfway before the shields failed completely."

"And then?" Chantrey prodded.

Planck closed his eyes and let out a deep breath. "Half the ship — the part still in Efferus — just vanished, severed neatly and cleanly like some celestial being had erased it out of existence. Or like it had come out the factory that way."

There was silence for a moment as the others contemplated this.

"You were there," Maker surmised. It wasn't a question.

Planck opened his eyes and looked at him. "Yes, and it was one of the most harrowing experiences of my life. I mean, my ordeal with the Vacra was horrible in ways I can't describe, but that was the one time when I not only came close to dying, but winking out of existence altogether. It terrified me like nothing before or since."

Planck suddenly shivered involuntarily, prompting Maker to lay a comforting hand on his shoulder, conveying both sympathy and understanding. He now had a greater appreciation of what Planck had suffered, and why his reaction to the cloud — Efferus — had been so visceral.

Maker tried to think of something soothing or encouraging to say, but before he could utter a word, Erlen let out a low, menacing growl. At the same time, klaxons began going off throughout the *Raider*.

"What is that?" Planck asked, sounding panicked.

"The Vacra," Maker replied solemnly. "They're here."

# EFFERUS

## Chapter 43

Maker raced back to the bridge, with Chantrey and Erlen right on his heels. On the way, he ran through their plan in his mind.

The Vacra were expecting Shoal, who — at this juncture — was probably back on Defalcator getting medical treatment. However, Maker and his team did have some still images of the Panthera that they could use for communication purposes. (If the Vacra were to wonder why the image seemed frozen, the explanation would be malfunctioning equipment.) Likewise, they had a voice modulator to mimic Shoal's speech pattern.

Needless to say, it wasn't a perfect plan, but it was the best they could come up with under the circumstances. Maker would simply have to bank on the Vacra's obsessive desire to get their hands on him (and by extension, Erlen) to overcome any flaws or shortcomings in strategy.

Upon reaching the bridge, Maker saw Wayne still on the scanners, while Diviana sat in the pilot's seat. Everyone else was at their appropriate battle stations, while Chantrey and Browing, as civilians, tried to make themselves as unobtrusive as possible.

"One ship just dropped out of hyperspace," Wayne called out without being prompted. "Conforms to Vacra design."

"Put it on the monitor," Maker said. "And kill the klaxons."

A moment later, the noise vanished, and the monitor screen switched to show an obviously alien vessel. Heavily outfitted with what appeared to be cannons, turrets, and the like, it was clearly a craft designed for battle.

Maker drew in a sharp breath. More than likely, Skullcap — his mortal enemy — was on that vessel. Now he just needed to get the insectoid leader to—

"Lieutenant," Wayne yelled, interrupting his thoughts. "I've just picked up a second vessel, same Vacra design, coming out of hyperspace. Now a third. A fourth."

"Shields up!" Maker shouted.

"Shields active at one hundred percent," said Loyola, who was manning the *Raider*'s defenses.

Maker felt slightly relieved. At least they had some kind of protection in place, although it wasn't likely to be of much benefit. Because of the sub rosa ship they had raided years before, the Vacra had tech that could cut through an ordinary shield like it was made of cobwebs. As if in confirmation of this, the lights suddenly began flickering.

"What the hell?" Maker said. "Somebody tell me what's going on with the lights."

"Some kind of system malfunction," Adames replied. "I'm trying to pin it down."

Maker turned to Loyola. "What about the shields? Are they still operable?"

Loyola nodded. "Shields still at full capacity."

The lights flickered again, accompanied this time by a growl from Erlen.

"Maker!" Browing shouted unexpectedly. "You need to get all your people into battle gear!"

"What?" Maker muttered as the lights continued to flutter off and on.

"It's an attack, you boneheaded Marine!" Browing replied. "They're targeting life support!"

"Not just that," Adames added. "The jump drive is offline."

Maker stared at him mutely for a moment. An inactive jump drive basically meant they were sitting ducks.

"Everyone needs to get into their armor!" Browing repeated, getting Maker's attention. "*Now!*"

Maker seemed to deliberate for a moment, then said, "Do it."

A moment later, everyone was hurriedly stepping off the bridge except for Maker, who took the pilot's seat, and Erlen. Maker strapped himself in and fired up the ship's normal-space engines. He then flipped a nearby switch, turning on the intercom.

"This is Lieutenant Maker," he stated, his voice booming through the enclosed halls and passageways of the *Raider*. "Everyone is ordered into battle armor — no exceptions."

That last bit was mostly for Fierce and Planck in the medical bay. It was a sure bet that they didn't know exactly what was going on, but they — like everyone else —needed to prepare for the worst.

"We're about to engage in evasive maneuvers," Maker continued on the intercom. "Put on your gear as quickly as possible."

Without warning, a body flopped down in the seat next to Maker. It was Chantrey. As Maker turned the intercom off, she quickly and methodically began strapping herself in.

"What are you doing here?" he asked as he began sending the ship into motion. "You need to be putting on your battle gear. The armor has its own life support system. It'll keep you alive if we lose life support on the *Raider*."

"What about you?" she asked.

"What *about* me?"

"Don't you need to be putting on armor as well?"

"No, what *I* need to do is put this ship through some loop-de-loops, barrel rolls, and anything else that will shake the Vacra off. I've transferred all the controls to me here and Browning's right — whatever they're doing is targeting life support. It's down to eighty-two percent."

As he spoke, he noticed the Vacra ships starting to give chase.

"But why are they doing that?" she asked as the *Raider* shot forward, momentum pushing her into her seat. "I thought they wanted you alive."

"It's not me they want — it's Erlen," Maker admitted. "I'm just a stepping stone. Somehow they know he's on the *Raider*, so they don't even have to bother squeezing me for info about his whereabouts."

"But if they want him, won't taking out life support…"

She trailed off, but Maker understood that she was remembering something she had learned about the Niotan on their previous mission: Erlen didn't need life support. He could survive in the vacuum of space.

"I won't let them have him," Maker declared matter-of-factly, speaking more to himself than Chantrey. He then flipped the intercom on and said, "Everybody hang on. It's about to get bumpy."

\*\*\*\*\*\*\*\*\*\*\*\*\*\*\*\*\*\*\*\*\*\*\*\*\*\*\*\*\*\*\*\*\*\*\*\*\*\*\*\*\*\*\*

For the next quarter hour, Maker tried every trick he knew to shake the Vacra. He was a seasoned pilot, but he was trying to escape from four alien craft that admittedly had superior technology.

He tried firing on them several times. Although he scored a couple of direct hits, from all indications he inflicted no damage on any of his pursuers. On their part, the Vacra continued to hammer at the *Raider*'s life support systems. It was when said systems were down by two-thirds that Maker hit upon his plan.

At that juncture, everyone but Maker and Chantrey had donned their battle armor. Moreover, despite being tossed around like leaves in a tempest, they had all made their way back to the bridge, including Planck and Fierce. (Amazingly, Erlen somehow managed to remain glued in place no matter what type of aerial stunt Maker employed.) As each crewmember had taken their position at the various battle stations, Maker had transferred the appropriate controls back to them.

Browing, Planck, and Fierce (who had no bridge duties) strapped themselves into a couple of empty chairs set in an out-of-the-way place against a wall. Maker ceased the *Raider*'s wild flight pattern long enough for Chantrey to join them, thereby freeing up her seat next to him for Adames. It was when the NCO announced that life support was at thirty percent that Maker decided to tell everyone what he was planning.

"Our jump engines are dead and life support's failing," he said as he continued maneuvering the *Raider*. "When that gives out, we won't last much longer, even with battle armor. We've got to get away from them — some place they can't follow."

There was silence for a moment as everyone digested his words. Then Planck, obviously discerning Maker's intent, began shouting.

"No!" he shrieked, fighting against the harness that held him where he was currently seated. "You can't! You'll kill us all!"

"Well, we'll die if we stay here," Maker retorted. "So it's a bit of a Hobson's choice."

And with that (as well as Planck gibbering madly), Maker guided the *Raider* straight into Efferus.

# EFFERUS

## Chapter 44

Based on what Planck had told him, Maker was certain of two things. First, the Vacra would break off their attack rather than follow the *Raider* into the mysterious cloud. Second, their shields would afford them some measure of protection and perhaps buy them a little time.

His first assumption turned out to be absolutely correct. The Vacra ships discontinued pursuit the second the *Raider* entered Efferus, and the effect was immediately evident.

"Life support now at twenty-five percent and holding," Adames said, almost with a grin.

Apparently they were safe on that front; if the Vacra were still attacking the *Raider*'s systems, their efforts weren't penetrating the cloud.

At that point, however, Maker saw his second assumption strongly challenged.

"Shields have dropped to ninety-four percent," Loyola stated. "Ninety. Eighty-eight."

At that rate, the shields would last no more than a few minutes — *if* they were lucky.

"Is there any way at all that you can communicate with whatever's in here — let it know we're not a threat?" Maker asked over his shoulder, pushing Loyola's steady reporting to the back of his mind, even as she declared shields to be at eighty-one percent.

"That kind of thing really isn't in my wheelhouse," Diviana bluntly admitted.

Maker turned and stared at her for a moment, giving her a sobering look. "I need you to try."

Diviana nodded and Maker sensed that, within her armor, she had closed her eyes, concentrating.

"Seventy-five percent," Loyola said softly.

The entire bridge was silent, but even with their armor on, it was evident to Maker that everyone was clearly on edge. It suddenly occurred to him that he hadn't heard Planck since just before they entered the cloud. Frankly speaking, he expected the man to be screaming his head off by now. However, when he looked in Planck's direction, Maker noted that he seemed to be slumping, as though asleep.

*Probably passed out*, Maker thought.

"Shields at sixty-seven," Loyola reported.

Maker, sparing a glance for Diviana, caught movement with his peripheral vision. It was Erlen, making a soft rumbling sound as he stalked over to where Diviana was seated. With a start, Maker noted that the Niotan's eyes appeared to be glowing green.

"Fifty-nine percent," said Loyola, somehow managing to keep her voice even.

Diviana still hadn't moved or said anything. In his mind's eye, Maker envisioned her frowning deeply, with beads of sweat breaking out on her forehead. The Niotan sat on his haunches in front of her, still making the rumbling noise. It was obvious to Maker that his companion was doing something, and — having a vague idea of what it was — he stayed silent.

"Forty-eight percent," Loyola announced.

Maker, however, wasn't really listening to her any more. Like the others on the bridge, his attention was focused on Diviana and Erlen. (Presumably everyone else had noticed the change in the Niotan's eyes, but no one had mentioned it thus far.) Mentally, he crossed his fingers, hoping for some kind of breakthrough on their part.

"Thirty-eight percent," noted Loyola.

"Maker," Browing hissed, getting his attention. "Whatever this gas is, it's making mincemeat of our shields. We need to leave."

"And go where?" Maker asked rhetorically. "We can't jump to hyperspace, and the Vacra are out there just waiting to pounce. This gas is all that's protecting us at the moment."

"Twenty-seven percent," said Loyola.

With Browing decked out in armor, Maker couldn't see his face, but he got the impression that the man was fuming. No one else said anything, but the tension was almost palpable.

"Eighteen percent," Loyola declared, still managing to speak in a calm manner.

Maker let out a sigh. It appeared that his plan was a failure. He glanced around at everyone, feeling that he should say something and suddenly bothered by the fact that he couldn't see their faces. In a few moments, they would all be dead — snuffed out of existence, if Planck had it right. It didn't bother him so much that this was his own fate, nor with respect to Erlen (whom he knew would rather die than end up in the Vacra's hands). As to his people, well, they were Marines; they knew that every mission could be their last. And with respect to the three civilians—

"Eighteen percent," said Loyola, cutting into his train of thought.

Maker blinked, not sure he'd heard her correctly. "What did you say?"

"Shields holding at eighteen percent," she repeated, her voice sounding almost giddy.

# EFFERUS

## Chapter 45

The sense of relief that flooded the bridge was almost tangible, with everyone suddenly cheering Diviana. Maker assumed that, within her armor, the psychic was probably blushing; he'd always gotten the sense that she didn't care much for accolades.

"Are we safe, Diviana?" Maker asked, cutting into the celebratory atmosphere.

She nodded. "I think so. The, uh, life-form in here…it won't harm us."

This set off another round of cheering.

"Okay people, we're not out of the woods yet," Maker announced, reestablishing order. "I want shields back up at a hundred percent asap. Life support, too. Also…"

Maker continued giving commands until every Marine found themselves with a chore to do. However, he did give them ten minutes to get out of their armor, which they all decided to take advantage of. As they were leaving, however, he asked Diviana to remain behind for a bit.

In addition to Diviana, Chantrey also didn't leave. Like Maker, she had never donned her battle gear and therefore had none to get out of. Not to be outdone, Browing stayed as well, taking off his helmet and running a hand through his hair. After a few seconds, the four of them were the only people on the bridge (not counting Erlen, who stood next to Maker).

For a moment, Maker considered ordering Chantrey and Browing out. He had wanted a short debrief in private with Diviana and hadn't really wanted anyone else present — especially not civilians. However, so much of this mission had gone sideways that simply staying alive seemingly gave everyone a need-to-know with respect to every bit of intel. That being the case (and considering how much the two already knew), he decided not to make their presence an issue.

"I know you said we're safe," Maker began, speaking to Diviana, "but I need a better understanding of what we're dealing with."

"I'm not sure how to describe it," she said, removing her helmet. "It's a life-form, but not like anything we're familiar with. However, I think it feels the same way in regards to us."

"But you were able to reach it?" asked Chantrey. "Speak to it?"

Diviana frowned. "I'm not sure how to explain it to someone who isn't a psychic. It was like I was an amoeba trying to get a person's attention. I don't think it saw me initially — I was way beneath its notice. And then, I got a…boost."

She glanced at Erlen, then bent down and scratched his head, smiling. It was probably the first time she'd shown the Niotan any overt sign of affection. She obviously realized that he had helped her and was grateful. Maker profoundly understood what she had experienced, as Erlen had once helped him fend off a psychic attack in a similar manner.

"What happened next?" Browing inquired as Diviana rose back up.

"I, or rather, *we*, were able to get its attention," she replied. "It was like we'd been floundering in the dark and suddenly someone shined a spotlight on us."

"And then you were able to talk to it?" asked Maker.

She shook her head. "Not exactly. But it seemed to sense that we were in distress and was able to divine the source. It then stopped whatever was attacking the shields and tried to comfort us."

"Comfort you?" Chantrey repeated, confused. "Is it psychic as well?"

"Not exactly. It's more like it's empathic — it can sense and broadcast feelings to a certain extent. The main thing, however, is that it won't hurt us."

Maker and the two civilians took a few seconds to absorb this information, while Diviana reached down to pet Erlen again.

"Okay, thanks," Maker said, prompting Diviana to stand back up. "That'll be all."

She nodded, then turned and left the bridge.

"You're getting lax," Browing commented after Diviana was gone.

Maker gave him a curious look. "What do you mean?"

Browing gave him a smug look. "Watching you and Diviana just now, I couldn't help but notice the lack of military courtesies that would normally take place between a superior and subordinate. No salutes, no order to be at ease or at rest, no formal dismissal…."

Maker let out a snort of derision. "Thank you for keeping tabs on that, Browing. I appreciate your concern, so I'm sure you'll be pleased to know that in battle mode or under threat conditions, the commander has the authority to dispense with typical military conventions. You don't want a guy standing on the bridge waiting to be dismissed when he should be racing to the engine room to put out a fire. I consider this entire mission since the *Raider* and the *Mantis* parted ways to be under threat conditions, so forgive us if we're not observing all the minor courtesies you elitists expect, like wearing a monocle or lifting our pinky when we drink tea."

"Stop it," Chantrey interjected. "Both of you. We were close to dying just minutes ago, and here the two of you are arguing about things that are completely inconsequential."

"I'm not the one keeping a tally of exceptionally minor infractions," Maker insisted.

"Fine then — let's talk about the big stuff," Browing countered. "What about you telling your friend here" — he pointed at Erlen, who growled softly — "to communicate with whatever this thing is you flew us into?"

"What?" Chantrey intoned, clearly caught by surprise at this statement. Maker, on the other hand, merely stared at Browing, plainly unsure of how to respond.

"When he shouted back asking about communicating with whatever this life-form is, he wasn't talking to Diviana," Browing said, his gaze fixed on Maker. "He was talking to Erlen."

"How can you possibly know that?" Chantrey asked.

"Initially, I didn't," Browing replied. "But then I saw Erlen's eyes — we all did — and I remembered Maker telling us that his little friend had helped him once before when he was under psychic attack. Plus, what he was asking wasn't something Diviana is capable of."

Chantrey looked expectantly at Maker, waiting for him to say something.

Maker sighed. Previously, in a tit-for-tat exchange of information, he had indeed made Chantrey and

Browing privy to certain information about Erlen — including an anecdote about the psychic attack.

"Yes," Maker finally admitted, "I was talking to Erlen, but Diviana mistakenly thought my question was directed to her. She can sense thoughts, but what I was asking — reaching out mind-to-mind — isn't one of her talents. Still, I was proud of her for making the attempt."

"And with Erlen's help, she was able to do it," Chantrey realized. She glanced at the Niotan. "As she put it, he boosted her natural abilities."

"Maybe that's one of the reasons the Vacra want him," Browing suggested. "There's so much about that animal that we don't know."

"The same could be said of you," Maker noted.

Browing's eyes narrowed. "I'm listening."

"You knew before anyone else that the Vacra were attacking our life support systems," Maker said. "And what they were using wasn't a conventional weapon — not the way it completely sidestepped our shields. So the question is, how did you know?"

Browing suddenly looked annoyed. "I assume you have a theory."

"I might," Maker hinted.

"Then let me save you the rest of the litany, *detective*," Browing intoned, the last word dripping with sarcasm. "Yes, I knew what was happening, and I knew it was the result of the Vacra using the sub rosa tech they stole from us."

"But it's not just that," Maker said. "You've got the inside scoop on *everything* they took. Not just what it was, but how it works, what it does…everything."

"Admitted," Browing said casually.

"What?" Chantrey uttered in a somewhat stunned tone. "How?"

"That's easy," Maker answered. "Planck."

Browing didn't volunteer anything this time, while Chantrey looked confused.

"Planck was the lead scientist on that sub rosa ship the Vacra raided," Maker continued. "That makes him a high-value asset. That being the case, I found it bizarre that he was just left on the *Mantis*. I mean, no special ops team came to retrieve him, no high-ranking officer came to debrief him on the sub rosa tech, no handler showed up to make sure he stayed in line and didn't say the wrong thing to the wrong people. But that's because he already had a handler. He already had somebody in place who had debriefed him on the relevant subject matter. Somebody who was already on the *Mantis*."

Chantrey gave Browing an incredulous stare. "You?"

Browing didn't answer her. Instead, he looked at Maker and asked, "When did you figure it out?"

"All of the pieces were in front of me for a while," Maker said. "I was just too preoccupied with other things to give it much thought. But when you knew what was happening when the Vacra attacked, it all fell into place."

"So what now?" Browing asked.

"I told myself I'd kill you if it even looked like you were going to betray us again," Maker said, causing Chantrey to draw in a harsh breath.

"I haven't betrayed anybody," Browing insisted. "Like I've said before, I'm just a man following orders —

not much different than you, except I don't wear a uniform all the time."

Maker made a dismissive gesture. "Maybe if you'd ever worn the uniform, you'd understand the difference between your actions and mine."

Maker then turned and walked away, without waiting for a reply.

## Chapter 46

Chantrey and Browing left the bridge immediately following their impromptu conference. The latter was probably going to get out of his armor, while the former may simply have wanted time to deliberate on everything she'd heard. With so much going on that she hadn't deduced, she had to be feeling out of the loop.

Within the allotted ten minutes, however, the Marines were back on duty, hard at work on their assigned tasks. Although it took about an hour, they eventually had most of the *Raider*'s systems back up to par.

While his team was effectuating repairs, Maker spent the time watching the Vacra ships on the monitor and trying to come up with a viable plan of action. From what he could tell, the insectoids' ships stayed well back from the outer edges of Efferus, but beyond that they didn't seem to move.

After receiving the last of the repair reports, Maker called the entire crew to the bridge.

"I need to brief all of you on our current status," he said after everyone was assembled. "But we're in a hostile environment, with enemies and other potential threats nearby, so we're doing it here — with the requisite people at their duty stations — instead of the briefing room."

Maker paused, noting several of those present nodding in understanding.

"First of all," he continued, "I think by now all of you know that the Vacra's ultimate aim, with respect to us, is Erlen."

Almost all eyes in the room shifted to the Niotan, who as usual was by Maker's side.

"Moreover," he went on, "I don't think I have to tell any of you at this point that Erlen is special — in quite a number of ways — but we don't have time to go into that now. Just suffice it to say that the Vacra are willing to do almost anything to get their hands on him. That's why they've got four of their ships hounding us, waiting for us to come out of this cloud. That, of course, brings up another issue."

Maker then spent the next few minutes telling them about Efferus and Planck's previous experience with it. Like everyone else, Planck was present, and in an ideal world Maker would have stepped aside and let him brief the issue of Efferus himself. However, after one look at Planck, Maker knew he wasn't up to it. The man had a sickly pallor to him, and looked as though he might keel over at any moment. Apparently the *Raider* being inside Efferus was taking its toll on him.

"So, this entity actually consumes whatever it comes into contact with?" Snick asked when he'd finished.

"I don't think that's exactly right," Maker said. "But I can't argue that the end result isn't the same."

"And the Vacra ships — what are they doing right now?" Loyola asked.

Maker shrugged. "Probably wondering why we haven't been vaporized or something yet, since they know what Efferus can do. But they essentially haven't moved since we entered the cloud. They're just watching and waiting."

"In short," Adames added, "we've got a ways to go before we can consider ourselves safe."

Fierce cleared his throat. "What about the jump engines? Can't we just bring them back online and then jump home — or at least someplace safe?"

Maker looked at Wayne, who lowered his eyes momentarily and then said, "The jump engines aren't just offline. They're fried. It'll take weeks to repair them."

"But we're fine for now," Maker assured them. "Apparently, the Vacra can't get to us inside Efferus."

"This entity — Efferus," Browing said. "How much can we trust it?"

Maker rubbed his chin for a moment. "That's really a question for Diviana, in my opinion."

All heads turned in Diviana's direction, who didn't seem to care for all the attention.

"It seemed sincere," she said after a moment. "I trust it. I…" Her voice trailed off and her eyes suddenly seem to be staring at something in the distance.

Absolute silence enveloped the bridge as everyone waited for Diviana to complete her thought, but she remained silent.

After about ten seconds, Loyola called her name. "Diviana," she said. "What is it?"

Her roommate didn't immediately respond, but Maker did.

"It's Efferus," Maker stated plainly, looking towards the ceiling. "It's here."

## Chapter 47

The rest of those present followed Maker's gaze upward. There, through a vent in the ceiling, a blue-white gas similar in appearance to that outside the *Raider* was slowly floating down into the bridge. There were a few harsh intakes of breath, and Planck started whimpering.

"Nobody move," Maker ordered. At that point, Maker noted that the vapor was coming in not just through the ceiling, but through some of the wall panels as well.

"Where's it coming from?" Browing asked beneath his breath.

"From outside," Maker muttered impatiently. "Where else?"

"But how is it getting it in?" Browing clarified.

"Apparently the *Raider* isn't completely airtight," Wayne explained. "Maybe something the Vacra did is causing a minute percentage of leakage."

"Or maybe since this thing is alien, it has modes of entry we haven't contemplated," Adames offered.

"That too," said Wayne, in agreement.

As Maker watched, it became even more evident that this wasn't some ordinary gas; it moved with purpose, with portions of it bulging out in random spots like a pseudopod as it seemed to inspect things. He saw it touch the back of a chair, an instrument panel, and other items.

Planck was now making odd distressed sounds, almost like a wounded animal, as the gas moved closer to him.

"Planck!" Maker hissed angrily. "Hold it together, man!"

Oddly enough, his words seemed to have some effect, as Planck suddenly stopped mewling and looked at Maker. Visibly trembling, the man closed his eyes and seemed to bite his lip. And then Maker could spare him no more attention as a portion of the gas swirled up in front of him.

Maker didn't move — didn't even avert his eyes. The gas was somewhat like smoke, such that Maker could actually see through it. Frankly speaking, seeing it like this, he had difficulty contemplating it as a sentient life-form — until a pseudopod suddenly formed and extended towards his forehead.

If Planck were right, the thing could basically poke a hole through his head (and brain) if it so desired. But it hadn't harmed any of the chairs, instruments, or anything else it had touched thus far. Of course, none of those things were living, either. Nevertheless, Maker steeled himself and decided not to move.

Much to his surprise, just before the pseudopod touched him, Erlen strode forward, not just walking towards but *through* the gas.

"Erlen, no!" Maker shouted, practically leaping toward the Niotan. At that point, however, Erlen had already made contact with the vapor, as had Maker himself when he'd tried to come to Erlen's aid. Much to his relief, neither he nor his companion seemed to suffer any ill effects. In fact, the smoky substance simply seemed to whip around them for a few seconds, like a miniature twister, and then it began to withdraw. But it didn't just withdraw from them — it left the entire bridge. In a few seconds, it was like it had never been there.

Maker scanned the faces of all his people, trying to make sure everyone was okay. He stopped when he got to Diviana, who still had a faraway expression on her face. Maker stepped quickly towards her.

"Diviana," he said softly, then gently touched her shoulder.

She immediately blinked, seeming to come back to herself. "Sorry," she murmured apologetically. "I felt Efferus coming on board and then…then it tried to communicate with me, but I think we had trouble making a connection."

"Well, it's gone now," Maker assured her.

Rather than acknowledge this, a strange look came over Diviana's face. Then she began to slowly shake her head.

"No, it's not gone," she declared with certainty. "It's here."

She raised a finger and pointed towards the entry to the bridge. Looking in the direction indicated, Maker saw Jerry, Wayne's homemade robot. Then his eyes widened as he saw blue-white wisps of a gaseous substance surrounding it. As he watched in fascination, the vapor then slid quickly into the robot through openings near its various connecting joints, as though sucked inside by a vacuum.

# EFFERUS

## Chapter 48

"What was that?" asked Adames.

"I think Efferus — or a portion of it — went inside Jerry," Wayne replied.

As if in confirmation of this, Jerry began making peculiar noises, and a diode near its head started flashing.

"Looks like Diviana's new friend may have corrupted your toy in some way," Browing chimed in. "You might want to get it out of here before it explodes."

"It's not going to explode," Wayne said dismissively as he began moving cautiously towards his invention.

The little robot appeared to track Wayne's movement, its head turning slightly to watch as he approached. When he got close, Wayne knelt down in front of it. Jerry reached a hand out toward its inventor; at the same time, it began making even more of the curious sounds, with the diode near its head flashing crazily.

"Be careful," Loyola advised.

It wasn't clear that Wayne heard her, however. Rather than respond, he spent a moment visually inspecting his creation, a smile slowly creeping onto his face.

"I think..." he began, almost nervously. "I think it's trying to communicate."

"Communicate?" repeated Chantrey, plainly a little astounded.

"Yeah," Wayne said. "I believe that Efferus is trying to use Jerry to talk to us."

"I think you're right," Diviana added. "I can sense in its thoughts an effort to...interact."

236

Several of the others, like Chantrey, expressed surprise at this. Maker ignored their comments, as an idea had suddenly occurred to him. Glancing at the monitor, he saw that the Vacra ships were still outside the cloud, apparently still waiting on the *Raider* to stick its head out, so to speak.

"All right," Maker said, coming to a decision. "Wayne, take Jerry, uh, Efferus…whatever the heck it is…and try to get a dialogue going. Diviana, go with them and see if you can help out."

Wayne and Diviana both quickly acknowledged the command and then hustled off the bridge with Jerry in tow.

"The rest of you, back to your stations," Maker commanded.

# EFFERUS

## Chapter 49

Following the integration of Efferus and Jerry, for lack of a better term, time seemed to tick by incredibly slowly on the *Raider* — mostly because there wasn't much to do. Once the bulk of their systems were back to normal, there was only so much busywork Maker could assign, and only so many viable threat scenarios they could run.

Of course, the jump engines still needed to be fixed, but Wayne was their chief engineer and Maker wanted him involved in any repair effort. Right now, however, Maker was hesitant to take the young Marine off translation duty, as he thought of it. For what he had in mind, it was important that they be able to communicate with Efferus.

And so, roughly a day after giving Diviana and Wayne their most recent marching orders, Maker found himself wondering how much progress they had made. At the time, he was on watch with Snick on the bridge, having left Erlen in their quarters. Unlike a lot of people Maker had been on watch duty with in the past, Snick didn't have the need to engage in idle chatter. He mostly left Maker to his own thoughts, which Maker found extremely beneficial under the circumstances.

Thus, it caught Maker a little unexpectedly when Snick suddenly asked, "So, what's your plan, Lieutenant?"

Maker gave him a grin. "Which plan are you referring to?"

"You gave Diviana and Wayne the task of determining how to communicate with the cloud entity. You didn't do that out of whimsy or mere curiosity."

"So you're assuming I have a practical application for their efforts — if they're successful."

"It would be in line with your personality."

Maker almost laughed. *Was there anybody on this ship who wasn't psychoanalyzing him?*

"Okay," Maker said. "I do have a reason: the four Vacra ships still out there."

As he spoke, he pointed to the image of the ships on the monitor. Frankly speaking, he always made sure the *Raider* kept them in sight.

Snick frowned. "I'm not sure I follow. How will communication with the cloud help us?"

"Wayne stated that it'll take a week to fix the hyperspace engines," Maker said. "But when that happens, I don't think we'll just be able to jump home — or anywhere. At least not from inside Efferus."

"What do you mean?"

"Think about it. If we jump from inside the cloud, it's almost a certainty that some portion of it will get trapped inside the jump field and travel with us. Not only do I not know what that will do to Efferus, but I don't know what the effect will be on the *Raider*."

"You're concerned that some portion of it — any portion of it — that jumps with our vessel could possibly consume the ship."

"And us," Maker added.

"So the obvious solution is to exit Efferus and make the jump."

"Yes, but the second we're free of the cloud, you can bet the Vacra ships will start converging. In fact, they don't even have to wait until the *Raider* is fully clear of Efferus — they can just blast any part that coasts out into the clear, disrupting our life support a second time, taking out the jump engines again, etcetera."

"Hmmm. So how does communication with Efferus fix any of that?"

"I'm hoping to convince it that we're the good guys. And you saw the way it moved when it boarded us. It can extend portions of itself outward."

Snick nodded. "I think I understand. You want it to reach out and destroy the Vacra ships."

"Well, I'm certainly not adverse to the notion, but I don't know how Efferus will take to the idea. That being the case, I only want to ask it to reach out and scatter them — frighten them into motion. Basically, keep them occupied enough with their own survival that they forget about us for a few minutes."

"Long enough for us to get clear of Efferus and jump," Snick concluded.

"Exactly."

Snick seemed to contemplate for a moment, then said, "It would seem to be a reasonable plan."

"Thanks. It's about all we have to hang our hats on at the moment."

"Lieutenant, I think I'd like to go get some water," Snick declared unexpectedly.

"Ah, sure," Maker said, thinking the conversation had suddenly gone on an odd tangent. He glanced back as Snick was leaving the bridge — and saw that Chantrey had entered. Seeing her, it became blatantly obvious why Snick had quickly excused himself.

She came over and sat down next to Maker.

"You've been avoiding me," she said without preamble.

"Not true," he retorted. "We have different shifts for watch duty."

"You selected the personnel for those shifts."

"Well, Diviana and Wayne are out-of-pocket. Planck's a mess, and Fierce needs to keep an eye on him in sickbay. That leaves six of us for watch duty. I didn't like the idea of two civilians on watch together, so I paired you with Loyola, and Browing with Adames, who will keep a close eye on him. That left me and Snick."

"With three teams, watch shifts are eight hours each," she replied. "That means there should have been at least eight hours when we were both off duty."

"Being off *watch* duty doesn't mean completely *off* duty."

"I get it — you've got a full plate. But you're the one who said we needed to talk."

Maker rubbed his eyes with his thumb and middle finger for a second. "You're right. I did say that."

"So talk."

Maker stared at her for a moment. "Are you sure you want to do this?"

"Absolutely," she replied without hesitation.

"All right, cards on the table," he said, crossing his arms. "You're a beautiful woman, Ariel, and I admit that the notion of being more than just your colleague has a certain amount of appeal. But you were in my life before I even knew you existed, manipulating me from behind the scenes for years. How am I supposed to deal with that?"

"First of all, it may have started years ago, but what I did in regards to you wasn't continuous. It wasn't constant or routine, so I wasn't some puppet master pulling your strings on a day-to-day basis. Second, just like you, I was merely following orders. Third, all I did was predict your behavior, so stop talking like I was controlling you."

"The military gave me orders — assigned me missions — based on your predictions. You had to know that would happen, and it's the same as controlling me."

"It's not the same at all. There was no guarantee that they'd even take my analysis seriously, let alone use it."

"If they weren't using it, you wouldn't be here. And that's the real problem."

Chantrey gave him a look of confusion. "What do you mean?"

"Look, I understand that you were just doing your job. I can get past that. I don't like it, but I wouldn't let it get in the way if there was something between us."

She reached out and took his hand. "There's no question that there's something between us, but I'm still not seeing the issue."

Maker let out a deep breath. "If we're involved romantically, you become tainted. Your reports may be perceived as useless because you're in a relationship with me. It's a clear conflict of interest. You may lose all credibility."

Chantrey laughed. "How about you let *me* worry about my credibility?" She then leaned forward and kissed him.

He returned the kiss for a moment, then drew back, even pulling his hand from hers.

"I'm serious," he said. "If you lose credibility, if your reports aren't worth anything, then why have you here? Do you understand? They'll transfer you."

"Wow," she muttered. "You really *are* serious."

"Of course I am."

"You're seriously going to miss me if I'm transferred," she said with a wink.

Maker shook his head in frustration. "Forget it. This is nothing but a joke to you."

"Oh, honey," she murmured softly, taking his hand again. "Nobody cares — ask Fierce and Loyola."

"Everybody knows about Fierce and Loyola because they're a package deal. If you take one, you get the other."

"Well, if it makes you feel any better, it can be our little secret."

"You can't keep secrets on a boat this small," he insisted.

"Really?" she remarked, raising an inquisitive eyebrow. "I'm sure Erlen would beg to differ."

Before Maker could reply, a cough sounded from behind them. Looking back, Maker saw that Wayne had entered the bridge.

"Excuse me, el-tee," he said, "but is now a good time for you to speak with our host?"

## Chapter 50

There were five of them currently in the briefing room: Maker, Diviana, Wayne, Chantrey, and Browing. Erlen was also present, lounging in a corner, and on the center of the briefing table was Wayne's robot, Jerry. At the moment, Jerry had a number of wires running from his head to a small computer tablet that Wayne held.

"So you've really learned to speak with it?" Maker asked.

"It's not what I'd call perfect," Wayne admitted. "The translation isn't always exactly right, but yes, we can speak to him now."

"'Him?'" echoed Browing.

"Efferus," Wayne clarified. "From what we've been able to glean, it doesn't really have a gender as we understand it, but to make things easier I'm going to refer to it in the masculine."

"How'd you do it?" Chantrey asked. "Open a dialog with him?"

Wayne smiled. "We started with math."

"Math?" Browing repeated. "What do you mean?"

"Math is the universal language," Wayne explained. "It's the one constant among all sentient beings. For instance, two plus two is always four, no matter your race, language, species, or planet of origin."

"Got it," Maker said.

"That helped us establish a baseline. From there, with Diviana's help, we were able to formulate a few basic concepts: here, there, up, down, big, small, and so on."

"To be honest, though, I had a little help myself," Diviana admitted, glancing at Erlen.

"Anyway," Wayne went on, "from those humble beginnings, we were able to build an elementary vocabulary and things just expanded from there until we were generally able to communicate with each other."

"Great," Maker intoned. "Now, what can you tell us about it?"

"Well, it's exactly what you see out there," Wayne said. "That immense cloud."

"Where did it come from?" asked Chantrey.

"It's not entirely clear," Diviana chimed in. "It sort of translates as the 'Otherwhere-When.'"

Browing frowned in thought. "So what's it doing here?"

"Again, not a perfect translation," Wayne stated, "but it comes across as something like 'knowing.'"

"Knowing?" Chantrey said quizzically. "Knowing *what*?"

"We're kind of guessing here," Diviana acknowledged, "but we think he's a scientist. We believe 'knowing' refers to the fact that he's been here studying something."

"Did he say *what* he's been studying?" Maker asked.

Wayne shook his head. "It's one of the things that's not very clear. We think it may be something on a level that's beyond our ability to observe. But we do know that he's been at it for a while."

"Quantify 'a while' for us," Chantrey said.

Diviana shrugged. "Hard to say, but it seems to be at least hundreds of years — maybe even thousands."

There was silence for a moment as this sank in.

"Going back to Efferus' scientific studies," Maker said, "is that what he was doing when he destroyed anything he came into contact with, like our probe?"

Wayne exchanged a glance with Diviana, then began to speak. "Here's where it gets a little tricky. Efferus never did any of that intentionally. The truth of the matter is that he has never recognized us as a life-form before."

Maker blinked, then rubbed his temple trying to get his head around what he'd just heard.

"What?!" he barked somewhat forcefully.

"Remember when I said I felt like an amoeba when I was trying to get his attention?" Diviana asked. "That's a very close analogy. Not to put too fine a point on it, but we were basically beneath his notice."

No one said anything for a moment, and looks of stunned disbelief settled on the faces of Browing, Maker, and Chantrey.

"But that's insane!" Browing suddenly bellowed.

"Really?" Diviana uttered sarcastically. "So how much thought do you give to amoebas in the water before you go swimming?"

Browing made a dismissive sound, but otherwise remained silent.

"So back to my earlier question," Maker said. "What's his explanation for disintegrating anything that touches him?"

"Apparently it's not a conscious act on his part," Wayne replied. When he got nothing but blank looks from Maker and the two civilians, he tried another tact. "Think of it like your stomach. When you eat something, the acid in your stomach will start trying to break it down. You don't consciously control the process, and the acid doesn't care whether you've eaten food or rocks or needles. It will simply try to break down whatever finds its way into your belly. Likewise, Efferus' body, for lack of a better term, did the same thing."

"So he *does* devour anything that touches him," Browing surmised.

Diviana shook her head. "No, he's not really eating it. He just sort of…vaporizes it."

"So does that mean we *are* or *aren't* safe here?" Maker asked.

"We're safe," Diviana assured him. "Efferus actually has the ability to consciously control the vaporization, if you want to call it that. He's shut it down with respect to the *Raider*."

Maker took a moment to think about this, then asked, "For how long?"

"It's a little hard to answer," Wayne declared. "His concept of time seems to be different than ours. Basically, he plans to leave soon — go home, actually — but we haven't been able to grasp what that means on our chronological scale."

"Let's forget about *when* he's going to leave for a second," Maker suggested. "Instead, let's talk about *how*. Does he have a spaceship out there or something?"

Wayne shrugged. "We haven't asked him that, but I guess we can."

"When?" Browing inquired.

"Right now," Wayne confirmed as he began tapping on the tablet. As he did so, Jerry began to make random sounds.

"So how does your little invention come into this?" Maker asked.

"Apparently Efferus needs an interface to communicate with us," Wayne answered as he finished entering data on the tablet. "Ideally, he wanted to use one of us, but didn't think we were suitable."

Chantrey's eyebrows rose at this. "What do you mean?"

"Based on what he said, Efferus has the ability to go into our bodies," Diviana said. "Our brains. Once there he'd sort of...merge — combine his consciousness with the person's."

"You mean like a symbiote?" Chantrey suggested, clearly ill-at-ease with what was being suggested.

"Something like that," Diviana stated. "It would have been the easiest way for him to communicate with us: go into someone's brain who already speaks the language, then use them as a mouthpiece. But, even though it would only have been temporary, he was worried our minds were too fragile and would be damaged."

"Thank heaven for small favors," muttered Browing.

"Ultimately, he settled on Jerry as a host," Wayne chimed in. He then turned his attention to the tablet as information began scrolling across the screen. He frowned. "With respect to leaving, he simply says he will 'transition.'"

"What exactly does that mean?" asked Chantrey.

Instead of replying, Wayne tapped on the tablet again, presumably passing along the question. His brow wrinkled as he looked at the data that came back to him seconds later.

"He says 'Transition is transition,'" Wayne observed. "But he's offering to give a demonstration, if we'd like."

Maker hesitated barely a second before saying, with utter conviction, "Tell him to do it."

"Hold on!" Browing exclaimed. "You don't even know what it is he's going to do!"

"You're right — I don't know what he's going to do," Maker admitted. "But here's what I *do* know: our hyperspace engines are shot, so we're going nowhere any time soon. Right now, the only thing keeping the Vacra from having their way with us is Efferus, and he's already announced that he's leaving. Bearing all that in mind, if he's got some mode of travel that might be of benefit to us, I'm interested in finding out about it."

Browing looked as though he had more to say, but Chantrey didn't give him a chance.

"He's right, Bain," she interjected. "Our situation may be desperate pretty soon, so we need to be willing to explore all possible options."

Browing clearly wasn't happy, but a look of resignation settled on his face. Maker turned to Wayne and gave him a nod, at which point the young Marine began tapping on the keyboard. After a few seconds, he stopped.

"Now," Wayne said, "I guess we just wa—"

Wayne was cut off as something extraordinary seemed to happen. From Maker's perspective, it appeared as though he was suddenly flung a thousand light years away. Everything around him suddenly receded from view — the briefing room, his companions, the *Raider*, even the solar system they were currently in... In a flash, the entire universe seemed to shrink down in size, first becoming small, then minute, and finally no more than a pinprick in size. Maker himself, seeming to float in darkness while this occurred, felt like he was staring at eternity — removed from creation. Before he could grasp what had happened, he seemed to shoot forward, with the universe once again assuming its normal dimensions and Maker back in his previous spot.

He shook his head to clear his thoughts, trying to make sense of what he had just experienced. However, before he could come to grips with anything, the process repeated itself, with the universe seeming to shrink and expand once again. This time, however, Maker felt incredibly disoriented when it was over. It was as though he had gotten caught in a whirlwind and spun around innumerable times before being dropped back to the ground. He staggered slightly, struggling to maintain his balance. Moreover, he saw that the same was true of the others in the room, with Wayne actually tumbling to the floor.

A few seconds later, Adames' voice came through over the intercom from the bridge.

"Can someone tell me what the hell just happened?" he asked.

## Chapter 51

"So we actually changed position?" Maker asked.

"Yeah," Adames confirmed. "It was only for a few seconds, but the instruments showed us moving a notable distance and back again, although we stayed within the cloud. Plus, I think we all experienced some weird type of...dislocation."

Maker silently contemplated what he was hearing for a few moments. He was back on the bridge, having run there after the demonstration of "transition" by Efferus. The others from the briefing room had followed right behind him, including Jerry and Erlen. Adames, Loyola, and Snick were already there.

The fact that Efferus could actually do what he claimed changed their outlook by an order of magnitude, in Maker's opinion. Needless to say, he didn't understand the science behind it (assuming it could be classified as science), but the ramifications were huge. Basically, the lack of operable hyperspace engines was no longer an impediment to travel. Of course, they still needed Efferus to work with them.

Maker turned to Wayne, who was making some adjustments to the wiring that connected Jerry to his tablet.

"Ask Efferus if he can transition us to a specific location," Maker said, "assuming we give him the coordinates."

"Will do," Wayne assured him, and then began entering information on his tablet. He stopped after a few seconds and started reading as data began appearing on the tablet screen.

"He says he can do it," Wayne stated. "However, he recognizes that we still have a bit of a language barrier, so there's a possibility that he may misinterpret something and take us to a place we have no interest in."

Adames snorted. "Unless he drops us into a black hole, it can't get much worse than our current predicament."

"Hmmm." Wayne muttered, frowning as more information flowed across the screen.

"What is it?" asked Diviana.

Wayne looked up. "Efferus says he's receiving a semaphore — and that it's directed towards us."

Upon hearing this, Maker's interest was immediately piqued.

"Ask him where it's coming from," Maker nearly commanded, although he had a pretty good idea.

While Wayne put the question to Efferus, Snick said, "I'm sorry, but what's a semaphore?"

"It's probably a poor translation of what Efferus meant," Diviana answered, "but a semaphore is a signal of some sort."

"He says it's coming from one of the four ships out there," Wayne said, cutting in.

"The Vacra," Maker practically hissed, his hypothesis now confirmed. "They're hailing us."

## Chapter 52

"Apparently their signal can't penetrate Efferus," Wayne noted.

"That's probably why their attacks ceased once we entered the cloud," Browing said. "It's not just their ships that can't come in here — their weapons-fire can't drill through either."

"Efferus wants to know if he should let it through," Wayne relayed. When he got nothing but blank stares, he said, "The signal. Should he let it through or not?"

Maker hesitated only a moment. After giving a short glance to Erlen, he said, "Sure — why not?"

"Is that a good idea?" Chantrey asked as Wayne passed along Maker's statement to Efferus.

Maker shrugged. "Maybe, maybe not. But I'm curious as to what they have to say."

A moment later, the comm — now set to broadcast audibly over the bridge's intercom — blazed to life. Although the system was synced with the monitor, no image appeared on the screen, indicating that communication in this instance would be audio only.

With that understanding, Maker listened intently, trying to ignore Erlen (who was emitting a low, menacing growl). He noted nothing but the soft hiss of static for a moment, and then a distinctly alien voice began speaking.

"Humans," said the voice, although it pronounced the word as "Hoo-mans" in an odd accent. "We would speak with you."

There followed a few seconds of silence, at which point Maker realized that the speaker was waiting for a response.

"We're here," Maker declared. "Speak."

"No," came the reply. "Not like this. Not with words ferried through the void, but through proximal articulation."

Maker frowned for a moment, trying to comprehend what the Vacra meant. Glancing at Chantrey, he saw her mouthing the words, "They want to meet."

Maker gave her a nod to show that he understood, then said, "It's a kind offer, but I'm not exactly sure what we need to talk about."

"The Senu Lia. It is in your custody, but you do not fully perceive or fathom what you possess. It belongs with the Vacra. It belongs *to* the Vacra."

Sensing what the speaker was talking about, Maker glanced at Erlen. The Niotan was still growling, softly but menacingly.

Maker cleared his throat. "Be that as it may, the most recent interaction between us would seem to indicate that a face-to-face meeting would not be in our best interest."

"We would convene under the auspices of the Grueyndon Barza. Thus, your safety would be guaranteed."

"Does that mean we would be meeting on our ship?"

"Neutral ground is preferable. We propose the planet in this star system."

"We would still be heavily outnumbered."

"You would be protected by the Grueyndon Barza, which no Vacra would dare violate. But if it gives you comfort, we will limit our assemblage to three individuals, if you will do likewise."

"And whom would we be speaking with?"

"Two subordinates, and myself."

"And who might you be?"

There was no verbal answer, but the monitor finally showed an image: one of the Vacra, wearing a particular suit of armor, with the skull of an animal embedded on the helmet.

Skullcap.

## Chapter 53

They broke off communications with the Vacra moments later, asking for time to consider the offer.

"It's obviously a trap," Adames said almost immediately. "I don't think these guys have ever made a deal that they didn't plan on breaking."

"I agree," added Chantrey. "Don't forget, not too long ago they were basically trying to choke the life out of us by killing our life support."

Maker looked at Browing. He couldn't believe what he was about to do, but he did it anyway, asking, "What do *you* think?"

Browing was obviously surprised to get the question. For a moment, it was almost as if he were stupefied, so he obviously recognized what it had taken for Maker to ask the question of him.

"I say we do it," Browing replied. "Let's not forget that one of our primary objectives is the stolen tech the Vacra have. If this gets us one step closer to finding or achieving that goal, I'm all for it."

"Plus," Maker added, "Skullcap will be there."

"Don't be dense," Chantrey advised, almost angrily. "Skullcap is just bait — they know he's catnip to you and you won't be able to resist the offer of a face-to-face with him."

"I'm not quite that obsessed with him," Maker assured her (and by extension, the rest of those present). Then, turning back to Browing, he said, "You negotiated with the Vacra before — what is this Grundon Bars he kept talking about?"

Browing shrugged. "Never heard of it. You'll need someone who's had more experience with the Vacra to explain that one."

Maker smiled. "Thankfully, we have somebody like that."

\*\*\*\*\*\*\*\*\*\*\*\*\*\*\*\*\*\*\*\*\*\*\*\*\*\*\*\*\*\*\*\*\*\*\*\*\*\*\*\*\*\*\*\*\*\*\*\*

"Grueyndon Barza," Planck said, correcting Maker's pronunciation. "It's basically a flag of truce."

"I sort of got that," Maker asserted. "I'm more concerned with whether it actually means anything to them."

"It's one of their sacred tenets," Planck assured him. "They won't violate it."

Maker nodded in understanding, thinking. They were currently in sickbay, where Fierce still had Planck under observation. In addition to the three of them, Adames, Browing, and Chantrey were also present.

"How long is this flag of truce good for?" Adames chimed in.

Planck seemed to calculate internally for a moment. "Their timetable is a little different than ours, but it's roughly just a little less than six hours."

"When does the clock start ticking?" asked Maker.

"The moment the parties actually meet," Planck responded.

Upon hearing this, Maker only pondered for a moment before saying, "Okay, we're going to this meet. They've asked us to limit it to three people, so—"

"I'm going," Browing interjected forcefully, making it clear that it wasn't a question.

Maker stared at him for a moment, then nodded in acquiescence. "Okay — it's me, you, and Adames. Go get your gear on, and we'll let our new friends know it's tea time."

With that, everyone except Fierce and Planck began to file out. Maker, however, hung back at Planck's request.

Once the others had gone, Planck cleared his throat and then said, "Lieutenant, I want to apologize again for my behavior earlier."

"If you're talking about when I flew us into Efferus, there's no need," Maker assured. "I can guarantee you that we were all feeling a little terrified at that point. It was only natural under the circumstances."

"I agree that *feeling* terrified was acceptable, but *acting* terrified was not. No one else panicked the way I did."

"Well, I'm a Marine, which means I'm too stupid to act scared unless a superior orders me to," Maker said, getting a rare chuckle out of Planck. "The rest of my people just followed my lead. As for Browing, he's just a cold-hearted S-O-B who'd have to buy feelings in order to have any. Chantrey's simply too analytical — she'd spend more time dissecting the notion of fear instead of actually experiencing it."

Planck gave him a grateful smile. "Thanks. I appreciate you trying to make me feel better, but the truth of the matter is that I'm only here because I allegedly have value for your mission. If I'm going to go to pieces every time there's a crisis, then I'm useless. I may as well have stayed on the *Mantis*."

"You're being too hard on yourself," Maker insisted. "Despite whatever issues you may have, they haven't kept you from contributing — from telling us about Efferus to advising us about this flag of truce."

"It's nice of you to say, but we both know the truth: I'm a coward at heart. But I don't want to be. And the only way to change that is to start facing my fears."

Maker frowned. "What are you trying to say?"

Planck took a deep breath, clearly tapping into some internal reserve, then flatly stated, "I'm saying that I want to come meet the Vacra with you."

## Chapter 54

Maker found Dr. Chantrey waiting for him when he left the medical bay.

"I know we never finished talking," he began as soon as he saw her, "but it'll have to wait."

She gave him a slight smile. "I'm glad you're still thinking about it, but that isn't why I was waiting to speak with you."

"Then I suppose you want to tell me again that I'm walking into a trap."

"Not exactly. I wanted to talk to you about Planck. He asked to come with you, right?"

Maker gave her a look of surprise. "How'd you know that?"

"It's my job to know things like that," she insisted. "I know you don't like me predicting the behavior of others — especially yours — but it's what I do, and I'm damned good at it."

"Well, if you're aware of the fact that he asked, I suppose you already know my answer."

"You agreed, of course."

"With Fierce's blessing," Maker added, reflecting on the fact that he had gotten the Augman to medically confirm that Planck could participate in the meeting with the Vacra. "But the truth of the matter is that his knowledge and experience regarding the Vacra can't be dismissed out of hand."

"This is the same conversation we had back on the *Mantis*," Chantrey said. "Physically, this meeting might not be an issue for Planck, but psychologically, this will probably be a crisis point."

Maker frowned. "What do you mean?"

"In deciding to go with you, Planck's choosing to face his fear. Even if he never says a word while you're down there, this meeting is going to tip the scales for him one way or another. Either he'll hold it together, in which case his mental health is likely to improve significantly — maybe even approach something akin to normal at some juncture. But if things go bad, he could easily go to pieces."

"In which case he'll end up like Humpty Dumpty," Maker concluded, "and never get put back together again."

\*\*\*\*\*\*\*\*\*\*\*\*\*\*\*\*\*\*\*\*\*\*\*\*\*\*\*\*\*\*\*\*\*\*\*\*\*\*\*\*\*\*\*\*\*\*\*

After parting ways with Chantrey, Maker decided to make a pit stop by Browing's room. There were a couple of things he felt they needed to discuss before they met with the Vacra. Given their history, he was quite unprepared when Browing not only civilly ushered him into his quarters, but opened up the conversation with an expression of gratitude.

"I just wanted to say thanks," Browing began.

"For what?" Maker asked.

"Not fighting me on being part of the team to meet the Vacra."

Maker shrugged. "You've got experience with them. It makes a certain amount of sense."

"That might be the first time we've agreed on something," Browing acknowledged with a grin.

"Well, don't expect it to become a habit," Maker jibed.

"Duly noted," Browing quipped. "Now, I know this isn't just a social call, so what's on your mind?"

Maker let out a deep breath. "I'm not completely sold on this 'flag of truce' notion."

Browing nodded. "That's understandable."

"You've negotiated with them in the past. What kind of *auspices* did you meet under previously?"

Browing frowned. "I didn't correct you before, but you're exaggerating my role in the process. I didn't personally participate in the initial negotiations. As I keep saying, I was just a guy on the back end with orders to make sure the deal closed."

Maker gave him a somber look. "There has to be more to it than that, Browing. I look at you, and I see a guy who's clearly plugged in at a fairly high level — probably as a result of family connections."

"You're right to a certain extent," Browing admitted, "and I don't apologize for my family's contacts or the fact that I've taken advantage of them to advance. But family connections can only get you so far. After a certain point, you have to show you're competent — that you merit the confidence being shown in you. Just like soldiers in the military, you have to step up and take on the tough assignment if you want to get promoted."

Maker blinked, as certain pieces of the puzzle started falling into place for him.

"The tech the Vacra took from that sub rosa ship..." Maker muttered.

"Yes," Browing said. "Getting it back was — is — the test of my mettle. Previously, the easiest method appeared to be cutting a deal with the Vacra."

Maker fought down an angry feeling that was rising in his gut — something he felt every time he dwelt too long on the bargain Browing had previously made to trade Erlen for the stolen tech.

"But the ringleaders who orchestrated that deal were all rounded up and dealt with," he protested.

"Don't be a fool," Browing scoffed. "Some scapegoats got served up on a platter to satisfy the general cry for blood, but the real masterminds are still out there, still calling the shots."

"And you've still got the same mission," Maker concluded.

"Not exactly. I'm to retrieve the sub rosa tech if possible. If not, I'm supposed to destroy it. Beyond that, I have two standing orders."

"Which are?"

"The first is not to compromise *your* mission. You've shown an innate — damn near uncanny — ability to track the Vacra down."

"And you have to find them before you can get back what they took."

"Correct."

"So what's supposed to happen now that we've done that and are about to powwow with them?"

"In an ideal world, I'd first try to keep you from going for the Vacra's jugular, and then I'd see if we could reach some type of accommodation with them." Then seeing the look on Maker's face, he swiftly added, "Something that doesn't involve handing over Erlen."

Maker seemed to ponder for a moment, then said, "Okay, let's do it your way."

"Huh?" Browing uttered, unable to mask his astonishment. "What do you mean?"

"When we meet with the Vacra, I think you should do the talking."

"I have to admit to being surprised," Browing admitted. "With a truce in place, I would have thought you'd relish the idea of being able to fling all kinds of verbal abuse on the Vacra."

"You can bet the thought definitely occurred to me. But plainly speaking, I don't trust them. I can't shake the feeling that somehow, some way, they plan to pull the wool over our eyes. With that in mind, I want to be able to ignore the chatter if necessary, and instead focus on them and everything going on around us."

"Got it," Browing said with a nod. "I'll engage in idle chitchat while you keep an eye out for danger. Anything else?"

"Yeah," Maker said. "Earlier, you mentioned two standing orders, but only talked about not interfering with my mission. What was the second order?"

Browing gave him a pensive stare for a moment, then said, "Not to let Planck fall into their hands again — by any means necessary."

## Chapter 55

The flag of truce appeared to operate as intended. The *Raider* was able to exit Efferus and head towards the planet without harassment by the Vacra ships. That said, the connection that Efferus had made to Jerry appeared to remain intact, despite the separation from the rest of his "body."

"No dangerous or corrosive elements in the atmosphere," confirmed Wayne, who was once again monitoring the scanners as the ship quickly descended to the planet's surface. "But it's not breathable, either."

"Shouldn't matter," said Maker. "All three of us will be in battle gear, so breathing won't be a problem."

In fact, he, Browing, and Planck were already suited up. They now stood on the bridge, watching on the monitors as the *Raider* approached the designated meeting spot.

As had previously been noted, the surface of the planet was mostly dry and arid. What garnered everyone's attention, however, were the myriad ships that littered the landscape. Although they knew what to expect, their previous observation from space did not do justice to what they were seeing close at hand.

First of all, there were far more ships than they had initially thought, as some appeared to have sunk below the surface, the only evidence of their existence being a bit of hull sticking out here or there. Next, the sheer variety of craft was incredible, not just in terms of use — such as pleasure yachts versus tankers versus warships — but with respect to origin. (For instance, Maker saw a pair of spaceships next to each other from two races that had been at war for centuries, and whose vessels would engage in battle as soon as one detected the other.) Finally, the vast majority of the ships seemed to have suffered no damage. In almost all instances where they employed their scanners, Maker's team could detect nothing to indicate that the physical framework of the ships was harmed or compromised in any way. It gave the entire landscape an eerie feel.

As they passed over a colossal Gaian warship, Wayne said, "Picking up life signs — three individuals. Vacra."

Maker nodded in acknowledgment, as this was expected. Upon receiving word that their offer to meet would be accepted, the Vacra had — as a token of goodwill — volunteered to send their people down to the planet first. A short time later, the crew of the *Raider* had observed one of the Vacra ships break away towards the planet's surface and then return almost immediately.

"Looks like they've kept their word so far," observed Adames, who was in the pilot's seat.

"Yeah, we'll see how long that lasts," Maker grumbled. "Sorry you aren't coming with us."

"*I'm* not," countered the NCO. "Now I get to see how the other half lives — staying back in the ship like an officer while sending low-ranking grunts out to get their butts shot off."

"Actually, you already got shot on this mission," Maker reminded him, "so this is just a little show of compassion until you're ready to take a bullet again."

Laughing, Adames set the *Raider* down in the shadow of the gigantic warship. It was close enough for the three-man delegation to walk to the meeting spot, but far enough back that the Vacra shouldn't get nervous.

"All right," Maker said to everyone in general, "Browing, Planck, and I are about to head out. Supposedly they won't violate this truce, but I wouldn't put anything past the Vacra. Stay sharp and be ready to fly out on a moment's notice."

He then gave a covert hand signal to Adames — which the NCO acknowledged — that basically said, *If anything goes haywire, don't wait for us. Leave.*

## Chapter 56

It took them about five minutes of walking over sandy ground to reach the meeting spot. As they were striding along, Maker and his companions tested their comm systems and he was pleased to see that everything was in working order. He could communicate jointly or individually with Planck or Browing, as well as the ship. Although they had tested everything before leaving the *Raider*, planet conditions — especially on an *unknown* planet — had been known to interfere with communications before, and Maker wanted to confirm that there were no issues in that regard.

"Tell me again why we're loping across this place on foot instead of just having Adames drop us off where the Vacra are waiting?" Browing asked.

Maker let out an exasperated sigh. "Our battle suits need time to get acclimated to the environment — gravity, atmospheric pressure, and so on. They'll make the necessary adjustments so that our movements — as well as regular body functions, such as oxygen intake — remain as close to normal as possible. I'm surprised you don't know this, given how expensive that personal armor is you're wearing."

"Look who's talking," Browing countered. His comment was directed at the fact that Maker's armor was custom-made (although he'd built it himself from scratch) and even had an image of Erlen engraved on it as the sigil.

Maker decided against further commentary as they began quickly closing the remaining distance between themselves and the Vacra. As expected, there were three of them — one standing in the fore, with the other two on either side of him and slightly in the rear.

Physically, as always, their six-limbed segmented bodies reminded Maker of ants. Looking at them now, he noted that the two in the rear appeared to be wearing what he thought of as standard Vacran armor. The one in front had the anticipated skull on his helmet, as well as the ring of skulls embedded in his armor, and finally, the deformed middle arm.

It was Skullcap.

The Vacran leader's helmet momentarily swiveled slightly in Maker's direction as they approached. Maker smiled; Skullcap had obviously seen the image of Erlen on Maker's armor, so the Vacran leader now had a pretty good idea of who was in the delegation before him. (Of course, if this was a trap to lure Maker out, Skullcap knew by now that he had succeeded.)

Maker's team stopped when the two groups were about five feet apart. Browing was in the center — directly across from Skullcap — with Maker and Planck flanking him.

There was silence for a moment as the two parties sized each other up, then Skullcap began speaking.

"Humans," the Vacran leader began, "we are grateful that our invitation to meet was well-received. We noted you making ready to depart and wished to converse with you before you did so."

*Depart?* Maker thought, confused. And then he almost laughed as understanding dawned on him. The Vacra had witnessed Efferus "transition" the *Raider*. They were operating under the assumption that Maker and his team were on the cusp of jumping home.

"As promised," Skullcap continued, "only three of us are before you. The first" — he indicated the Vacra to his rear left — "is a warrior of note who has distinguished himself in numerous campaigns, beginning with the battle of…"

Maker tuned Skullcap out as he switched to internal communications and reached out to Planck.

"Is there a reason why he's giving us his underling's curriculum vitae?" Maker asked.

"It's standard with a meeting like this," Planck answered. "The intent is to let us know that we're engaging with peers — members of the Vacra who are at our level."

"How long will this go on?"

"Hard to say. Could be five minutes, could be five hours. That said, Skullcap — as you call him — tends to be brief."

Mentally groaning, Maker severed the comm link. He assumed — and hoped — that Planck was exaggerating about how long it would take for Skullcap to make the necessary introductions. Five hours would be the bulk of the time under the truce. But maybe that was the plan: get the crew of the *Raider* down to the planet, spend hours and hours yakking about nothing, and then attack when the truce ended.

Of course, that was an improbable outcome, but the Vacra were a race that humanity had very little experience with (and the bulk of that experience was negative in the extreme). Who knew what they might expect?

Fortunately, Skullcap's recitation of honors and accolades – including his own – came to an end after about a quarter hour. The only part Maker had seriously paid attention to was when his archenemy had stated his given name: Ni'xa Zru Vuqja. In truth, however, this was information Maker was already aware of, thanks to Planck. (Needless to say, Maker preferred – and had continued using – "Skullcap" to refer to the insectoid leader.)

In response to the Vacra introductions, Browing merely laid a hand upon his chest to indicate himself.

"I'm Bain Browing," he said. "I'm accompanied by Dr. Planck and Lieutenant Maker." He gestured towards his companions as he spoke.

"Maker," Skullcap echoed, pronouncing the name as "Make-her," with two distinct syllables, as he turned his face in Maker's direction. "We are familiar with this one."

"As is he, with you," Browing chimed in. "Now, you said you wanted to talk."

"Yes," Skullcap announced. "We would speak of the Senu Lia with you." He pointed at the image of Erlen on Maker's armor.

"Go on," urged Browing.

"It is a creature of ancient lineage and incredible power," Skullcap went on. "It is a treasure meant for sovereigns, a mark of divine favor."

"Are you saying that possession of this Senu Lia somehow converts to an increase in status?" Browing asked.

"The possessor of the Senu Lia would be considered nothing less than a potentate," the Vacra leader answered. "And its return to the Vacran race would herald a new golden age for our species."

"It sounds as though it would be worth a king's ransom," Browing remarked.

"Such has been offered," Skullcap remarked.

"Browing!" Maker hissed over the comm. "What are you up to?"

"Just listen!" Browing shot back. "And if I get out of line, you can always kill me, like you promised yourself."

Shutting off communications with Maker, Browing turned his attention back to Skullcap.

"It sounds as though the possessor of the Senu Lia conveys sovereignty among the Vacra," he said. "But I've heard no indication that such a person has to actually *be* Vacran."

Skullcap appeared to do something akin to a double-take, which was followed by a fierce stream of chittering that Maker recognized as the Vacran language. A moment later, it was cut off, as Skullcap seemed to recognize that he was speaking in his native tongue *and* that he had been broadcasting to Maker's party as he did so. There was nothing but silence for the next minute, but Skullcap clearly seemed to be in conference with his compatriots.

Maker opened a comm channel to his two companions, at which point Browing asked, "What do you think they're talking about?"

"I'm guessing your statement threw them for a loop," Maker said, trying not to chuckle. "How'd you even come up with that?"

"Just a roll of the dice, really," Browing replied. "In all honesty, I expected him to laugh it off."

Before Maker could comment on this, Skullcap reopened the comm channel between the two groups.

"Only Vacran can rule Vacran," Skullcap announced. "We are a mighty race, born to greatness, with an inherent power and spirit that other species lack. We are the keepers of the egg-flame, the protectors of…"

Maker stopped listening as Skullcap waxed on about the ingrained greatness of the Vacra and their innate superiority over all other creatures. Instead, he focused on what he'd learned about Erlen and what it might mean.

He had a better understanding now of why the Vacra were so focused on the Niotan. (Assuming, of course, that what Skullcap maintained was actually true.) It suddenly occurred to him that it might be prudent to start implementing a few additional safeguards for Erlen's protection, and he spent some time working those out in his head. When he checked the time, he noticed that another fifteen minutes had gone by, and Skullcap was still praising the Vacran race to high heaven.

Maker frowned. Something about this didn't feel right. His instincts were starting to go haywire.

He opened a channel to Planck. "When Skullcap was making introductions earlier, was that long or short compared to what you've seen him do before?"

"He's usually pretty brief," Planck declared. "Much shorter than what he did today."

"And right now — have you ever seen him be this verbose?"

"Never."

"He's stalling," Maker said flatly, knowing it to be true. He then added Browing to their comm channel and announced, "They're up to something. Break this off *now*. We need to hustle back to the ship."

"We appreciate your sentiments," Browing interjected, cutting Skullcap off, "and wish to retire now to our ship to deliberate on what you have said."

They didn't wait for the Vacra to acknowledge Browing's statements; they merely turned and started walking away. It was all Maker could do not to march double-time back to their ship.

"Adames," Maker said, hailing the *Raider*. "We're on our way back."

"So, how'd it go?" Adames asked.

"Hard to say, but something's off," Maker replied. "Just fire up the engines and get ready to take us off this rock. As a matter of fact, meet us halfway."

"You got it," the NCO answered.

Maker felt tension he wasn't aware of starting to ease, but it was a short-lived experience as roughly thirty seconds later, Adames contacted him from the ship.

"Gant," he said solemnly, "the engines are dead."

## Chapter 57

"Apparently there's a microbe in the atmosphere of this planet," Wayne explained. "In and of itself, it's harmless, but apparently it affects the fuel cells in spaceships — renders them inert."

"That would explain the graveyard of ships on this planet," Snick said.

"It also explains why the Vacra wanted to meet here," Maker added. "And why their own ship dumped off the landing party instead of sticking around. They knew this would happen."

He was angry with himself. The meeting had turned out to be a trap after all, although it had taken something like an hour for Wayne to figure out exactly what the issue was. At present, everyone was on the bridge, where they were just learning the magnitude of the problem. (And, on Maker's order, they were all currently in their battle suits as well, *sans* helmets.)

"But what about the truce?" asked Chantrey.

"Technically they haven't violated it," Browing answered. "There's no argument that they tricked us, but the Vacra themselves haven't done anything wrong. That may change, however, when the truce ends. At that point, they can carpet-bomb us from space if they want to."

"That will never happen," Maker declared. "They want Erlen, and they want him alive. Thus, there won't be any bombing or anything of that nature." *They'll just resume attacking our life support*, he thought. *This time successfully.*

"What about Efferus?" Loyola chimed in. "Can we ask him again about 'transitioning' the ship like he did before?"

Wayne looked at Maker, who nodded, then spent a few seconds entering information on his tablet. Roughly fifteen seconds later, he announced, "Same answer as before — something's going on with the portion of his body that's still in space, and it's interfering with his ability to transition."

Maker frowned. Asking Efferus for help had been their first option, but apparently he had his own issues. Moreover, whatever those issues were, Maker was absolutely sure the Vacra were involved.

"But there are a lot of other ships around us," Fierce noted. "Any chance some of them have usable fuel cells?"

"If they did, they probably wouldn't be here," Wayne countered. "But it won't hurt to look."

"All right," Maker said. "Let's do it."

\*\*\*\*\*\*\*\*\*\*\*\*\*\*\*\*\*\*\*\*\*\*\*\*\*\*\*\*\*\*\*\*\*\*\*\*\*\*\*\*\*\*\*\*

An hour later — after sending teams to break into and search about a half-dozen nearby ships (including the mammoth warship) — it was confirmed: the fuel cells in all of them were inert. Once again, everyone assembled on the bridge, the mood more somber than ever.

"This is probably a very basic question," Fierce said, "but is there no way to make the fuel cells active again?"

"In very simple terms, fuel cells generate power from a chemical reaction," Wayne said. "With the right chemical elements we could probably fix the problem — but we don't have them."

Chantrey looked at Maker, catching his eye, then glanced towards Erlen, who was at Maker's side.

"No," Maker said, causing everyone else to stare at him.

"It's our only option," Chantrey said.

"It's *not* an option," Maker countered. "It's an exercise in futility."

"Um, I'm not sure what this conversation is about," Adames interjected, "so could someone clue the rest of us in?"

Maker let out a frustrated sigh. "Dr. Chantrey is suggesting we use Erlen to provide the missing chemical elements."

"Wait…" muttered Wayne, looking confused. "Can he… Can he do that?"

Maker nodded. "That, and a whole lot more. Remember when I said he was special? He's basically a living chemical factory. He can reproduce just about anything he's come into contact with, including the elements for the fuel cells."

"So what's the problem?" asked Loyola.

"The problem is that there's only one of him," Maker said. "Have you seen the fuel cells? They take up a massive amount of space. There's no way he can produce enough to make them all active. You'd need a thousand of him to make that plan work. So, rather than waste time on an idea that *wouldn't* work, I was trying to keep us focused on coming up with something that *would*."

"At the moment, Gant, it's all we've got," Adames said. "At the very least, we need to try."

Maker turned to Erlen, looking into his eyes. The Niotan made an odd noise, something between a purr and a bark that sounded half-pleading, half-compelling.

"All right," Maker said with a nod. "Let's do it."

# EFFERUS

## Chapter 58

"It's not working," Wayne said. "Or rather, it could work, but it's like the el-tee said — Erlen can't produce the requisite chemicals fast enough."

The young Marine had been working with the Niotan on the fuel cell issue for the better part of an hour before he decided to admit defeat. Now they were back to square one. As Maker had indicated, the effort had cost them valuable time, but he didn't see the need to blurt out any type of I-told-you-so.

"So what now?" asked Planck.

"The truce is still on for a little while," Maker announced. "We just need to get every possible idea on the table."

He looked around at his people. No one seemed to have any ideas, although he could see from a few faces that they were concentrating. That said, the mood was rather glum — even more sullen than it had been when they were seconds away from the shields failing and being devoured by Efferus.

Speaking of the cloud entity, Maker glanced at Jerry and saw the diode on the robot's head flashing wildly.

"Wayne, are we getting some kind of message from Efferus?" he asked.

Wayne glanced at the tablet. "Yeah, he's been reaching out for an hour or so, but I haven't paid close attention because of the fuel cell issue. I also killed his speakers because those noises were distracting."

Maker was curious. "Can you see what he wants?"

Wayne nodded, looking at his tablet. "He wants to know if we're returning to where his 'body' is soon because he needs to get back there."

"Tell him we'd love to," Maker said sincerely, "but we're having an issue with our fuel cells."

Wayne dutifully entered the info on his tablet. A moment later, he gasped and almost dropped the device.

"Efferus…" Wayne began. "He, uh, he…he wants to know if he should reactivate the fuel cells."

# EFFERUS

## Chapter 59

"Apparently we were right about Efferus being a scientist," Wayne said. "During the time he's been in this system, one of the things he studied was the microbes on this planet."

"And he can reverse the effect they had on the fuel cells?" Maker asked.

"So it seems. We did an experiment on a single fuel cell at first — just in case something went wrong — and he did exactly what he claimed. He reactivated it. He's in the engine room now, doing the same to the remainder."

"Any idea how he did it?"

"Not a clue," Wayne admitted, "but if I did, I'd be a very rich man."

They were currently alone in the briefing room. With everyone else on the bridge preparing for what they hoped was the eventual takeoff, it was the best place to talk. (Erlen, after discovering his services were no longer needed, had gone to their quarters for a nap.)

"So how long will it take?" Maker asked.

Wayne sighed. "It's probably going to be close, if I'm being honest. We'll probably bump up against the time the truce is set to expire."

"Can Efferus work any faster?"

Wayne shrugged. "I don't know. But he's clearly in distress because of what's going on with the portion of him that's still in space."

"And we don't have any inkling of what's happening up there?"

Wayne made a gesture of futility. "What can I say? Everything on this ship is powered by energy from the fuel cells. When those go, so do other things, like the scanners, and without those we're blind to just about anything you can't see with the naked eye. Unfortunately, the only thing to see around here is dead ships."

"Maybe that's all we *need* to see," Maker commented as a thought occurred to him.

"Sir?" asked Wayne, confused.

Maker smiled. "I have an idea…"

## Chapter 60

The attack came just as expected — at the precise time the truce came to an end. Other than Erlen, Maker was alone on the bridge at the time, dressed in full battle gear.

"We've got incoming!" Wayne's voice suddenly shouted over the comm. "Three Vacra ships just entered the planet's upper atmosphere."

Maker flipped a switch next to him that was supposed to bring the scanners online. Thankfully, they were operable again. He had actually been worried that they wouldn't be, because only half the fuel cells were functioning. To implement the plan he'd come up with, it had been necessary to stop Efferus about midway through the task of reactivating them.

"Get ready," Maker said over the comm link as he activated the monitor. On its screen, he saw the three Vacra ships flying in tight formation, approaching their position.

Maker assumed that the ships would once again target the life support system. It was the most sensible move if they wanted Erlen alive and unharmed. However, he didn't plan to give them the chance.

"Now!" Maker suddenly shouted.

A moment later, the *Raider* shook madly, rocked by a repetitive series of thunderous booms. On screen, the three Vacra vessels were pounded by a barrage of large-caliber weapons fire. The one in the center — its shields obviously failing under the unexpected bombardment — exploded in a ball of flame, raining scorched and twisted debris down towards the ground.

The two remaining ships fled back to the relative safety of outer space.

"Fierce!" Maker bellowed into the comm. "You're up!"

"I'm on it!" Fierce's voice boomed in response.

Maker immediately went into action. Sitting in the pilot's seat, he quickly had the *Raider* airborne and a moment later, it was swiftly circling the colossal warship that Adames had previously parked their vessel next to. Within a minute, he spotted what he was looking for: an open bay door on the warship. He quickly flew inside and set the craft down.

"The *Raider*'s in," Maker announced, locking the ship down to the bay floor. "Get us out of here."

Adames' voice crackled over the comm. "Good as done, el-tee."

Maker jumped up and ran for the exit, with Erlen on his heels. Moments later, they were outside the *Raider* and in the massive bay of the warship. The sudden sound of footsteps approaching drew Maker's attention, and he looked around to find Fierce running towards them. Like Maker, he was in full battle gear — despite the fact that he was staunchly opposed to using any of the weaponry at his disposal. Basically, there was a practical reason for Fierce to be in a battle suit at the moment: life support wasn't currently operating on the warship.

"Any problems?" Maker asked.

"Nothing I couldn't handle," the Augman replied.

"All right, then. Let's go."

With that, they started running, heading for the bridge of the warship. At the same time, the floor — the entire vessel, in fact — slowly began to tilt up at a slight angle, the movement accompanied by metallic shrieks and groans. They were taking off.

As they hurried along, Maker occasionally saw what appeared to be discarded suits of battle armor cast randomly about. However, he instinctively knew that — rather than being abandoned — each battle suit probably contained human remains. When her fuel cells became inert, the warship had lost power to the various systems — including life support. Many of her crew had made it into battle armor, but eventually those life support systems failed as well. It was a grim reminder of what awaited Maker and his own squad should their current stratagem prove unsuccessful.

With that in mind, he began reflecting on the plan they were effectuating. It was, in essence, a slight variation of what they had done at the Defalcator space station. The only difference was that, this time, the vessel assisting in their getaway was a gargantuan warship.

The idea had come to Maker while Efferus was reactivating the *Raider*'s fuel cells. If Efferus could do it for *their* craft, why not for a larger vessel? Plus, with Efferus insisting that something untoward was happening with respect to the rest of his body in space, it seemed to Maker that they needed to bring some back-up.

He'd had to halt the reactivation of the *Raider*'s fuel cells in order to send Efferus to do the same on the warship (which they were able to identify as the *Black Pearl*). Needless to say, getting all the *Pearl*'s fuel cells reactivated wasn't possible in the time they had available. That said, they didn't need power for everything on the warship. In fact, they only anticipated needing a handful of the *Pearl*'s systems to be functional — primarily, the weapons and the engines.

With that in mind, Maker had sent the bulk of his people over to the warship. They had previously scouted the interior while searching for active fuel cells and, despite being aged, found it to be more or less intact. Thus, while Efferus and Wayne had gone to the *Pearl*'s engine room to deal with the fuel cells, everyone else had devoted themselves to preparing the craft for takeoff as power was partially restored bit by bit: checking ammo, weapons systems, navigation equipment, etcetera.

As their plan was taking shape, there had been a slight temptation to simply abandon the *Raider*; it would essentially be only half-powered, and would be far from capable of taking on the Vacra ships. However, the majority of their gear — from medical equipment to weapons — was on board the *Raider*, and there simply wasn't time to move everything over. Thus the decision was made to park their craft in one of the warship's bays. The only problem was that they had no power to spare for the bay doors, which would therefore have to be operated manually. Unfortunately, the manual controls had rusted solid, another indication that the warship had been there for years. In the end, Fierce was the only person with the strength to operate the rusted controls, and so he had found himself saddled with that particular task.

Thankfully, everything had worked out almost perfectly. Maker smiled as he imagined how shocked the Vacra must have been to find the *Pearl*'s guns come alive and take aim at their ships. Maker didn't have nearly enough people to handle all the weapons on the warship, but he had enough to present a credible threat. (In support of that theory, the report alone from the *Pearl*'s oversized weapons had been loud enough to shake the

*Raider* when they first fired.) And Fierce had done an exemplary job of getting the bay doors opened and closed. All in all, Maker would have been hard-pressed to say how things could have gone any better.

As he, Fierce, and Erlen got close to the *Pearl*'s bridge, however, Maker realized that something was amiss. Rather than getting the sensation that the warship was steadily rising, he got the impression that it was somehow moored in place. Even worse, the vessel was starting to shake from top to bottom. Within moments, it was shuddering wildly, like a hairless dog in a blizzard.

Struggling to stay on his feet, Maker staggered onto the bridge, noting that all of his people were in armor and most of them — including the civilians — were at battle stations. The only people not manning weapons were Adames (who was piloting), and Fierce, who refused to engage in violence. Entering the bridge behind Maker, the Augman quickly buckled himself into a seat away from any of the weapon controls.

"What's wrong?" Maker asked without preamble as he made his way to the captain's chair and sat, with Erlen taking a position next to him.

"This warship's been here for ages," Adames replied, "and is partially sunk into the ground. She's having trouble breaking free."

Maker gritted his teeth. That was bad news, to say the least. Even a ship the size of the *Pearl* was nothing but a beached whale if it was immobile. They were dead meat if they couldn't move.

Suddenly, with a massive groan of strained metal (and as if in answer to a silent prayer), the ship apparently broke loose of the surface and began to rise. The shaking ceased almost immediately, and they quickly began to gain altitude.

Now that his eyes weren't being rattled out of their sockets, Maker took a moment to survey his new surroundings. As with everything else on the *Pearl*, the bridge was extensive — far larger than that of the *Raider*. It was pretty clear from the layout that the place was designed to accommodate a large bridge crew. His people seemed so spread out that he almost felt they'd need bullhorns to speak to one another.

Aside from scope, however, the bridge was very much along the lines of what he expected and was familiar with. There were the usual systems (like communications and navigation), ship controls, viewing monitors... In fact, each of the battle stations where his people were stationed had its own monitor (presumably so one could see what one was shooting at).

"I'm picking up more inbound ships," Wayne blurted out, interrupting Maker's thoughts. The young Marine was doing double duty — manning both weapons and the scanners. "This time an entire squadron — no, *two*. At least forty Vacra ships."

"*Forty*?" Maker repeated, surprised.

"Yes, sir," Wayne said, with Efferus/Jerry next to him. "They're closing fast. I'll put it on the screen."

A nearby monitor suddenly went from being a blank screen to showing a patch of sky that was currently occupied by a score of charging ships. These vessels were slightly different than the trio that had attacked a short time before — a bit larger and more aggressive in design, but still obviously Vacran.

"Everyone pick a target," Maker said. "Now, fire!"

# EFFERUS

It wasn't exactly a turkey shoot, but it was close enough. The *Pearl*'s guns were truly unlike anything Maker had ever seen, decimating protective shields and then punching through the Vacra ships like tissue paper. Truth be told, they were more like a force of nature than weapons — potent, unstoppable, and unrelenting. The Vacra ships that weren't destroyed outright tried to reform, only to have the warship smash through their lines and send them scattering.

Simply put, the *Pearl* was a juggernaut — so big and so powerful that almost nothing could stop her once she was set on a course. And that was without considering the firepower she wielded. The Vacra ships were like bumblebees, swarming around the warship annoyingly (and occasionally getting swatted).

Maker couldn't help but be impressed. He'd never even known that a ship of this class existed in the Gaian fleet. At a guess, he assumed that they didn't make this model any more, and — as evidenced by the age of the ship's controls and equipment — it had probably been stranded on that planet for a century or more. (Adames had initially described the ship's systems as "damned near archaic," but operable.)

That said, he had to grudgingly give the Vacra credit for trying. Despite the obvious futility of their position, their ships continued firing on the *Pearl* (and periodically got blasted apart for their efforts). However, there was little — if any — effect on the warship that he could see.

He briefly wondered whether their adversaries were attempting to use any of the sub rosa tech at their disposal, such as attacking the life support systems as they'd done to the *Raider*. Not that it would have mattered in this particular instance, since Maker's team hadn't bothered with restoring life support to the *Pearl*. (It was part of the reason they were all in their battle armor.) That said, the Vacra did have other sub rosa weapons in their arsenal, but they either hadn't used them or had found them to be useless against the warship.

"Leaving the upper atmosphere," Adames announced, bringing Maker out of his reverie.

The scene on the monitors now showed that they were in space, the planet of dead spacecraft falling away below them. Without being told, Adames made a beeline for the area where the rest of Efferus' cloudlike form was located. Seconds later, an image of their destination appeared on the monitors, and it became immediately evident what was causing Efferus such distress: most of his gaseous form was gone.

# EFFERUS

## Chapter 61

Maker simply stared for a moment, stunned by what he was seeing. Where — just hours before — there had been something like an immense, voluminous cloud in space, there now appeared to be little more than smoky wisps. The remaining vapor still covered a large area, but it was amazingly skimpy compared to the quantity that had been there before. Knowing that this was, in some way, a living creature made Maker feel slightly queasy.

"What...?" Diviana muttered from her battle station. "What happened to him?"

Wayne looked at his tablet, where data seemed to be scrolling across the screen. "Efferus says... He says he's been 'appropriated.'"

"What does that mean?" asked Chantrey.

"I think the explanation is on the screen," Maker replied, still staring at the monitor.

Wayne, perhaps picking up on what had caught Maker's attention, enlarged the image on the monitor. With a magnified view, they saw something extraordinary: Vacra ships were flying close to the portion of Efferus that remained in space and firing large metallic cylinders into the vapor. The gas would then be drawn into the cylinders as though sucked inside by a vacuum, and at that juncture the cylinder would be retrieved by the ship. After the cylinder was back on board, the vessel holding it would disappear — presumably having jumped to hyperspace. The entire process took approximately thirty seconds.

Just eyeballing the scene, Maker estimated there were hundreds of ships engaged in this "appropriation" technique.

"What are they doing to him?" asked Loyola.

"That's easy," Planck chimed in. "They're weaponizing him."

# EFFERUS

## Chapter 62

There was stunned silence for the most part after Planck's statement. Truth be told, however, it was actually what Maker had been thinking when he saw what the Vacra were doing. Efferus' gaseous form would make a formidable weapon — especially if, as had been indicated, it could basically wipe anything out of existence. And with that thought, a horrid possibility suddenly occurred to him.

"Wayne, ask Efferus if we're in danger from his gaseous form," Maker said. "Can it harm the *Pearl*?"

While Wayne put the query to Efferus, Adames — understanding Maker's concern — began to bring the warship to a halt.

"He says possibly," Wayne stated a moment later. "He says he's not in harmony with his constituent parts at the moment, so his ability to control that particular process is minimal."

"Great," Maker muttered sarcastically, watching as Vacran ships continued scooping up portions of Efferus. Despite the battlefield prowess of the *Pearl*, it was starting to look as though they might need to turn tail and run. If so, it would probably be a running firefight.

"What about firing on the Vacra ships?" Maker asked. "Will it harm him if we have to vaporize any that have appropriated other portions of his body?"

The answer came back almost immediately.

"He says it won't hurt him," Wayne relayed, "but it's too late for that."

"Too late for what?" Browing queried.

"It's too late to engage the Vacra," Wayne stated. "Efferus says he has to transition."

"Transition where?" demanded Adames.

"He doesn't know," Wayne insisted. "Wherever the Vacra are taking the rest of him."

"But why?" asked Maker.

Wayne shrugged. "It's not completely clear. It's somewhat akin to someone twisting your arm up behind your back. Once they do that, they can frog-march you anywhere they want."

"So wherever they're taking the rest of him, the portion in Jerry needs to follow," Adames summed up.

Wayne nodded. "In a nutshell."

"So he can transition now, but not when we were stranded down on that planet," Maker noted a bit testily.

"It's some kind of proximity thing," Wayne stressed. "The closer his various parts are to each other, the easier it is for him to transition. But the real question is whether we go with him."

At that juncture, Maker heard the phrase "What?" in stereo.

"He can either leave us behind or transition us with him," Wayne explained. "But he can better protect us if we're with him."

Looking at the Vacra ships continuing to scoop up the remainder of Efferus, Maker didn't have to ask what they needed protection *from*.

"Okay, we're in," he decided. "How soon do we leave?"

He got his answer a moment later in the form of a feeling — a force — that seemed to rip his soul from his body.

## Chapter 63

Maker found himself body-slammed back into existence, the transition effectuated by Efferus being much more jarring this time. He winced, finding himself burdened with a sudden and incredibly powerful headache. Moreover, the health monitor in his armor was going off, indicating some kind of physical trauma.

He didn't immediately notice anything wrong — none of his limbs seemed broken or impaired — so he simply shut off the health monitor and had the suit inject him with something for the headache. (He also noted an injury report which indicated that he'd suffered a nosebleed, but didn't have time to read more than that.)

Surveying the bridge, Maker saw that almost everyone else had fared worse than he had (not counting Fierce, of course). He couldn't see their faces, but the way that they were slumped over in their armor and groaning indicated that the transition had been harder on them than him.

"Report," Maker ordered, trying to get his people focused. "Where are we?"

Having a job to do seemed help bring them around. Adames, in the pilot's chair, began checking nearby instruments. He then did a double-take.

"Come on, come on," Maker demanded impatiently. "Where are we?"

"You're not going to believe this," Adames said. "But we're in Gaian Space. Pretty much at the Fringe, but still Gaian Space. We're home."

"Are you sure?" asked Snick.

"I checked it twice," Adames shot back. "There's no mistake."

"It's true," Wayne said. "Multiple long-range scans confirm that we're in our own neck of the woods."

Maker could sense the relief in the voices of his team. They could have ended up anywhere, but to actually wind up on their own doorstep was more than any of them expected — especially with the Vacra involved.

Maker suddenly drew in a sharp breath as he remembered that Efferus didn't just randomly bring them to Gaian Space; he was tagging along with the rest of his body.

"Scan for Vacra ships," he ordered. "Quickly!"

"Located them," Wayne said. "Putting them on screen now."

Maker looked at the monitor and audibly gulped. He wasn't certain what he had expected to see, but certainly not the sight before him.

There were hundreds — more like thousands — of Vacra ships nearby. They weren't just within shouting distance of the *Pearl*, but all of humanity. And, being aware of what they had just added to their arsenal, he knew that, in this instance, discretion was the better part of valor. Thus, he ordered the *Pearl* to head farther into Gaian Space at top speed. A moment later, they were on their way.

# EFFERUS

## Chapter 64

They didn't stop until they'd put a reasonable distance between themselves and the Vacra fleet (which was probably the best way to describe the assemblage of alien ships). Much to their surprise, they were neither pursued nor fired upon as they fled. In fact, from what Maker could discern as the *Pearl* moved away, the Vacra ships seemed to be holding their position.

Ultimately, they came to a halt in a semi-populous star system of five planets. Recognizing how fearsome the *Pearl* probably appeared, Maker immediately began hailing what appeared to be the capital world in an attempt to let whoever was in charge know that they were not a threat. After about five minutes of waiting (and wondering if their hails were getting through), they finally received a reply as the image of a well-dressed but visibly nervous middle-aged man appeared on the warship's monitor.

"H-H-Hello," the man began. "I'm Governor Moniz. How can I help you?"

"Pleased to make your acquaintance," Maker said. "I'm Lieutenant Arrogant Maker, Galactic Marines. I need you to contact the nearest military installation and let them know I have a high-priority message for the Upper Echelon — the military high command."

"O-O-Of course," Moniz stammered. "Right away." The monitor immediately went blank.

"He seemed a little out-of-sorts," Adames commented.

"You would be, too," Maker assured him, "if a warship the size of a moon suddenly parked on your doorstep."

That got a few chuckles from around the bridge.

"How long do you think it will take him to relay your message?" asked Browing.

Maker shrugged. "Who knows? Although with an alien armada banging on humanity's door, let's hope it's not too long."

\*\*\*\*\*\*\*\*\*\*\*\*\*\*\*\*\*\*\*\*\*\*\*\*\*\*\*\*\*\*\*\*\*\*\*\*\*\*\*\*\*\*\*\*

It turned out to be not very long at all. Within ten minutes of his conversation with the governor, a half-dozen battle cruisers dropped out of hyperspace around them, guns at the ready. Although sizeable, Maker was sure he could fit all six of them into the *Pearl*, and for a moment he daydreamed about what the outcome would be if a shootout actually commenced.

The sound of the comm receiving a hail cut into his thoughts, and a second later a man wearing a Star Forces uniform appeared on the monitor.

"I'm Brigadier General Roche," the man said in a gruff tone.

"Sir," Maker began. "I'm Lieutenant—"

"I've been made aware of who you are," the general interjected.

"Yes, sir," Maker stated. "Then you probably already know that we have a message—"

"I've heard about this message you have as well," Roche declared, again not giving Maker a chance to really speak.

Maker blinked, a feeling of frustration starting to build in him. Balling his fists, he tried to keep a civil tongue in his head, saying, "I'm sorry, sir. We seem to have gotten off on the wrong foot, which is not how I wanted things to go. I had—"

Roche held up a hand, effectively cutting Maker off with the gesture. "Let me explain how this is going to go, Lieutenant. In about five minutes, a crew of Star Forces personnel is going to enter that ship and take command. You resist them in any way, you hinder them in their duties, you so much as look at them crosswise, and I'm going to interpret it as a hostile act and treat you and anyone else on that ship as a hostile combatant. Have I made myself understood?"

Maker pursed his lips, then muttered between clenched teeth, "Yes, sir."

Roche gave him a curt nod and then broke the connection.

## Chapter 65

An hour after his conversation with Roche, Maker found himself occupying a cell in the brig of a Star Forces ship. He assumed that his people were all nearby, being held in similar accommodations, but he had no way to confirm that. Likewise, he had no real idea of where Erlen was at the moment, and that was of particular concern to him. Maker sighed, thinking how quickly things had gone to hell in a handbasket.

As Roche had indicated, his people had come aboard the *Pearl* and immediately assumed command. Maker had tried to talk to them — explain that he needed to make a report to the senior brass — but they essentially ignored him. Instead, Maker and his team were taken into custody, transferred to the vessel he currently found himself on, stripped of their armor, and finally, separated. (There had been a tense moment when Roche's people first attempted to split up Erlen and Maker — with the Niotan on the verge of clawing someone's face off — but fortunately Maker was able to calm his companion down and convince him to cooperate.)

Since then, Maker had been cooling his heels in a cell, wearing prisoner coveralls. He was trying to maintain a calm demeanor, but — knowing that the Vacra were not far away (and probably plotting something) — he was growing more impatient by the second.

Maker found his thoughts unexpectedly interrupted by the sound of a door opening nearby. A moment later, General Roche stood in front of his cell.

"I have some questions for you," the general said flatly, getting straight to business.

"I've already given your people the basic name, rank, and serial number info," Maker said testily, "as well as told them as much as I could about my mission. Now you need to let me send my message to the senior brass."

"As far as you're concerned, *I'm* the senior brass," Roche stressed.

"Look," Maker pleaded, "you *have* to let me send this report."

"I'm the ranking military officer in this region, so I don't *have* to do anything. Plus, you're in no position to make demands, especially after showing up in the midst of an alien armada, illegally barging through Gaian Space in a Mammoth-class warship—"

"Mammoth class?" Maker echoed.

"Oh, you didn't know? That makes two of us. To be honest, I had to have my people look it up to figure out what class of ship it was. Apparently they only made a handful of them, so they were never truly en vogue, and they were reportedly taken out of service about two hundred years ago. That's around the time that the one you showed up with disappeared."

"Sir, I appreciate the history lesson and normally I'd be fascinated, but given the circumstances I fail to see the immediate relevance."

"You want to know what I find fascinating and relevant? That the infamous Madman Maker — notorious for getting the entire crew of the *Orpheus Moon* killed — shows up on my doorstep with another ship full of bodies."

"What bodies?!" Maker demanded. "You mean the crew of the *Pearl*? They were already dead!"

"So what happened to the rest of them?"

Maker gave him an incredulous stare. "The rest of *who?*"

"The rest of the *Pearl*'s crew. Those skeletons we found in armor weren't nearly enough people to fully man a ship that size."

"How should I know?" Maker said in exasperation, shrugging his shoulders at the same time. "You yourself just said they disappeared two hundred years ago. If I had to guess, I'd say they buried them."

Roche frowned. "Explain that."

Maker wiped his face with his hand, groaning in irritation. "Their fuel cells became inert, which led to them losing power. Eventually life support failed, and they didn't have enough self-sustaining power armor for everyone. I'm guessing those in battle suits buried those who didn't have any rather than have to walk by and see their dead and decaying comrades every day until the life support in their own armor failed."

"That's a fascinating theory," the general remarked, rubbing his chin in thought.

"And completely inconsequential," Maker added, "considering the fact that we have a fleet of alien ships bearing down on us."

"Those ships haven't moved," the general stated casually, "so the only one that's been bearing down on us is *you.*"

"Don't be fooled," Maker warned him. "I've tangled with these guys before and they're incredibly cunning. If they're here in those numbers, it's for a reason — and I don't think it's to talk."

"Funny you should mention talking. That's actually all they've been doing."

"What?" Maker muttered, startled.

"It's just the same message, over and over," Roche said as he reached into a pocket and pulled out a slip of paper. Looking at it, he read, "'We demand the Senu Lia.'"

Maker frowned, thinking about the implications.

"Anyway," the general went on, "they'll find we're more than prepared if they try anything. I've got the entire Hundred-and-Twelfth fleet headed to their position. We'll outnumber them two-to-one."

"That's a mistake," Maker insisted. "The whole point of the message I want to send is to make sure we do *not* engage with them. It's not a battle we can win."

Roche harrumphed. "History will probably see it a little differently."

He then turned and left, leaving Maker fuming in frustration.

\*\*\*\*\*\*\*\*\*\*\*\*\*\*\*\*\*\*\*\*\*\*\*\*\*\*\*\*\*\*\*\*\*\*\*\*\*\*\*\*\*\*\*\*\*\*

Maker was still seething thirty minutes later when he received a second visitor. Oddly enough, it was Browing. Seeing him on the other side of the cell bars, Maker was hard-pressed to hide his surprise.

"I thought they had all of us locked up," he said. "How'd you finagle a get-out-of-jail-free card?"

"Roche actually hails from a very distinguished pedigree," Browing answered. "His family and mine go way back. When he realized who I was, he simply exercised a little discretion."

"I get it," Maker grumbled. "The good-ole-boy network is alive and well."

"Well, it's less of a network and more like a system of favors. Roche helps me out now, I help him

302

out at some point down the road. For instance, he let me check in on our people, and you'll be happy to know they're all fine. Locked up, but fine."

"Good," Maker said sincerely. "Now, will Roche do you the favor of letting you send a message to the Upper Echelon?"

Browing shook his head. "No. He's not letting anybody get near the communications equipment. In fact, he has a detail of armed guards watching it."

"What?" Maker blurted out. "Why?"

"Because he's taken the entire Hundred-and-Twelfth fleet to BatCon Four."

"Battle Condition Four?" Maker droned. "But that means…"

"Yes," Browing said as Maker trailed off. "He considers conflict imminent, so he's restricting all communications. Basically, he's ordered radio silence as he takes the battlefield."

"And they call *me* a maniac," Maker muttered, somewhat to himself. "Browing, if you've got any influence with this guy, you need to talk him down."

Browing snorted. "Odd words coming from you. Aren't you the man who's been itching for a chance to take on the Vacra?"

"Not with the current odds," Maker countered. "There's got to be some way to make him see reason."

"Don't you think I've tried? I've seen what Efferus can do, and if the Vacra have weaponized his body, it'll be a slaughter. But Roche won't listen to any of that. He's convinced that this is his moment."

Maker's brow wrinkled in confusion. "What do you mean?"

Browing sighed. "Remember when I mentioned how family connections can only get you so far? That beyond a certain point you have to show you're competent in order to advance further? Well, Roche is one of the incompetent ones."

"Okay, but there's a difference between incompetent and stupid."

"I don't think he's stupid," Browing countered. "He's just obsessed with history and his place in it. He's basically been waiting for his moment to shine — to show his mettle — and he thinks this is it."

"Great," Maker muttered sarcastically. "A glory hound."

"Exactly. That being the case, I don't think anyone could get him to change his mind at this point — me included."

"So is that why you're here, Browing? To tell me all the things you can't do? How you can't get a message off, can't talk sense into Roche, can't chew gum and wa—"

"It's Erlen," Browing interjected. "I'm here because of Erlen."

Suddenly, everything else fell into the background. Roche's ineptitude, Browing's cronyism, the Vacra fleet, his own incarceration… In Maker's mind, they all became minute — minor inconveniences — when weighed against the notion of something happening to Erlen.

"What's happened to him?" Maker practically whispered, struggling to stay calm. "Is he okay?"

"He's fine. Locked in a cage, but fine."

Maker let out a sigh of relief. "Okay, so what's the problem?"

"The problem, as usual, is that the Vacra want him."

"I know. They've been broadcasting that they want the Senu Lia since we appeared."

"Yes, but the Vacra have more than just standard comm links for sending messages. There are back channels of communication, and covert methods for sending long-range coded missives to certain individuals."

"And you think they're using them."

"I don't know for sure but that would be my guess. There are some very powerful people who are practically foaming at the mouth to get back that tech the Vacra took. If the only cost of that is handing over Erlen, my assumption would be that, behind closed doors, a deal's being made. Sooner or later, despite the order for radio silence, word is going to come down to hand him over — assuming Roche doesn't get us killed first."

Maker stood there in stunned silence, not quite able to process what he was hearing.

"I'm sorry," Browing went on apologetically. "But I thought you'd want to hear it from a friend."

"We're not friends, Browing," Maker said testily.

"From an acquaintance, then," Browing retorted. "Someone who's on the same side."

"You're on no one's side but your own," Maker shot back. "If you *were* on my side, you'd stop this."

"I *can't*," Browing stressed. "I can't even reach the right people to let them know I'm in the middle of all this, although they're probably aware of it by now."

"Then do me a favor," Maker pleaded. "Check on Erlen and make sure he's okay."

"Sure. I'll make sure he's being properly cared for."

"No — not some flunky," Maker stated flatly. "You, personally. At least that way he gets to see a familiar face, if not a friendly one, before you sell him off."

Although he clearly didn't like Maker's tone, Browing nodded. "All right. I'll go do it now."

## Chapter 66

Roughly two hours later, Browing returned — this time with two Star Force guards and wearing a heavily tinted pair of sunglasses. The guards headed to a nearby wall with a recessed panel containing a keypad and screen. Each pressed a thumb to the screen, which Maker now realized was a scanner of some sort. The screen began to emit a soft glow as it seemingly read and verified their thumbprints. A moment later, one of the guards typed in a code on the keypad, and the door to Maker's cell slid open.

"Thank you," Browing said to the guards. "That'll be all."

The guards took their leave as Maker stepped out of his cell. He eyed Browing warily.

"You suddenly develop photophobia or something?" Maker asked, staring at the sunglasses. "Is the light in here bothering you?"

"No," Browing replied stonily, removing the eyewear. "Your pet monster bit me."

With the sunglasses removed, Maker got a good look at Browing's eyes and saw that they were glowing red. He started laughing.

\*\*\*\*\*\*\*\*\*\*\*\*\*\*\*\*\*\*\*\*\*\*\*\*\*\*\*\*\*\*\*\*\*\*\*\*\*\*\*\*\*\*\*\*\*\*\*\*\*\*

As they walked through the ship, Browing — now with his sunglasses back on — led the way, while explaining to Maker what had happened.

"I went to check on Erlen, just like you asked," Browing said. "Since they couldn't classify his species, he was being held in a cage in a quarantined room — just in

307

case he had some type of unknown disease. When I walked in, he was already out of the cage. The bars on it had been dissolved, as if by acid."

Maker smiled. It wasn't hard to figure out that part. Erlen, able to create just about any chemical imaginable, had apparently produced a compound to eat through the bars of the cage holding him.

"I was barely over the threshold when he jumped me," Browing said. "He chomped down on my arm."

"And?" Maker asked.

"As if you don't know," Browing replied. "A minute later, I had my brainpower magnified a hundred times over. I could remember everything that I'd ever done — everything that's ever happened to me."

Maker understood exactly what Browing was going through. He had experienced the same thing himself on several occasions, including the glowing red eyes.

"Erlen's bite injected you with a mental stimulant," Maker said. "Gave you total recall."

"Yes, but it wasn't just memory. It was a complete brain boost across the board. High-level math, advanced chemistry and physics, nanotechnology… I understand it all now." Browing chuckled. "I just came up with an algorithm that would earn me a fortune in the financial markets."

"Sounds great," Maker chided. "If only you live to enjoy it."

His comment, intended to focus Browing on their current situation, had the desired effect.

"I haven't forgotten about our current predicament," Browing assured him, although he spoke in a tone that implied he found it a mundane topic. He guided Maker towards a door set in a side wall of the corridor they were in. "Come on — let's talk in here."

The room they found themselves in appeared to be some kind of study nook. Roughly one hundred square feet in size, it had floor-to-ceiling bookshelves filled with thick, black binders on each wall. The center of the room held a modest rectangular table with three chairs on each side.

Taking a look at the binders, Maker suddenly realized that they were reference manuals — instructions for maintaining, repairing, and troubleshooting problems on the ship. It made sense; if you started having issues with, say, the ship's power, you might not be able to pull up a digital copy of the repair manual.

Browing took a seat on one side of the table. Without waiting for an invitation, Maker sat down across from him.

"Before I get sidetracked," Maker began, "where's my squad?"

"In the mess hall," Browing replied, "getting something to eat. Erlen, too. They've all been released. Satisfied?"

"I suppose."

"Good," Browing said. "Now, back to what I was saying earlier: I haven't forgotten that we're in the thick of things, and I was able to get a message off to the Upper Echelon."

Maker was impressed. "How'd you manage that? Did your big brain help you convince Roche to let you break radio silence?"

"No, his orders are still not to let anyone use the comm," Browing replied with a grin. "So I built my own."

Maker raised an eyebrow. "Really?"

"Well, it was actually more of an auxiliary comm unit. It acted as a remote link and let me tap into Roche's communications array."

"Where'd you get the parts?"

"The quartermaster — she had everything I needed. Of course, she didn't do it out of the goodness of her heart."

"I see. How much did it set you back?"

Browing laughed. "A cask of Amontillado."

Maker frowned. "I don't get it."

"You and Adames are behind the times." Browing chuckled. "Using cash as an" — he spent a moment searching for the right word — "*incentive* in certain situations is passé. It's far too easy to track, among other things."

"Oh? So what's the current medium of exchange when it comes to bribes?"

"Do you remember all that expensive bubbly that you didn't want me bringing aboard the *Raider*?"

"Wait a minute," Maker uttered, a little astounded. "That's what all that stuff was for? Graft and kickbacks?"

"*Incentives*," Browing stressed. "It's almost just as easy to motivate someone with a bottle of champagne worth a year's salary as it is with the cash, and it invites far less scrutiny. I had to get someone to take me by shuttle to retrieve it — which cost me extra — but it was worth it."

"So this is how the upper crust does it," Maker noted. "Instead of paying money *under* the table, it's wine and caviar on *top* of it. And here I was thinking that you just couldn't live without the finer things in life."

"I told you that you'd misjudged me," Browing reminded him. "But at least now you know what all that special food and drink was for."

"Well, if we get out of this, I'll personally build you a wine room to keep all of your spirits at the perfect temperature."

"Wow," Browing muttered, mostly to himself. "I've just thought of a wine preservation method that will keep an opened bottle as good as new indefinitely." He looked at Maker. "It's incredible — having my mind opened and expanded like this. I mean, I saw it happen to you before, but I never thought about what it would be like."

"I know," Maker said with a nod. "It's like you're Gulliver and everyone else is a Lilliputian."

Browing laughed. "That's actually not a bad comparison."

"Now," Maker said, switching gears, "as to giving Erlen to the Vacra — do you want him boxed or just with a ribbon around his neck?"

Browing frowned. "We can't hand him over. He's not a gift, a commodity, or an anomaly. He's a weapon."

Maker nodded. "Now you get it. With him, the Vacra would have the means to develop weapons that would make the sub rosa tech they stole look like toys for infants."

"That brings us back to the subject at hand — the Vacra and the message I sent."

"I'm listening."

"I told them what was going on — that the Vacra had an armada at the Fringe. They were already aware of the situation, and had previously sent word for Roche to take a defensive position well back from the front line and wait for reinforcements."

"I hope you passed on to them that he's not a good listener."

"They know he's disobeyed the prior mandate and is practically eye-to-eye with the Vacra. They've been trying to reach him and order him back, but all of the ships in his fleet appear to have initiated closed-circuit comms."

"So they can still talk to each other, but no outside communications can reach them," Maker summed up.

"Not without getting within extremely close range."

"What about the reinforcements?" Maker asked. "When are they arriving?"

"They're not," Browing replied. "I didn't give a lot of detail, but I relayed to the Upper Echelon that the Vacra have what might be considered a doomsday device. Anything that gets close to it is going to get atomized. That being the case, they're not sending any more ships at the moment."

"So they're just going to let the Hundred-and-Twelfth get wiped out of existence?"

"There's nothing they can do. Roche isn't obeying orders."

"Can't they strip him of command?"

"They already have — he just doesn't know it."

Maker couldn't hide his surprise at this. "So who's in command?"

"Yours truly," Browing said. "How do you think I was able to get you and everyone else released?"

Maker gave him an incredulous look. "They put a civilian in charge of a fleet?"

"It will probably come as a shock to you, but I'm actually a commissioned officer in the Reserves."

"You're kidding."

Browing gave him a sideways glance. "I can have you locked back up if you need further convincing."

Maker ignored the jibe. "If Roche had made the ship's comm off-limits, how'd the Upper Echelon get a message through about a change of command?"

"I had my auxiliary comm, in case you forgot."

"And the crew here just took your word that commands coming through a homemade comm device were bona fide orders from high-ranking military officers?"

"Actually, no. But after some debate they decided to verify it by using the ship's comm. After they received confirmation, I assumed command."

"So where are we exactly?" asked Maker. "I mean, this ship obviously isn't with the rest of the fleet, or the closed-circuit comm would have prevented you from sending that message to the Upper Echelon."

"Correct," Browing stated. "This is really a supply ship, so it has no place on the front lines. Doing that would just get the ship's crew killed."

"The crew of every ship in Roche's fleet is going to get killed if we don't do something."

"Again, there's nothing to be done."

Maker frowned, thinking intently. "What if we send a ship in close enough to coalesce with the fleet's closed-off comms and transmit an order to stand down and withdraw?"

Browing snorted. "Roche is deliberately disobeying orders as we speak. What makes you think he's suddenly going to start complying?"

"The order to stand down wouldn't be for *him*," Maker clarified. "It would be directed to the individual ship commanders. They're only following Roche's orders because they don't know he's been relieved of command."

Browing pondered for a moment and then said, "That might work."

"It has to. Otherwise everyone in the Hundred-and-Twelfth is going to die."

"Understood. But just delivering the order is something akin to a suicide mission if the Vacra open fire. Where are you going to find a maniac willing to volunteer to do that?"

Maker smiled. "A maniac? I have an idea of where we might get one…"

## Chapter 67

"I want to go on the record as saying that this is madness," Adames declared.

"So noted," Maker replied with a grin.

The two of them and their crew were back on board the *Pearl*. It still wasn't operating at one hundred percent, but — after Maker and his team had been taken into custody — Roche's people had put some time into powering up many of the warship's systems, including life support. Ultimately, that meant that on this particular voyage, they didn't have to man the bridge dressed in battle armor.

Planck, Chantrey, and Browing (whose eyes had returned to normal) were with them as well. Browing, of course, being in command, was the one who had authorized them to take the *Pearl*, which Roche had actually impounded. Frankly speaking, Maker was amazed Browing had decided to come with them on this "suicide mission," as he'd called it (and was equally astounded that Browing acquiesced when Maker insisted on being in command).

After he and Browing had finished talking in the study nook, they had gone to the mess hall. Once there, Maker had presented his idea to the rest of his squad. He hadn't made participation mandatory, but every one of his Marines had volunteered without hesitation. So had Chantrey and Planck. It was then just a matter of hustling over to the *Pearl* (which still had the *Raider* in her landing bay) and preparing to leave.

Now on the bridge, they were simply waiting for Roche's people to vacate the premises before they departed. It meant sitting idly for only a few minutes, but it felt like far longer.

"If they're really going to take on the Vacra," Wayne said, trying to make conversation, "I'm surprised they didn't take the *Pearl*. Even as old as she is, she could probably withstand more than any other ship out there."

"Everything on this ship is ancient," Adames retorted. "It should all be fully tested before being sent into battle."

The NCO's statement was absolutely true, and made them all realize how fortunate they had been that everything had worked out in their favor during their maiden voyage on the warship.

"She *is* pretty old," Loyola agreed. "But everything seems almost pristine — like she's barely aged."

"I'm guessing they applied a special coating wherever possible," Wayne said. "Something to keep everything here from aging, rusting, and so on."

"Tell that to the bay doors," Fierce said.

Maker chuckled. "I suppose that was an out-of-sight, out-of-mind issue. They probably never used the manual system, so they never thought about or implemented any of the safeguards or protections on it that they applied elsewhere."

Others began to chime in, giving their opinion about various features of the *Pearl*. Maker only half-listened as he noticed Chantrey unexpectedly walk towards the bridge exit and then motion for him to come with her. Telling Erlen to stay put, he went to join her. On the way out, he passed Efferus, who was still inside Jerry and attached to Wayne's tablet.

Once outside, Chantrey gave him a very frank stare and said, "Is this wise?"

"What do you mean?" he asked, plainly confused.

"Racing to the front lines with a firefight looming on the horizon."

"What do you think we should do, then? Just let all those people die?"

She crossed her arms and stared at him. "This isn't going to bring them back, you know?"

"Huh?" he muttered, frowning. "What are you talking about?"

"The *Orpheus Moon*."

"Now I get it," Maker said, nodding. "You think I'm doing this out of some misplaced notion of guilt. I couldn't save the crew of the *Orpheus Moon*, but I can save thousands more here. Is that it?"

"You have to agree it makes sense."

"I can understand how you'd get that idea, but maybe I'm just a guy who doesn't like leaving a man behind. As far as I'm concerned, everyone serving under Roche's command is being left behind because they're following the orders of a rogue commander. So, if you'll stop trying to analyze me and predict my behavior all the time, maybe you'll see me as a guy just trying to do his job."

He turned and headed back to his place on the bridge without waiting for a reply.

"All of Roche's people are gone," Adames stated a moment later.

"Excellent," Maker said. "Get us out of here."

# EFFERUS

## Chapter 68

General Colin Roche was beyond excited. He had spent his entire life dreaming of glory and grandeur, and now he was on the cusp of it. His family connections had helped him make general, but for some reason it seemed that he could go no further: a dead-end post in the middle of nowhere, where nothing ever happened...until now. Destiny had given him an opportunity for greatness, and he would not be denied.

He looked at his monitor, noting the vast array of battleships that made up the Hundred-and-Twelfth fleet that he commanded. At the same time, he spied the alien ships of the Vacra — another hideous race of bugs — not too far away. He felt a bit proud of the fact that, as he had told Maker, they probably had the Vacra outnumbered two-to-one. That said, he kept his flagship (where he was currently located) well back from the front lines.

Those fools in the Upper Echelon had tried to hold him down — hinder his march towards history. They had wanted him to wait for "reinforcements," as they put it. In other words, someone else wanted to share in the glory that was rightfully his alone. Well, that was *not* going to happen...

"Sir," said the young officer manning the scanners, "I'm picking up a large warship coming in on our flank, at the far end of the fleet." The officer studied her instruments for a moment, then added, "It's the *Black Pearl*."

"The *Pearl?*" he repeated. "What's it doing here?"

"It looks like it's conjoining with the closed-circuit comm," someone replied. "They're trying to send a message to our ships."

"Let me hear it," the general said.

A moment later, a voice that he recognized as belonging to Lieutenant Maker echoed through the bridge, saying, "—lieved of command. Repeat. General Roche has—"

"Kill that and block the rest of the *Pearl*'s communications," Roche ordered, in the back of his mind wondering why Maker wasn't still locked up.

"Done, sir," one of the bridge crew responded a second later.

"Now, open a fleet-wide channel," Roche ordered. After receiving confirmation that this was done, he cleared his throat and said, "Fleet, this is General Roche. A rogue ship has managed to infiltrate our comm network. We are currently jamming them, but — should that fail at some point — all personnel are to disregard any orders that originate outside the Hundred-and-Twelfth. Anyone who disobeys this command will be court-martialed. Over."

A moment later, someone acknowledged that his message had been sent to the fleet, at which point Roche turned his attention back to the monitor.

"Now, with respect to…" The general trailed off as he saw what was happening.

The Vacra ships had started moving forward, plainly ready to engage his fleet.

\*\*\*\*\*\*\*\*\*\*\*\*\*\*\*\*\*\*\*\*\*\*\*\*\*\*\*\*\*\*\*\*\*\*\*\*\*\*\*\*\*\*\*\*\*\*\*\*

Maker was incredibly vexed. Although close enough that they should be able to access the closed-circuit comm of the Hundred-and Twelfth Fleet, it wasn't happening. They were being shut out.

"We're being jammed?" he asked in astonishment. "But we're on the same secure frequency as the Hundred-and-Twelfth. How's that possible?"

"I don't think you want the full technical explanation," Wayne said. "The gist of it, however, is that it's not that hard given how old the *Pearl*'s systems are."

"Huh?" Maker murmured. "Not too long ago you were talking about how pristine everything here is."

"Yes, from a *manufacturing* standpoint it's like a lot of this stuff is fresh off the assembly line — just made yesterday," Wayne agreed. "But it's two hundred years out of date. It's like they made it and then sent it forward through time a couple of centuries."

"So physically it's like new," Diviana surmised, "but in terms of practical utility, it's old."

"Exactly," Wayne effused. "From a *technological* view, it's ancient. It's not up to par with current software, infrastructure, and so on. So with respect to being jammed, it's like we're an antiquated landline trying to communicate with a wireless system. All they've got to do to keep us out is cut the cord."

"And you don't need high tech to do that," Maker concluded. "You can go old-school and do it with a pair of scissors."

"Well, we're speaking metaphorically," Wayne said, "but that's essentially it."

"I think we can forget the metaphorical and focus on the actual," Adames chimed in. "Look."

He pointed at the main monitor, which showed the Vacra fleet starting to move.

"Start hailing Roche's flagship," Maker ordered. "Now!"

\*\*\*\*\*\*\*\*\*\*\*\*\*\*\*\*\*\*\*\*\*\*\*\*\*\*\*\*\*\*\*\*\*\*\*\*\*\*\*\*\*\*\*\*\*\*\*\*

Roche found it hard to hide his incredulity. "So we're jamming Maker's communications, and he's still finding a way to message us?" he asked, speaking of the urgent, high-priority hail his flagship was receiving from the *Pearl*.

"It's a special channel," his Comm Officer explained, "meant only for flagship-to-flagship messaging between fleet commanders, and apparently the *Pearl* was designed to be a flagship. However, he can't use it to reach our other ships."

"Then ignore it," Roche said. He was fed up with Maker's shenanigans. Even if he wasn't, he didn't have time to deal with the fellow now — not with armed conflict practically staring him in the face.

"All ships, prepare to engage," he commanded, then listened as the order was relayed to the fleet.

Roche smiled to himself, having trouble containing his excitement. Everything he did from this moment forward would be analyzed by historians, future battle commanders, and so on. He had to make sure everything looked good for posterity, from the fit of his uniform to exuding a commanding presence.

"Sir, enemy ships have fired projectiles," one of the crewman announced.

"All shields up!" Roche commanded, then asked, "What type of warhead?"

"It's weird, sir," came the answer. "There's no weapons signature."

"Huh?" Roche mumbled. "There must be some mistake."

"No mistake, sir. Scanners indicate that enemy projectiles contain no chemical, atomic, or explosive charge."

The general frowned. "Then what did they fire at us?"

"Some type of canisters, but they don't seem to contain anything assessable as a threat."

Roche let out a dissatisfied grunt. His flagship was far enough back that the canisters wouldn't reach his position, but — had he known this was all the fleet was likely to face — he would have gotten closer to the action. Now, of course, it wouldn't look as good in the history books (especially with the other side flinging the equivalent of sticks and stones), but it would still be a victory over hostile aliens. That being the case, he'd take it.

"Ready weapons on all ships," Roche ordered. "Fire on my mark."

\*\*\*\*\*\*\*\*\*\*\*\*\*\*\*\*\*\*\*\*\*\*\*\*\*\*\*\*\*\*\*\*\*\*\*\*\*\*\*\*\*\*\*\*

"The Vacra ships have halted, but have fired the cylinders containing Efferus," Adames said, essentially relaying the action on the monitors.

Maker stared at the scene, feeling impotent as the cylinders flew toward the ships of the Hundred-and-Twelfth. They had no idea of what was headed their way, and — with Roche not only jamming them but refusing to acknowledge their hails — he wasn't sure what to do next.

"Maker," Browing called out. "It's over. We tried, but there's nothing more we can do here."

Maker's face conveyed his resentment — not just due to his inability to do anything, but also because Browing was actually the voice of reason. All that he would accomplish by keeping the *Pearl* in her present position would be to get his people killed.

"Get us out of here," he said to no one in particular.

"It may be too late for that," Wayne decreed, looking at his tablet.

"How so?" asked Loyola.

"We're close enough now for Efferus to sense the parts of himself in the Vacra cylinders," Wayne said. "He says that those portions have been 'agitated.'"

"What exactly does that mean?" demanded Adames.

Wayne studied the tablet for a moment. "Apparently the effect we first observed, where Efferus basically consumed whatever he came into contact with, is going to occur — but to a far more extreme degree."

"And in layman's terms?" Snick asked.

"It means Efferus, once released, is going to claw through the shields of that fleet out there in a nanosecond," Planck interjected. "They won't have the luxury of seeing their defenses slowly diminish and maybe have a chance to get away. They're going to be vaporized, atomized, disintegrated — whatever you want to call it — before they even know what's happening."

"Not only that," Wayne added, "but Efferus says the agitation will affect his physical scope. In other words, he expects to expand farther than he did before — very far, very fast."

Maker rubbed his chin, thinking furiously. "Can Efferus stop it — like he did before, with us?"

Wayne shrugged, still looking at the tablet. "He anticipated that question and says that it's a proximity thing to some degree. To the extent he can assert control, it'll be greatest where he — meaning the fragment of his essence that's in Jerry — is physically located. He wants to know if we want him to try."

"Yes, dammit!" Maker barked. "Absolutely, without question, we want him to try!"

As he spoke, he saw the Vacra cylinders — now very near Roche's fleet — forcefully expelling the rest of Efferus' gaseous form.

\*\*\*\*\*\*\*\*\*\*\*\*\*\*\*\*\*\*\*\*\*\*\*\*\*\*\*\*\*\*\*\*\*\*\*\*\*\*\*\*\*\*\*\*\*\*

Roche rubbed his eyes, unsure of what had just happened. The canisters from the aliens had started shooting out a gas in the direction of his fleet, and then there had been a bright flash.

"Status report!" he bellowed, finally looking around.

"The alien armada hasn't advanced any farther," came the reply.

"And the fleet?" Roche asked.

There was silence for a moment, and then a tentative voice said, "Uh…I'm not… It's not… There's no…" There was suddenly a harsh intake of breath, followed by a stunned announcement: "All ships destroyed, sir."

"What?!" Roche screeched.

"The entire fleet's gone, sir."

"That's impossible!" Roche cried. Then he looked at the monitors and was completely stunned by what he saw. Where just moments before there had been the glorious Hundred-and-Twelfth fleet, there now appeared to be nothing. The alien armada was still there, of course, but his own ships were gone — vanished like a puff of smoke.

"How...?" Roche mumbled, staggering slightly as the magnitude of what had just happened hit him.

His rightful place in history was gone now — wiped out. His military genius (his strategic brilliance!) would go down unrecognized, unadmired, and unacknowledged. Rather than being honored as an exceptional military commander, he'd be lucky not to have his name mentioned in the same breath as that idiot from Old Earth... *What was his name? Mustard? No, Custard? No, that still wasn't quite right...*

"Are you certain about the readings?" Roche asked pleadingly. "They're all gone?"

"Yes, sir," came the response. "All ships..." There was a slight pause, and then, "Correction, sir. One ship remains. *The Black Pearl.*"

# EFFERUS

## Chapter 69

"What the hell…?" Maker muttered as his vision cleared.

There had been some kind of flash as the Vacra cylinders expelled Efferus' body — presumably a reaction of his gaseous form being "agitated," swiftly expanding, or maybe just interacting with the shields of the ships from the Hundred-and-Twelfth. They probably would never know the exact answer, but the effect on their eyes passed quickly enough and within moments, his vision was back to normal.

"What's the status of the *Pearl?*" Maker asked.

"She's intact," Adames replied. "No damage according to the systems I'm reading."

Maker nodded. "And the Hundred-and-Twelfth?"

At that juncture, a quick scan revealed precisely what everyone present had anticipated: Roche's fleet had been annihilated. The only ship remaining — besides the *Pearl* — was the general's flagship, which had been far enough back to avoid the fate of its comrades. (In fact, as he watched, Roche's ship began beating a hasty retreat.)

Wayne stared at his tablet as information began scrolling across it. "Efferus apologizes, but says he was only able to exert enough control to spare the *Pearl.*"

"Understood," Maker remarked stoically. They had just witnessed death and destruction on a cosmic scale, but he didn't have time to dwell on it.

The Vacra were still there; in a moment, they'd presumably begin scooping up Efferus again. In his mind's eye, Maker could see exactly what the future held: the Vacra would cut a swath through Gaian Space — obliterating any resistance they encountered the same way

326

they'd just eradicated Roche's fleet — and no one would be able to stop them.

"Efferus says he has to go," Wayne said, interrupting Maker's thoughts.

"Excuse me?" Maker said.

"He says that with his body no longer encapsulated, our current proximity allows him to transition."

Maker spent a moment thinking about what this meant. "So he can go home?"

"Yes," Wayne replied, "but not to the place we initially encountered him. His *real* home. The Otherwhere-When. And if he doesn't do it now, he may not be able to. Whatever the Vacra are doing when they encapsulate his body — it's killing him. He has to transition before they take him again."

"Then tell him to go," Maker said.

It was coming a little too late for Roche's fleet, but Efferus' departure would take away the Vacra's doomsday weapon, as Browing had dubbed it. However, they'd still have the sub rosa tech, and the *Pearl* was the only ship between them and the rest of humanity.

"Wayne," Maker said excitedly, as a thought occurred to him, "when Efferus leaves, can he take anything with him?"

Wayne looked confused. "Like what?"

"Ships," Maker clarified. "Can he take spaceships with him?"

"Now hold on a second," Browing began, but Maker shushed him as Wayne began typing the question.

There were some odd looks traded among the others on the bridge, but no one said anything. Maker, eagerly anticipating the answer, could barely contain his emotions for the few seconds it took to get a response.

"He says he can," Wayne confirmed. "But he would not advise that we undertake transition."

"Not *us*," Maker clarified, cutting off the comment he felt — as well as saw — coming from Browing. "The Vacra. Ask him if he can take them." On the monitor, he noted that the Vacra cylinders were once again starting to collect the cloudlike portion of Efferus.

"He can take them," Wayne confirmed a few seconds later, "but he'd have to take us as well."

"Why is that?" asked Loyola.

"Because, as a result of what the Vacra have done to him, he doesn't have full control at the moment," Wayne replied. "His ability to transition at such a nuanced level has been compromised."

"So he can't cherry-pick in terms of transitioning," Maker concluded. "It's all or nothing."

"Correct," Wayne affirmed. "Right now, asking him to take them and not us is like giving him a cup of coffee while he has the shakes, then filling it to the brim and telling him not to spill any. He can't do it. But even if he could, there's also another wrinkle."

Maker frowned. "Go on."

Wayne sighed. "Human beings apparently don't handle the transition process very well. There's some kind of adverse neurological effect on us, and the damage it does compounds with every transition. Based on what he's observed so far, Efferus thinks that, with a couple of exceptions" — he glanced briefly at Fierce and then Erlen — "we won't survive another transition."

Maker glanced at the screen again, noting the Vacra cylinders sucking in Efferus' body. The window for making a decision was small to begin with, and shrinking by the second.

He looked around at his crew, men and women who had faith in him. He had taken risks with their lives before — as he had with his own — but in each of those instances, there had always been a chance of success, a possibility that everything would turn out okay. That they would survive. Rarely had there been a situation where death was essentially guaranteed.

Looking at them now, however, he saw conviction on their faces. Hardened resolve. They knew as well as he did what would happen if the Vacra weren't stopped. They also knew that, as formidable as the *Pearl* was, she posed no threat to the Vacra as long as they had Efferus as a weapon.

"Tell him to do it," Maker said flatly.

Moments later, he felt himself being yanked out of his body, as before — only this time it was going to be permanent.

# EFFERUS

## Chapter 70

A short time later, Maker was amazed to find himself rejoining the living. He came to in the captain's chair, on the *Pearl*'s bridge, with Erlen next to him. There was a dull but recognizable ache in his right forearm. Being familiar with the sensation, he knew that — at some point — Erlen had bit him, but when he checked the arm he saw no wounds. That, however, wasn't unusual; if he wanted to do so, the Niotan could include a healing element when he bit someone, such that any scars would vanish in record time.

Looking around, he noticed the rest of his people slowly regaining consciousness — all except for Fierce, who was not only awake but apparently checking on everyone else.

"How are they?" Maker asked the Augman.

"All alive," Fierce stated as he took readings from a medical device that was currently floating over Chantrey's head. "And apparently with no ill effects."

Maker was suddenly alarmed. "So what happened? We didn't transition?"

"Well, from what the instruments say, we're in a region of space with no known stars, constellations, or astronomical phenomena," Fierce said. "Bearing that in mind, I'd say we definitely transitioned."

"And we're still alive?" Maker asked incredulously.

"You don't have to sound so happy about it," Fierce joked, "but yes, we are. That said, *my* survival was never in doubt. As to you and the others, I have to admit surprise."

330

"Now who's sounding happy about it?" Maker quipped.

Fierce merely grunted in response, but Maker could tell he was amused. Erlen opened his mouth and yawned; Maker reached out and scratched the Niotan's head. How they had survived was no mystery to him: Erlen had injected everyone with some compound that decreased (or possibly eliminated) the effects of transitioning. The thought suddenly brought to mind their current circumstances — and the fact that not only they, but the Vacra as well, had been transitioned by Efferus.

Sitting up in alarm, Maker swiftly looked towards the main monitor. On the screen, he saw something unusual: an immense, gaseous form that almost completely permeated the field of view.

At first, he assumed that what he was seeing was Efferus — that his vaporous form had somehow expanded during the transition to the place he called home. Upon closer inspection, however, he realized that what he was seeing was actually not just one form but several. A number of them appeared denser than Efferus had been; others were darker or a different color altogether. With a shock, Maker suddenly realized that there wasn't just one Efferus — there was an entire race of beings like him.

Moreover, as he watched, he noted within several of the cloudy beings some familiar objects: Vacra ships. However, the insectoids seemed to be zipping around crazily, flying in mad haste but in an odd fashion — as if they had no real destination in mind. It was almost as if they were lost (or couldn't see, since they had several near-collisions just in the time that Maker had been observing them).

And then one of the Vacra ships simply disappeared — vanished in its entirety, as if it had never existed. Suddenly, Maker had a new perspective on what he was seeing. The other beings of Efferus' race had the same "devouring" effect the he did on most objects. At the moment, the Vacra ships all appeared to be within these beings. (They were so vast and extensive, Maker didn't see how anything he could currently see on the screen was "out" of any of these life forms.) Presumably, the mad dashing about that the Vacra ships were engaged in was an attempt to find the "exit" before their shields failed. And fail they did, time and again.

"Wow," said a voice close to Maker in near-awe. Turning, he saw Wayne — now fully conscious — watching the monitor, along with the other members of their team.

"Any chance of that happening to us?" asked Chantrey.

"No," replied Wayne, who was already tapping on his tablet. "Efferus is protecting us, and has spread the word to the rest of his people that we aren't to be touched."

Maker simply nodded at this. He had assumed something along those lines — otherwise the *Pearl* would have winked out of existence like so many of the Vacra ships had.

"All right, people — break's over," he said. "Let's start working on a way home."

# EFFERUS

## Chapter 71

As relayed by Wayne, Efferus felt that he would be able to transition them home in roughly three days (which was the amount of time it would take for his gaseous body to fully recover from what the Vacra had done). However, if Maker and his people were impatient, Efferus was willing to let one of his fellows take them sooner. It was an offer that was immediately declined, despite the fact that Fierce had cleared them all medically to undertake the journey and stated that none of them had any neurological damage.

"No offense to the rest of his people," Maker had said, "but this is really a devil-you-know situation. That being the case, we'll wait for Efferus to escort us home."

That, of course, left them with three days to kill. Maker almost wished that some of the Vacra ships had survived; it would at least have given them something to focus on. However, none of the insectoids' vessels had lasted very long after Efferus brought them all to his "home." (Apparently the transition process had done something to their jump engines, although Efferus gave a cryptic response when asked whether the effect had been deliberate.)

Ultimately, with almost nothing to do (and with everyone lounging about and engaging in idle chitchat for a few hours), Maker declared three days of R-and-R. The only caveat was that there would still be two-person teams on watch duty at all times. Maker himself took the first rotation, assigning Browing to join him.

Upon the announcement that official watch duty was about to begin, everyone except for Maker, Browing, and Erlen began to file out. Chantrey, however, hung

333

back for a moment, getting Maker's attention. Hurrying over, he joined her as she left the bridge.

They stood there silently for a moment, giving everyone else a chance to disperse, and then she turned to him.

"Look, I can take a hint," she began.

"What do you mean?" asked Maker.

"Well, you had a chance to spend time with me before by giving us watch duty together and you declined. You had a second opportunity just now and picked Browing. Knowing the animosity you two have for each other, if you'd rather spend eight hours alone with him rather than me... That obviously tells me something."

Maker gave her an inquisitive look. "Which is?"

"That you're uncomfortable with the idea of us being more than just colleagues. That you'd rather—"

The rest of what she was going to say was cut off as Maker leaned in and kissed her. She kissed him back, eagerly and longingly for a moment — and then pulled away.

"Well," she said nonchalantly, "that didn't take as long as I thought."

Maker frowned. "Wait a minute. Did you just... Did you know I was going to kiss you?"

She gave him a coy smile as she put her arms around his neck. "You mean, did I predict your behavior?"

"Yes."

"Of course not," she insisted, but in a tone that suggested that was exactly what she had done.

"Good," Maker said with finality. "Because you're terrible at it."

"Well, in that case, maybe I'll give it another shot later," she said before leaning in to give him a quick peck. "Now go to work. I'll see you soon."

She dropped her arms from his neck and gave his hand a squeeze before walking away. Maker watched her go, then returned to the bridge.

Browing was sitting in the co-pilot's chair when he came in. Maker sat in the pilot's seat next to him.

Browing looked at him, then asked, "What are you grinning so broadly about?"

"Huh?" Maker said, suddenly realizing that he had been daydreaming about Chantrey. "Uh, nothing. Just a joke I heard."

"Anyway," Browing continued, "I know you didn't ask me to be on watch with you because you enjoy my company. So what is it?"

Maker drummed his fingers for a moment before speaking, wondering how to phrase his question. "Back when I decided I wanted to try to save the Hundred-and-Twelfth, I essentially demanded that you put me in charge of the mission. You had the authority to tell me to go take a flying leap, and considering our history, I expected you to. But you went ahead and conceded to my demands. Why?"

"It sort of goes back to what I said before about being competent. Part of that is knowing your strengths and weaknesses. I'm in the Reserves, but I've never been in a battle — not the way you have. We were heading into a military situation, so we really needed someone with a military mind at the helm. Turns out it was the right decision."

Maker nodded, but didn't say anything. This was more of an admission than he had expected from

Browing. There were obviously more levels to the man than Maker had initially assumed.

Erlen, sitting next to Maker, suddenly stretched and let out an audible yawn.

Browing glanced at the Niotan and then said, "By the way, your friend bit me." He pulled up the sleeve of his left arm, revealing two small puncture wounds.

Maker was caught by surprise. It was probably the first time Browing hadn't referred to Erlen as a pet.

"Uh, yeah, I know," Maker replied. "It's how you got that big brain boost before."

Browing shook his head. "No, that's when he bit me *here*." He thrust out his other forearm, showing two similar bite marks on that one as well. "I suppose you have an explanation."

"Yeah," Maker stated. "That second time, Erlen didn't just bite *you*. He bit all of us, during the last transition — presumably after we passed out. It healed us from the negative effects of traveling that way."

"I figured as much. However, I checked with everyone else, and — while some of them feel a slight tingling in their arm — none of them have any bite wounds. Why is that?"

Maker debated for a moment, then simply decided to go with the truth. "Erlen let you have puncture wounds because he wanted you to know it was him that saved you. Despite the fact that you've called him a pet, treated him like a dumb animal, and tried to sell him to the Vacra, he still saved you."

"So, does he think that I owe him now?"

Maker shook his head. "No, Erlen doesn't think that way. And, of course, if *you* owed him, everyone on board would owe him."

"Except maybe Fierce," Browing countered. "I don't think he got bit. However, he did say he passed out, but it was odd."

"Oh? How so?"

"He said he was fine on the other occasions when we transitioned, but this time — he said it was like someone put a pillow over his mind and suffocated his brain until he was unconscious."

"Hmmm," Maker said. "Interesting."

"Yes. I've heard of psychics being able to accomplish things like that," Browing said, looking pointedly at Erlen.

The implication was not lost on Maker. Browing knew that Erlen was psychic — at this point Maker's entire team probably knew — but had stopped short of actually saying anything accusatory.

"Well, I suppose if a psychic were to render someone unconscious under the circumstances we were in, I would assume that — if they were one of the good guys — they didn't want someone to see what they were doing and get the wrong impression."

Browing appeared to ponder this for a moment, then muttered, "Makes sense." He then glanced at Maker and asked, "So what's next for you?"

Maker gave him an odd look. "What do you mean?"

"Well, you've hunted down the Vacra, seen them take some terrible losses, and finally gotten your revenge — assuming that's what you were after."

"I don't know," Maker admitted. "Something's changed. Before, the Vacra always took precautions to make sure they could capture Erlen alive. This last time, however... My gut says that they knew he was on the

*Pearl* and they attacked despite that fact. Maybe even because of it."

Browing concentrated in thought for a moment. "You think they want to kill him now?"

"I think that they realize what having him means, and they'd rather kill him than let him fall into anyone else's hands."

"And that's why they attacked — released Efferus — after the *Pearl* showed up."

"Yes. After you released me from the brig, you mentioned that we couldn't give Erlen to the Vacra because he was a weapon. I'm assuming that your assessment somehow got back to the people who sent you to recover the sub rosa tech. If they then rebuffed the Vacra request to hand Erlen over…"

"Then the Vacra might have decided to destroy Erlen rather than let humanity have him," Browing finished. "There is a certain logic to it, but we turned the tables on them. They've suffered massive losses, didn't get what they wanted, and that one you've been obsessed with is finally dead."

Maker frowned at the term "obsessed," but didn't dwell on it. "That all sounds good on paper," he said, "but I'm not sure about the reality. For instance, it seems weird to me to think of Skullcap as dead. I mean, I've imagined his death in a thousand ways, but nothing like what occurred today. I just can't see him going out like that. He's kind of like this ship — the *Pearl*. It would take something extraordinary to bring him down."

"Or something extra *ordinary*," Browing suggested.

Maker, somewhat confused by the comment, said, "You'll have to explain that."

"Didn't you find it odd that the Vacra didn't use any of the sub rosa tech on the *Pearl* when we first pulled the ship out of mothballs? They've used all kinds of stuff on us before — weapons that cut through shields like they were wet tissue, devices that disrupted life support, and so on. But on the *Pearl*, nothing."

"It *is* a little odd when you think about it, but I chalked it up to them not wanting to hurt Erlen at the time."

"Well, after your friend gave me a brain boost, I spent a little time thinking about it."

"And what did you come up with?"

"My theory is that they *did* use sub rosa tech on the *Pearl*, but it was mostly ineffective."

Maker shook his head. "I find it hard to believe that a two-hundred-year-old ship is more advanced than sub rosa tech — especially when I recently got a briefing on how outdated everything in here is."

"But its very age is what protected the *Pearl*."

Maker didn't even try to hide his confusion, stating, "You're going to have to explain that."

"Okay, think of the battle armor that you wear. It's an advanced piece of technology, right?"

Maker nodded in agreement. "Yes."

"Now think of a medieval knight who also wears armor."

"Okay," Maker said, not sure where this was going.

"Now you're both in armor, but let's say that someone sets off an electromagnetic pulse or does something else along those lines. It takes your battle armor out — renders it ineffective. But the medieval knight doesn't have that problem."

Maker nodded, catching on. "Because — even though he's armored just like me — he doesn't have anything built-in that would be affected by an EMP."

"Exactly. His low-tech equipment isn't hindered or hampered by the device that took out your battle suit."

"So you're saying that the sub rosa tech is intended to affect more advanced equipment than what's on the *Pearl*. So even though the Vacra probably tried to use it on us, it failed because our ship was a dinosaur."

"Well, it's just a theory, but yes."

"It's a good one, in my opinion," Maker said. "Nice to know you put all that extra brain power to use on something other than wine preservation and goosing the financial markets."

"Yeah," Browing said, turning his eyes once again to Erlen. "It was incredible. I mean, my mind was only expanded for a short period, and I was able to do amazing things — come up with fantastic ideas."

Maker grinned. "And now you remember that you had these remarkable thoughts, but can't recall exactly how they work, or were put together, or what have you."

"Exactly. But it makes you wonder what a person could achieve if he had Erlen's brain boost injected in him constantly, flowing through him all the time. To be Gulliver, as you put it, all the time while everyone else is a Lilliputian."

Maker burst out laughing, causing Browing to look at him strangely.

"What?" Browing asked, almost in irritation. "What's so funny?"

Finally getting himself under control, Maker — still grinning — said, "You obviously didn't fully utilize that big brain when you had it."

"What do you mean?"

"Because there actually *is* somebody who has that brain boost running through them all the time."

"Who?" asked Browing, clearly interested.

"Think about it," Maker responded as his p-comp chirped softly, indicating that he had received a private message.

Stepping away for a moment, he tapped the screen to bring up the communiqué. It was from Chantrey and read:

*I thought I would make another attempt to predict your behavior. This time, I anticipate that you'll be racing to your quarters on the* Raider *at top speed less than a minute after finishing this message.*

The verbiage ended, but then a two-dimensional picture of Chantrey began to scroll up on the screen. It started at her head, first revealing her hair, then her face, her neck…

*She must be wearing something extremely low-cut*, Maker thought as the image got to her bare shoulders and then scrolled lower. *Oh my…*

Maker felt himself growing hot and flushed as the image continued scrolling. Truth be told, Chantrey was *not* wearing something low-cut. In fact…

"Okay, tell me," Browing said, interrupting Maker's thoughts.

"Huh?" Maker said, looking around in embarrassment and at the same time closing the message Chantrey had sent. "Oh, I, uh, need to step out for about an hour. To check on something."

"No problem," Browing assured him, "but before you go, tell me."

Maker was perplexed. "Tell you what?"

"You said someone actually has Erlen's brain boost running through them *constantly*," Browing said impatiently. "Who is it?"

Maker didn't say anything; instead, he merely cut his eyes at Erlen. Obviously confounded, Browing stared at the Niotan for a moment — and then his mouth dropped open and his face took on a stunned expression as the full implications of what Maker was saying hit him.

Maker burst out laughing again. He clapped a still-shocked Browing on the shoulder and said, "Welcome to Lilliput." Then he went racing off the bridge.

THE END

Thank you for purchasing this book! If you enjoyed it, please feel free to leave a review on the site from which it was purchased.

Also, if you would like to be notified when I release new books, please subscribe to my mailing list via the following link: http://eepurl.com/C5a45

Finally, for those who may be interested, I have included my blog, Facebook, and Twitter info:

Blog: http://kevinhardman.blogspot.com/

Facebook: www.facebook.com/kevin.hardman.967

Twitter: @kevindhardman

Made in the USA
Columbia, SC
27 March 2023

14371832R00209